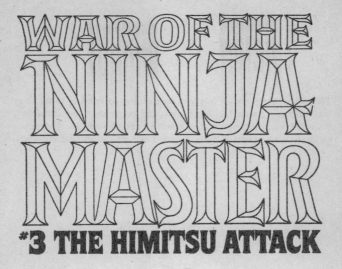

WAR OF THE NINJA MASTER
#3 THE HIMITSU ATTACK

WADE BARKER

D1559637

WARNER BOOKS

A Warner Communications Company

This stuff happens. What you are about to read is true; only the author's name has been changed to protect the innocent. As always, characters speak with forked tongue. Volume estimated by weight. Product may have settled during shipping.

WARNER BOOKS EDITION

Cover design by Andrew Newman

Warner Books, Inc.
666 Fifth Avenue
New York, N.Y. 10103

A Warner Communications Company

Printed in the United States of America

First Printing: August, 1988

10 9 8 7 6 5 4 3 2 1

The Most Dangerous Woman on Earth

➤   ➤   ➤

"I am death," he said, his arms going out slightly from his side, his palms toward her. He took his first step down the hall as the tiny steel tongue snapped out from under his left palm.

Rhea's head jerked when she heard it. Her eyes gleamed when she saw it. She looked radiant. She laughed with total delight.

"No, you are not," she answered. "But you'll have to do."

➤   ➤   ➤

The first Hanzo Razor shot from her hand and sped at his face. He went under and caught it with his wrist-knife as his left arm shot up. The spike sank into the corner where the wall met the ceiling, but he kept coming. He grabbed her still-bladed left wrist with his right hand, practically falling upon her.

She couldn't get the other Razor up and his knife was coming down at her throat...

WAR OF THE NINJA MASTER
#3 THE HIMITSU ATTACK

To Phil DeGrave, Ann Paris,
and the 1985 Turkey Quest.

Mange la porte.

ACKNOWLEDGMENTS

To Stephanie, Nathalie,
and all the empty faces.

Buban Ichi

"BOS"

"When sorrows come, they come not single spies,
 But in battalions...."
                                        —William Shakespeare

"Honour but an empty bubble;
 Never ending, still beginning,
 Fighting still, and still destroying...."
                                        —John Dryden

1

"Luck rules life, as does the will of heaven," said the Face and Hands mystic on the corner.

The words gave Michael Shaw pause. The tall, half-British, half-Chinese police detective stopped and turned: a risky thing to do on any Hong Kong street during the morning rush hour.

But the rest of the populace was nimble. Years of navigating the narrow sidewalks and dodging the mass of cars, buses, trucks, scooters, and bikes made them agile. The people behind Shaw danced around him with millimeters to spare, and those beside him made just enough room.

Shaw retreated two steps, hands digging into his pocket for change. As he stepped before the crouching old man he dropped several coins into the worn, bent, padded plate. The hunched man—knees on either side of his bent head—fiddled with his rusting can of burning incense and the pile of prayers written in red ink on yellow paper before glancing up.

He did a double take, then had to crane his neck farther back than usual. "Ah," he cackled in English, "a tall drink of water." But he sucked in the last syllable when he saw the Eastern eyes on the Western body. He immediately

quelled his *gweilo* tourist patter and looked humbly down at
the cracked sidewalk.

"Come down here," he muttered in Cantonese, waving
Shaw lower with one hand while nimbly pulling a rubber
band off the piled prayers. "I get dizzy with your height."

Shaw went to his knees. The mystic avoided the plainclothes
policeman's eyes for the moment, still shamed by his
mistake, but his long, wrinkled, wizened brown hands
sought Michael's own.

The mystic was preparing to gasp when their flesh touched,
but when the sound came, it was not artificial. The mystic
was surprised by the strength of his new patron's energy. He
immediately looked up into Shaw's face. So strong yet still
so young. So purposeful, but growing in understanding. The
mystic looked down at Shaw's hands with the anticipation
of a bibliophile opening a great book.

He was not disappointed. The flesh lines swallowed him
up. Suddenly the mystic was flying, like a great explorer
soaring through the sky. He sailed across Shaw's life,
through the white of his present and the blue of his future.
The mystic's eyes filled with tears of gratitude. He caressed
these large, strong hands like the great treasures of Quantung.

"*Mmm-goy,*" he whispered. Thank you.

The man must be hard up to be so grateful, Shaw
thought. Little wonder. With Face and Hands mystics on
almost every corner of the Wan Chai section, money was
scarce. And small wonder if all this particular old man did
was rub hands and bow submissively.

The mystic knew he was taking too long. But he also
knew he had to be very careful. He mustn't let an errant
word distract this man from his chosen path. He forced
himself to let go of Shaw's hands and grabbed a series of
prayers. He placed them atop Shaw's money on the plate
and set them smoldering with an insense stick. He took
them by the base and shook the pile of burning yellow
parchment, mumbling prayers for Shaw's ancestors.

Only then did he look back into Shaw's questioning eyes.
"You have had a great adventure," he said, bathing in the
man's deep eyes as if they were the smooth, shining China

Sea. "You have suffered, but you have emerged triumphant, glistening, and proud. You have fought the good fight and won. You have faced great danger, but you have been protected by the light of righteousness."

Shaw did not stir. These were grand words, and not inaccurate ones. Into his mind came the faces of the men he had just fought. They were nameless faces that roared at his mind's eyes as if shot from a cannon. But then, overwhelming the others, came the face with a name: Chiang Li, the Triad gang leader Shaw had been forced to kill.

Then more faces. On them expressions of intolerable hatred. Triad forty-niners, the soldiers whose job it was to eliminate anything in their Big Brothers' way. Their looks were for Shaw because it was he who stopped them at the Kai Tak Airport. And finally there was another face into which all the other faces fell. It was a young face of an old man whose thin lips were set in a wide smile. It was the face of the man they called Rover, whose crystal-brown eyes never smiled. The man whose hard, dead eyes looked at Shaw with deadly promise. . . .

Shaw came out of his reverie to see the Hong Kong shaman looking at him with sympathy and care, as if reading Michael's mind. It was then that the cop knew his disbelief had been breeched. His sense of karma upon hearing the mystic's come-on was justified. He listened carefully to what the mystic was saying.

"You must seek the light," the old man said slowly, distinctly, "for it is not over. You must face these dangers again. These are not the dangers you face every day. These are the dangers you already know, which are distinct from your day-to-day life."

Shaw nodded. He faced danger every day as a policeman.

"Seek solace in the ocean of your strength," the mystic suggested. "Seek strength from your comrades in arms. Seek serenity from your memories. You are destined . . . and others with you. Stand tall. Never look down. Fly above us. We will look up to you . . . and cheer."

For a moment Shaw did fly. But in his mind the white sun was her face and the red sky her hair. Shika: the woman who had left the airport in the company of a gweilo and a child. The woman who had saved his life. The woman he had saved. The woman who still haunted his thoughts.

Shaw felt the mystic let go of his hand—almost reluctantly. He looked down at his own long fingers, and when he looked up again, the mystic had turned away, his eyes closed.

"W-will you not bless me, *sifu*?" Shaw stammered quietly.

"I . . . I cannot," the mystic admitted sadly.

Shaw thought about that for a moment before he straightened. He took another moment to look down on the suddenly motionless man before continuing his walk to police headquarters. His long legs took him from the corner in seconds, and he was soon swallowed up by the mass.

He never saw the mystic look after him, his eyes wet. He never heard the mystic speak.

"Would it be that if only *you* could bless *me*. . . ."

2

The topless woman held up the small woven basket in one elegant hand, and the bone dice in the other.

She seemed to shimmer in mist, her smooth, buttery-yellow skin even softer for it. Her small, strong, round breasts jiggled as she threw the dice into the basket and brought the basket down to the floor in one motion.

She froze in that position, and the entire room seemed to swim in space.

As in space, where was no up or down. This cube of a room could have been anywhere for all the difference the city and country around it made. It was but four teak-and-paper walls with a *tatami* floor and ceiling.

She was a goddess of gambling, and those around her worshiped her. They worshiped with their money and with their eyes. She kneeled before them, her oval face and almond eyes serene, her long, straight black hair glistening, her chest strong, her stomach flat, a skirt affixed around her narrow waist, her right leg crouched in the cloth's slit.

She raised the basket slowly. Only then did their eyes leave her. They gasped and groaned as the dice told their story of loss and gain.

Shintaro Ichi's eyes never left the woman. "We are shamed," he said quietly, the fingers of one hand kneading the floor mat as if they were already filled with her flesh. He sat in one corner, away from the others, a small teak table beside him, on which was a single saki bottle and cup.

Asao Katsu was closer to the small floor strip that bisected the room, and upon which the gambling took place. He was facing the opposite wall so Ichi could look upon his profile. His hands were within his kimono, his shortened pinkie fingering the white wood scabbard of the short *tanto* blade. It was what they called "Yakuza masturbation."

"*Hai*," Asao said softly and deeply.

"The Gaijin made fools of us all," Shintaro said mildly. "He made promises, put us in his debt, and then disappeared."

Asao gave only the smallest of nods. He held his questions back. His sensei was speaking.

"We might forget if promises were all"—Shintaro sighed, pouring himself another cup—"but we have been compromised."

Asao hadn't forgotten the slaughter in the Shibu department store, which had placed them under police scrutiny, as the rest of the populace had seemed to. Highly publicized tragedies were like that. The more the headlines and television heads screamed, the less believable their ravings became. Soon these stories became the plot lines for movies, making them all the more fictional.

The Ichi gang had been found blameless, much to the police force's frustration, but such close inspection had caused other activities to suffer. It was only now that the gambling could resume without threat.

The woman held the basket and dice up again. The men

put down their bets. They nervously fingered their shirts and puffed on their small, noxious cigarettes.

"My brother must still be restrained." Shintaro frowned. "He sought to make things right."

Asao pursed his lips. That meant only two things. The Gaijin would be killed . . . or Tomisaburo Ichi would kill himself.

"I promised our mother my brother would be safe," Shintaro said, sipping the sake and watching the woman idly. "I have put these lives in your hands since you share a kinship with the Gaijin."

"I am honored," said Asao Katsu, bowing deeply, his hands on either side of his head. Both men were aware of the shortened final finger on his left hand. The digit the Gaijin had removed.

The other men ignored them. They did not wish to see one man bowing in loyalty to the other.

"You will have whatever you want," said Shintaro. "Whatever you need. Find the Gaijin. See that he seeks the assassin's road."

The assassin's road. The road Itto Ogami, famed Shogun's headsman, and Miyamoto Musashi, famed swordsman, had taken. The road to Hades.

Asao Katsu stood, straightened his kimono, and left the small room by the sliding door behind the gamblers' backs. They did not turn to see him go, nor did he turn to take a final look at the gambling goddess. He marched down the long hallway, the late-afternoon light streaming in the far side like a blind man's probing fingers.

He stopped at the small closet near the glass street door, blinking into the crisp sunshine. He removed his kimono to reveal the light gray suit beneath. Now, even with the tanto shoved into his waistband, he looked like any other salaried man. He no longer looked like the avenging yakuza, which was what he was.

In Italy they had a word for it. *Vendetta*. It was a word that meant death everlasting. It meant that it would never be over as long as there were those who took vengeance.

In Japan it meant that someone had to die. Either the

Gaijin or Asao Katsu. And Asao did not want to die. He pushed open the glass door and walked out onto the wide sidewalk, in the shadow of the Tokyo Tower, his face set.

He remembered the Gaijin's calm, sure face. He remembered how the Occidental had clipped Asao's pinkie right at the joint with such precision and skill. Their souls had clashed, and Asao's was found wanting. He would not make that mistake again.

When next they met, Asao would not confront the man directly. If he did, he would lose. Asao could not lose again, unless at the cost of his own life. It must be the Gaijin who died this time. Asao must send that perfect soul to its rightful resting place.

Only then did Asao think about how he would achieve this. He knew he would not want for any travel or equipment. Now it was a matter of brains. If his soul was weak, maybe his mind would be stronger. Maybe the key to discovering the Gaijin's weakness was in answering one question.

Why?

Why did the white man offer them Chinese riches, risk death, hack off his own final finger to ensure their cooperation, then disappear? Why did he insist upon their participation, then double-cross them? Why did he incur the Ichi brothers' wrath, seemingly for no purpose? Why?

It made no difference to Asao Katsu that the question's answer had eluded the greatest minds of history. He was driven to seek it with his very life, something no armchair philosopher had done. He would meet the Gaijin again. He would know why.

But where to begin? Where could the man be? Out of all the countries in the world, where could Asao Katsu start?

The yakuza gangster slowed, letting the businessmen sweep around him. Signs of the city were everywhere. The wide, multilaned street was congested with tiny cars, buses, and trucks. The sidewalks were choked with businessmen on their way to mama-san bars in the side streets where the yakuza had come from, and early dinner meetings at the three-star hotels across the way. Behind him were the walled gardens of the Imperial Palace.

Asao Katsu looked over his shoulder at the looming Tokyo Tower: that one anomaly in a downtown filled with black glass skyscrapers and eccentric architecture.

The Tokyo Tower, an exacting replica of the Eiffel Tower.

3

Paris was a soul sandwich. The sky was gray, the walks were gray, most of the buildings were gray, and his soul was gray. Daremo didn't know what reflected what. Was the mirror beneath his feet or above his head? Was the world or the heavens real? Did he stride on solid ground, or was it all dark imaginings? Did it make a difference?

No, it didn't make a difference.

He walked under the chestnut trees, seemingly against the tide of human endeavor. Everyone else seemed to be going in the opposite direction. And why not? It was the end of the working day, and the rain that had been threatening the city in daylight started to spit upon them at dusk.

They rushed from their offices to the nearest entrances of the Métro, which was where Daremo had been coming from. They walked as Parisians did; heads down, collars up, marching. Their hands were either clenched around them or alternately holding their hats down and umbrellas up.

Not for them the glory of their city—they had seen it before. They had to live in it. It was often said, "*Paris est la monde*." It was not a city. It was a world. It was all they knew, so why stare at it?

They didn't notice Daremo. He moved among them like a passing cloud. He danced within the ceiling of caps and berets, dodging the stodgy wingtips as well as the leather pumps. The men's legs were wrapped in regulation brown tweed. The women all had the uniform of white stockings with white dots underneath rustling skirts of every description.

Some of the women did a double take as the mist that was Daremo passed. It was only in their peripheral vision that the image of the serene, hard face with the short copper-colored hair and the steel-gray eyes came into focus. Then he was gone, like so much smoke. It was a game he liked to play with them.

Only one woman, a tall Asian with smooth, creamy, margarine skin and long, black, silky hair, stopped and stared purposefully at him. She was amused, then frightened, by the way he drifted through the crowd. His expression was the same as Fred Astaire's when the master danced by himself. Totally relaxed yet totally concentrated. That made her smile.

Her lips sank as his head seemed to come off his body and float down the street against the human traffic. His fists seemed to swing off his arms and weave around the people by themselves. And his feet seemed to slip through legs by popping off the ankles, then reaffixing themselves on the other side.

The Asian girl exhaled in relief. She was not going mad. It was just the way the handsome man was dressed. On his head was a black racing cap. On his hands and feet were gloves and shoes in a matching color. He even wore a plain, long-sleeved, black T-shirt. But over and under that was a zippered jacket and pants of gray.

It was a color that blended in with the walls and walks around him. So when he moved from intersection to intersection, his body seemed to wink in and out of existence. He was like a chameleon, literally blending into his surroundings.

But then the Asian girl was bumped by three of her school friends, who continued giggling and talking. One chastised the Asian for standing out in the rain, then they all swept along with the crowd to the Métro entrance.

Daremo waited until they had gone several yards before stopping near the wall and looking after his witness. He decided that she was what she appeared to be, a young,

slightly horny student. Rain? he thought. You call this rain?
Tears of the gods. Some few drops to commemorate this
grand occasion, then on to other worldly things. Daremo put
the young Asian girl's face out of his mind, then danced on.

My, they grow them big here, he thought, humming it to
himself. She was the tallest Asian he had seen since his
companion, and she was not alone in this town. He was
initially put on his guard by the number of Japanese and
Chinese in Paris. But they were no more "Asian" here than
the blacks were Southern. Paris made every race its own after
a while. The food and wine cleared their skin, strengthened
their teeth, straightened their spines, and stretched their
bones.

The raindrops came in on sheets of wind, cutting diago-
nally along the streets. It didn't detract from the city's
beauty. In fact, it enhanced it. These were streets that were
meant to be wet. It added to the further reflection of
Daremo's gray soul.

He hummed along, oblivious to the moisture that beaded,
then rolled, off his clothes, until he reached the Buci
Market. There the quaint, warm little stone-faced shops
gave way to the open-air selling of fruits, vegetables,
cheeses, and flowers. The scent of chestnuts roasting on
carts gave way to a rainbow of scents that painted the inside
of Daremo's nostrils.

The citrus were the lighter colors—the bright yellows and
the oranges. The tomatoes and peppers were the deep reds
and greens. The cheeses ran the gamut of white; from beige
to bone and everything in between. The flowers were
especially heady for Daremo's heightened senses. They
exploded like fireworks in his mind.

He almost felt like whistling. He hadn't felt so . . .
Wallacey . . . since his first death.

The death of Brett Wallace, and the man he had been
before everything Brett Wallace was had been destroyed.

He felt nearly light-headed. It could have been all the
booze he had sucked up on the plane, but he doubted it. He
had been drinking heavily all year, and it never made him
feel like this. He felt . . . good. This was a nice place.

Good? Satisfactory in quality, quantity, or degree? That was a condition he hadn't known for two years. By all rights he shouldn't be feeling it now. Not after what he had done. It wasn't that he had stopped killing. Killing he was used to. But purposely destroying people's lives was fairly new.

He had inadvertently been doing it all along—just by the nature of his existence. Even the most horrid among us had a mother. And if not, then a neighbor, companion, associate, or friend. If not, the media would have no one to interview after an arrest. But now Daremo was reveling in manipulation. He had made it interesting—like moving a chess piece just to see what would happen.

Even so, he had never felt good about it. Until Paris. He tried to figure out why as he passed the market and made his way to the Scandinavia Hotel.

It couldn't be just the city, although each building came in one of two categories. It was either a beautiful baroque stone that oozed history, or an ultramodern glass and white-wood monument. But every place had a grandeur, even if the stone was chipped and the paint was peeling.

It couldn't be just the people, who patently ignored him. Could it be the women? Hardly. They were tall and elegant, covered in leather and canvas, and seemed to wear their sex like an award—but he was beyond that pursuit.

By the time he reached Le Temps Perdu, a restaurant, he had come up with two reasons. It was a city of walls and gates. He liked that. It suited him. And here, unlike anywhere else he had been, he didn't have to fit in.

It was a ninja curse. That sect prided themselves on infiltration. In all the other countries he had visited, Daremo had to concentrate on not being seen. Here he felt he could do jumping jacks naked in the Louvre, and it would be a couple of minutes before anyone saw it. In New York they'd notice but ignore. Here, they'd literally not see it. That freed Daremo to truly see . . . maybe for the first time.

Spotting his contact was certainly no trouble for anyone who cared to look. With the intermittent rain there were only a few people seated beneath the umbrella-shaded tables outside the establishment. The man in question sat at the table farthest away, in the corner, next to the restaurant's front window. He was sipping from a steaming mug and reading a paperback as the waiters buzzed around him, seeking to roll out a plastic awning over a number of green metal supports.

He was dark-skinned, with a thick black mustache and heavy eyebrows. His actual coiffure, however, was expertly groomed, and his outfit was elegant. He wore a dark suit under an expensive overcoat. Daremo decided to stand just outside the restaurant's perimeter to see how long it would take before the man noticed him.

It was a minute and seven seconds. Not bad. Daremo just stood as he had been, arms slightly out from his sides, fists clenched, legs spread, when the man looked up, started, then smiled. As Daremo separated himself from the mass of oblivious passersby heading for the underground trains, the man put down his book and reached for his napkin.

Daremo stepped among the tables and made his way toward the back as the man wiped the hot-milk foam from his lips and stood up.

"*Quel temps sale,*" Daremo said as he approached, and the man laughed.

They greeted each other like familiar acquaintances. There was no hug as if they were friends, but a strong handshake, and the man clapped Daremo on the back.

"Obviously you have been in the City of Lights long enough," the man said, his voice lightly accented and urbane. It was not a French accent, although his French was excellent.

"It wasn't hard," Daremo said, sitting back. "They don't say hello here."

"No," the man agreed. "Just 'what weather.' That is all you hear from October to April. What weather. One says it. The other uses it as a reply. They both agree, using no other words. '*Quel temps sale.*' Would you like something? Coffee?"

"Something warmer." Daremo grinned. "Ask them to make me a blackout."

"What on earth is that?"

"One and a quarter ounces Absolut Peppar and a quarter ounce coffee liqueur in a shot glass."

"Good lord!" the man said as he signaled a waiter who

had just affixed the awning to the last upright, closing in the sidewalk café from the rain.

"Keeps me warm," Daremo defended.

"I would imagine," said the man before giving the order.

Daremo waited until the waiter, in the classic uniform of white shirt, black pants, bow tie, and apron, left before speaking again. "Thank you for agreeing to see me."

"Agreeing?" said the man. "I *had* to see the man with the perfect papers."

Daremo smiled, sprawling in his chair. To all the rest of the world he appeared to be the man of leisure, so totally sure of himself that he could completely relax in the bleakest of surroundings. "I was hoping they'd do the trick."

"Of course I demand all my contacts show me proof of identity and nationality," said the man, returning to his coffee. "But your passport and visa duplicates were beautiful. The best I had ever seen." He cocked an eye at Daremo. "Fake, of course. Or do you have the fakes?"

Daremo's smile widened. "We both have the fakes."

The man laughed. "Wonderful!" he cried, slapping the table. "Wonderful!" He calmed as the waiter returned, holding Daremo's drink out at arm's length and averting his head. Peppar is a Swedish vodka made with peppers.

Even the man at the table turned his head away slightly as Daremo sipped the concoction. "What a terrible shame," he tsked. "To do that to your interior here."

"What do you mean?" Daremo asked.

The man answered that question with another question. "What is Paris famous for?"

"Rudeness?"

The man waved that away. "Not at all. The French are not rude. They are romantic. It is foreigners like you and me who are rude. The French are only a reflection of an unromantic world attacking them on all sides."

Daremo put down his drink and straightened in the seat. "So they roll over. Paris is the rollover city."

"Paris is the center of romance," the man countered.

"If you call black marketeering romantic," Daremo said pointedly.

The man put up his hands and sat back. "Guilty as charged. But perhaps we can amend your estimation somewhat. Paris is the overlook city. They overlook you. They overlook me."

"Agreed."

The man smiled. "You see? And, yes, indeed, I consider black marketeering romantic. Would I have devoted my life to it if it was not? Would I live here if it was not?"

"*Touché,* for the want of a better French word," said Daremo. "And if I had not wanted to meet with the greatest of all black marketeers, would I have come here to see the magnificent Cristobal?"

The man laughed with honest mirth. "Now you are getting the hang of it. Let the words flow from your tongue like a crystalline waterfall. Let the compliments come easily and honestly from your heart. When you look at the world from your heart rather than your head, you shall soon see why Paris must overlook it all. Overlook it or live in despair. You see? I am already making a mistake."

"What is that?" Daremo asked, his stretched-out form suddenly becoming still.

"I am laughing. The French do not laugh, unless they are trying to impress a woman. That marks me as an outsider as surely as my skin, my voice, and my hair."

Daremo relaxed again. Cristobal's "mistake" was not a threat. "Would you change that?" he asked lightly.

"I wouldn't have to, if only I would master the look."

"The look?"

"The Paris look. It is simple. It is the face of everyday sadness and infinite apathy. See." Cristobal's face was suddenly devoid of all tension. His eyebrows and lips drooped, and his eyes became slightly watery. He reminded Daremo of that little cartoon dog with the melancholy voice.

"Droopy," he remembered aloud.

"Yes," Cristobal answered in recognition. "He is very popular here. They have Droopy books and Droopy clothes. For adults."

Daremo laughed this time. The men understood each other. "That is why you live here, eh?"

"Yes," Cristobal agreed surprisingly. "For that. For the sense of agelessness and youthfulness. For the love of food and the love of films. The love of life . . . and the wine."

The light went on over Daremo's head. "*That* is what France is famous for. The wine."

Cristobal nodded. He swung a hand at Daremo's murky brown drink. "Why coat your stomach with that when you could have a remarkable Dagueneau Pouilly-Fumé or a superb white Aligote, to name just two?"

"Why, indeed?" Daremo asked before swigging the black-out. "Bring on the *vino classico*!"

"Ah, my good fellow," Cristobal commiserated. "There may be a time when we can sample Paris's wealth together. But first . . . I think you came to plunder Paris, did you not?"

Daremo leaned back, letting the Absolut and liqueur give his stomach a glow. "Oh, no. I came to let you plunder Paris, then pay you enormous amounts of money for it."

Cristobal leaned in. "Now there's something I can do." He considered Daremo carefully. "Perhaps we can share a bottle of wine as we talk," he decided.

Daremo leaned in to meet him. They smiled at each other, cementing their immediate empathy. They were alike, these two, and they recognized that in each other. They might have even liked each other if either was capable of it any longer. "With pleasure," Daremo agreed.

Cristobal ordered a *moules brûlés doigts* and a *salade frisse au thon* along with a bottle of 1983 Château Etoile Bordeaux. A cast-iron pan covered with open mussels and a plate of fresh tuna cubes with shallots and endive were placed along with the wine, and Cristobal set right in with his fingers. Daremo joined him, and by the time the two had finished sharing, they were talking like longtime conspirators rather than new acquaintances.

"I am shameful," said the man, pouring more wine. "I mix the meal with merry abandon, seeking to take in as much as possible in one sitting. I would shock my French friends. This meal with this wine. . . ."

"I am not a French friend," Daremo reminded him. "I may be your partner."

"Perhaps," Cristobal agreed, ruminating. "Hong Kong dollars, Hong Kong dollars . . . what shall I do with Hong Kong dollars? What do you want for them?"

"Trust," said Daremo.

"A terrible commodity to come by," Cristobal said sadly. Daremo leaned in earnestly. "I want to do something unheard of. I want to use your goods to enter a country."

"Enter a country?" Cristobal echoed. "What country needs entering? That must mean . . ."

"The greatest country for black marketeering in the world. I have the passport. I have the visa. I need the materials once I'm in. I need the system to get whatever I want in there when I need it."

Cristobal stared at Daremo, then leaned back and gave him a ho, ho, ho. "What are you saying? Are you talking about what I think you're talking about? Fresh fruit and soft toilet paper, is that what you're talking about?"

"And car parts and televisions and audio components."

Cristobal's eyes focused. He looked at the remnants of the food and wine, then back at his supper companion. "This is not a game just to smuggle state secrets, is it? For if it is, I will crucify you on the Champs-Elysées and slit open your stomach."

"No," said Daremo.

Cristobal stared at him some more. "You do not frighten me," he finally said. "I do not know what it is, but it is not fear. I am not afraid because I read nothing in your eyes or on your face that you do not wish me to read. I trust you because there is no falseness there. But there is nothing there, and it does not frighten me, and I don't know why."

"Do you believe me?"

Cristobal thought carefully before he spoke. "It is not a matter of belief, and you know it. I know this is not all you wish to accomplish, this entry. But I can also see no way your ultimate fate ties in with mine"—Cristobal's face finally lost its wishful expression—"except the million or so ways in which the entire plan could explode in my face.

But that is usual. That is standard operating procedure.''

"Will you do it?"

Cristobal poured himself the last of the wine. "You do not mind," he asked in a way that was not a question. "I deserve this." He sipped the wine and thought aloud. "The black market is a response to the state's inability to satisfy the needs of the masses. This is the ultimate state-versus-citizen conflict. It is a challenge."

"It is the ultimate challenge," Daremo told him. "It would be the culmination of your career."

"You do not need to tell me that," Cristobal rumbled. "I have always fought hunger and misery. From South America. From here. And now..." He looked back at Daremo, his eyes hard. "Hong Kong money. That garbage."

Daremo shrugged. "And perfect papers."

Cristobal's eyes grew distant again. "There is that," he agreed.

Daremo knew he had him. Cristobal had always wanted to try what Daremo suggested but never had any reason to until now. The risks to himself had always been too great. But here was a man sitting across from him who offered to take all the risk—take the point, as it were. He was also going to take a lot of the financial responsibility.

Cristobal was getting older. He didn't have much time left before his senses and instincts would dull. He knew that. Daremo knew that as well. Although the possibility of failure was great, the allure of attempting the greatest accomplishment in black-market history before retirement was strong.

Cristobal sipped the wine in the fine bistro, wearing his beautiful clothes and feeling itchy. He realized that he had been out of the trenches a long time. His friends in Peru would not recognize him now. Nor trust him.

Cristobal put down the wine and nodded. "Perhaps some *quatre-quarts aux poires* to chase all this down," he suggested. "And some coffee to chase that?"

"With something in it," Daremo added.

"With something in it," Cristobal echoed. "If you insist." He signaled the waiter over and gave him their order of luscious pear tarts before leaning back with satisfaction. "Something to eat while we talk," he told Daremo. "Planning is hungry work."

Daremo mirrored his new partner's moves. He had been right. Right to come to Paris. Right to meet Cristobal. Right to send the others away. Now there'd be months of planning and organization, all in the comforting confines of this spectacular city. He could finally still his hands. He could finally take them from their baths of blood.

He felt the warmth of the leather flat against his right forearm. He felt the weight of the steel inside it, and the coiled springs below them. It was comforting to know that these vipers could rest for a while. It would make them hungry, but the sleep would do them and their master good.

Let Hama have the time to collect as many U.S. dollars as possible. Let the others get what peace they could before the big push. They would need all their strength for what was to come.

But that was months away. Now it was time to use their minds, not their blades. Daremo looked away, under the dripping awning, to the famous rooftops of Paris. Cristobal was right. It was a supremely romantic city. It overlooked everything—stupidity, cruelty, evil. It ignored them and went on its sad way. It was a perfect place to be.

Daremo smiled happily. After all the death and difficulty, he would get a respite. He heard words in his mind he never thought he'd hear again.

"This is going to be easy."

4

The fun would be over soon. Le Tenter silently cursed the words that played around the outer edges of his ego. They were always there, like the whispers of Caesar's prized servant as he marched into yet another conquered city.

"All glory is fleeting."

Caesar paid the slave to say this into his ear even as the laurel wreaths were being placed upon his head. Only Le Tenter's servant was smaller, with hummingbird wings and a triangular devil's face. It had red skin and a Sardonicus grin. It lived inside his head and was invisible.

It's over soon. The fun is over. Like a dandelion seed sweeping out from under the hand as the fingers clenched it, the fun was marked by its end. To achieve it was to end it.

Le Tenter ignored the taunt. He savored the sweetness of conquest instead. His head reared back, his eyes closed, and he tasted the heady bouquet of innocence and ripeness combined, of sophistication and immaturity mingled, of lust and fear. All were combined; all were always combined in the bodies of young French girls.

A drop of water smacked into his forehead, breaking the spell. His eyelids snapped open and his head craned back onto his neck. There, the actual vision made his heart swell.

Here he was in the sewers of Paris—*les equots*. Here he was, motionless, standing on the narrow walkway in the darkness, beneath the feet of the city's occupants. They walked blithely overhead, unaware of him and his ecstasy.

He stood in one square foot of the system's one thousand three hundred and five miles. He stood among the sodden, moss-draped halls and curving ceilings. He stood amid the sweating cables stuck onto the dripping walls like coiled tree roots and octopus arms.

And there she was. Standing before him. Blind. Mute. Hearing only the bellows and shrieks of the giant concrete ball-plungers on either side of them. The gigantic cement stones were wrenched up and pushed down to control the direction and speed of the sewage.

Her arms were out, seemingly seeking to twist among the cables, seemingly holding herself there in a crucifixion . . . for him.

The rubber-coated wires were only apparent upon closer examination. They blended in with the black leather gloves she wore, which went to her upper arms. The wire coiled around her wrists and elbows. She twisted in them, gripping the cables with her short fingers. She pulled at them achingly, but she wasn't going anywhere.

Le Tenter watched her attempts to regain control through veiled eyes. She was not trying to escape. She knew that was beyond her. He watched as she pulled at the bonds longingly, the dainty feet in the elegant high heels stepping forward to keep her balance.

She was not awkward, like a frisky colt. She was self-aware, like a mare, moving her body this way and that—the forces of her femininity moving in a counteracting ballet. Her torso would be thrust forward, and then her flanks, their roundness shimmering with the single glowing yellow light at the curve of the tunnel.

Le Tenter remembered when he had selected those shoes. He remembered it all, like a film that played in his mind all at once, rather than scene by scene. Seeing the girl, meeting her, shopping for her in the Rue de Seine, seeing the shoes in the window as if they were the only ones there, picking her size perfectly, using just his memory of her.

Her face: round, fresh, unblemished. Her eyes: bright, small, light brown with amber flecks. Her hair: lustrous, unkempt, rich, dark. Her lips: full, dark pink, soft. Her image played in his mind.

He fed his recollections by drinking in the sight of her now. Arms outspread, feet placed carefully. Legs stretching from beneath the hem of her party dress. He remembered buying that for her too. He remembered getting the complete package, using only his encyclopedic knowledge of women to choose the perfect size. The size that would hold her round, firm torso in black suede. The size that would cup her growing breasts in the strapless top. The size that would give hint of her strong legs beneath the billowing crinoline of the skirt.

He had even bought the lingerie. But it was not that box he presented to her at his apartment. He remembered her standing there, between the two tall, open windows, in the corner of the high-ceilinged room. The sunlight moved across her as the afternoon rain clouds fought their heavenly battles with it.

She was youth in her T-shirt, denim skirt, and jacket. He was wisdom and experience in his suit and his sixteenth-arrondissement apartment. He held the rectangular box wrapped in the shiny blue paper out to her. She almost squealed when she saw the black silk stockings inside.

She was not squealing now. She was making another noise as she slowly pulled on her bonds. A sound somewhere between a shout and a moan emerged from the padding covering her lips. He could see her lips there, the yellowing light playing across them as they were detailed beneath the skintight plaster tape.

Her eyes, too, seemed to glow gold, but she was not a princess of the Egyptian sands. Two small squares of the tight, reflective, glue-dripping tape had been placed over her closed eyes, molding them into semicircular orbs.

It made her seem to be this mythical goddess, captured by man and held in unnatural captivity on Earth. Trapped in the bowels of the city, she ever yearned for escape to the skies. But the wire held her there, crucifying her before him.

He stood, still resplendent in the suit, watching her, and remembering as she playfully put the stockings on for him. He remembered her watching him carefully as she pulled up her skirt to affix the garter belt over her blue panties. She was always testing him, teasing him, both hoping that he would do something and that he would not.

He remembered the curl of her lip and the gleam in her eye as he watched her from across the room, never approaching. In her eyes was the acknowledgment of their relationship. Trust. Maturity. They were both adults, weren't they? Wasn't she?

Then the stockings went on. She had placed her dainty foot upon the seat of the Louis XVI chair as if she were already in high heels and caressed the silk up her leg. She luxuriated in it, keeping in her mind's eye his look of respect and appreciation. Appreciation—not that she was doing this for him, but for her very existence as a beautiful woman.

Not girl: that was what she was to others her own age. To him she was a woman, and he treated her accordingly.

Le Tenter knew those same stockings and garter belt were under that rustling skirt now. He knew that the panty was different, but he knew what that looked like too. He could see it just as clearly in his mind as if he had lifted her skirt.

There was time enough for that.

He had bought everything she wore that night, including the diamond drop earrings that flashed on either side of her sealed mouth, and the tricolored gold necklace that hung under her shining throat and over her heaving chest.

They had eaten in his apartment, on the little round table in the other corner, the monuments of Paris stretched out beyond them. He had placed a white tablecloth over it and candles on that. He had served lamb in lime-pesto sauce—a fitting meal for his sacrificial virgin. He had served the wine, a full-bodied Beaujolais . . . in her honor. Dessert was cheese and fresh berries, which they ate with their fingers.

And tonight would be *le grand jeté*.

Talk of it had been mischievous at first. She had mentioned how much she disliked people her age shortly after their meeting. She had responded quickly to his treatment of her as an equal. As, of course, he knew she would. He had been able to choose her out of dozens from a myriad of clues. Her posture, her bone structure, her expression, her wardrobe, her habits, her movements . . .

So he talked to her of sophisticated things. Art, music, manners, society, sex . . .

She had responded, naturally, with mock maturity, attempting to convince him, no doubt, of her worthiness. There was no hint of sarcasm in his attentiveness. He listened and accepted her precisely as she was. More so, he actually seemed to appreciate her just that way, so each subsequent meeting became a conspiracy. Everything in which he initiated her seemed an unspoken agreement between them; as if only he knew what she actually wanted.

That did not mean he agreed with everything she said. He would surprise her whenever she would test him. She would speak of her latest lover and how he condemned the weak government, the Fascist government, and the corrupt government. He had agreed with the young man's fiery politics, and then went on to reveal things that neither she nor her last lover had thought of.

He had not fallen for her jealousy trap. He had involved the two of them instead. He had made her look better in her young lover's eyes when she relayed this tutored information, and impressed the young man with his conviction. It was the first of several steps to intimidate the young man subtly, so he was hardly aware of his balls being cut off.

The conversations deepened in meaning and purpose. He was a well she could return to again and again, without fear of it going dry. And she was young and round and female, so it was of no surprise when the talk turned to flesh.

Then she heard of *le grand jeté*. Heaven on Earth. The true purpose for existence.

She had felt the tearing of her inner skin and the pulling of her interior flesh as her young friend sought to relieve himself. She had made love but not felt it. She had felt passion and desire instead. That is what he had told her, and what she believed. She was unfulfilled. Always unfulfilled. Trying to get through to her young man was like throwing pats of butter at a wall. They would stick, then dry up or fall off.

That was right, she agreed, nodding.

She spent more time with him, telling her parents she was with her boyfriend, telling her boyfriend she was busy. They would talk for hours, never touching. She would yearn for him, and he would treat her like an adult. They would not hold hands. He would put her arms in his. They would not hug, they would embrace. He would caress her neck with the back of his hand and kiss her earlobe with a nibble as he put on her coat.

She felt herself throbbing, as if the dormant furnace inside her had finally lit. She had to start taking responsibility for her own laundry, lest her parents suspect.

Le grand jeté. Would she ever feel it? Perhaps, he said. When the time was right. If she was ready to accept it.

What would she need to do? Her mind and body would have to be ready. Both. Not one or the other.

How? She would have to accept truth in all things. She would have to know right from wrong and be willing to fight for it. She would have to free herself in mind and body.

She had gone into his bathroom as a teenage girl. She had emerged a woman.

"You are ready," he had said quietly.

She was in ecstasy throughout the meal. She felt the explosion building up inside of her. But, incredibly, he had her laughing by dessert. He had even let her feed him some berries, plopping them into his open mouth. She had never felt so accepted, so wanted, so trusted.

He had served her cognac, then finally leaned down to place his lips on her neck. She had moved her head aside and put her hand on his face. She had closed her eyes and sighed.

That was when he had suggested they take a walk.

He had presented her with a stole and the gloves. She had carefully walked with him until they reached the corner where the Quai d'Orsay and the Pont de l'Alma met. He had gone down the steps of the sewer entrance and held his hand out to her.

She looked both ways. No one was in sight. For the first time in hours she had felt indecision.

"You must know hell to understand heaven," he said. Daring words? He did not think so. Looking at her now, he believed he could have said "Eat the door" and had the same effect.

He had seen her gather her courage, before she inevitably went down the stairs and placed her gloved hand in his.

He felt her excitement as they stepped into the tunnel. He placed his hand on her neck. He felt her yield to him, expecting a caress.

He carefully placed his forefinger and thumb, then squeezed.

She sighed and leaned against him, all strength to her limbs stilled. He wrapped his arms under her shoulders and thighs. He lifted her in his arms and walked to where he had left the wire, the tape, and, incongruously, the ice-filled decanter with the bottle of champagne.

"You were not ready," he said to her once she awoke. "Your mind was still ballasted to Earth. You could not fly."

Her wrists twisted in the rubber-coated wire. She leaned forward, her breasts filling the cups of the dress to overflowing. Her flesh gleamed. She tested her voice. She hummed beneath the plaster strip.

"You must be free to feel," he said, stepping forward. His leg went between hers. His right hand rose. His left hand sank. "You are trapped. You have no choice. You can do nothing . . . but feel."

The fingers of his right hand went into her hair. His head lowered to her neck. She cringed when his lips touched her flesh, but he pulled her head to the side. Its trip was not completely unwilling.

His left hand rested on her hip. He suddenly surged against her, pressing her to the wall. She tried to cry out and move away, but she could not. He held her, kissing her, and felt her body moving like the surf. Her arms twisted, her back arched, her legs slowly scissored.

"You will feel," he whispered to her, "inside yourself. Within your world you will know all. You are free now. Remember, you are free."

Her lips sought his, her sealed mouth rubbing against his face. Her fingers clawed the air for him. Her legs gripped his.

"Feel," he said. "Do not fight. Feel." One hand snaked into the top of the dress. The other lifted the skirt. His hands pressed what he found there. The nipple was already hard. The panty was already wet. Her leg muscles started to spasm.

She was drunk and hysterical. One of her last coherent thoughts was that he wasn't sharing. He didn't want her to pay him back. That was why he stilled her limbs. He did not want her to hold him. That was why he had sealed her lips. He did not want her to kiss him. He only wanted to give to her, not take from her. So she would be free to feel.

"The fun is almost over," said the tenter demon. "Get it while you can," it said, buzzing around his head as he expertly excited the teenage girl. "Because after this comes

the work. After this she is yours forever. After this you will
not be preparing her, you will be containing her. It becomes
much harder then.''

Her panty fell to the sewer walkway with a wet whisper.
He held her to him with one arm and drizzled ice gems and
champagne on her while they danced. The wine droplets
were in her hair like dew. The diamonds of frozen water
moved across her skin and down her bodice. They moved
together rhythmically.

Every muscle on her body was tensed, and she did not
even know it. All her muscles moved in perfect harmony
with him, and she was no longer in control. He had
achieved what he had set out to do. She was on automatic. He
had done what he said he would. He had freed her. She
soared within her own head now.

It did not come to him naturally. He had spent years
honing this skill. She was but a lucky recipient. How many
like her were there who were not so lucky?

''Be careful,'' said the demon. ''They might gather and
rise from the sewage any second, their decaying arms coming
from the sea of refuse like spears, their hands like claws.''

How many? How many necks were broken rather than
caressed? How many throats were crushed rather than kissed?
How many were strangled rather than rendered unconscious?
How many were buried when he failed to win their hearts and
minds? How many were expendable guinea pigs to this success?

''The fun is over,'' said the demon. ''Even now, as you
bring her to the first climax. Now it will become work as
you move to the next step. Creation and destruction.''

''It is as Napoleon says: 'Destroy to create, create to
destroy.' They follow one another naturally, as day to night,
sun to moon. She is yours, but you cannot keep her.''

The tendons on her neck stood out, like support beams
for her skull. The skin around the edges of the plaster tape
stretched. Her red-painted fingernails scratched the sewer
wall, digging among the cables. Her legs stiffened at their
widest aperture.

She bucked, her head moving, her hair flinging madly.

''Look,'' said the demon, ''at the hands, which would

soon be put to work on other things. At the legs, which would run to prevent capture. At the body, which would not know party dresses or evening gowns for many weeks, months, and maybe years to come.

"Do you like what you see? She is yours, to be used as a source of your power. Rejoice. Her bonds will always be there, tying her to you."

The girl fainted, overwhelmed at the depth and strength of her feeling.

Le Tenter, the Tempter, stepped back, holding on to his belt so his pants would not gather at his ankles. He was breathing deeply through his nose, letting the stench of the offal and the aroma of her perspiration mingle in his nostrils. He did not choose this location errantly. He would never be able to smell her again without thinking of the sewer.

Her flesh glowed in the yellowing light, and she hung from the wires, her head down, her legs bent and to the side. Her hair obscured her face. The Tempter was struck by the awful beauty of the sixteen-year-old in woman's clothing.

Earth to earth, ashes to ashes, dust to dust; in sure and certain hope of the Resurrection unto eternal life. So sayeth the Bible. But it also said, "Give unto them beauty for ashes, the oil of joy for mourning, the garment of praise for the spirit of heaviness."

The Tempter stood in the sewers of Paris and prayed before the cross of a young girl's soul, so she would not be cursed to eternal damnation for what he was going to have her do.

5

They grew much faster here, Daremo thought as he walked across the city. They grew faster in body and mind, he decided, resting his eyes on the young people who went by. So serious they were, so empty of anything save energy.

"You will see," Cristobal had told him. "In a few days time you will get used to the common, everyday grandeur of this city and see it for what it is."

"And that is?" Daremo had inquired.

"*Fatigué*," said Cristobal. "*Très fatigué*."

Daremo saw it now. Browns and rusts mixed in with the grays. The fetid crusts of something that caked the edges of the sewer drains. And the people weren't merely sad and romantic. They were tired, as if the coming winter weighed heavily on their shoulders—as if the white season were personal packs strapped on by God.

They wrapped fashionable coats around themselves and swept their legs forward. This feeling of oppression added to their sophistication. Their faces had the vapid look that came from knowing everything or knowing nothing. It was a fifty-fifty proposition.

But most of them were tall and most of them were thin. They were fashionable whether they wore the thinnest canvas or the thickest fur. They defined the word *metropolitan*, not to mention *cosmopolitan*. "It was the best of times, it was the worst of times"—if Dickens had not been writing about Paris, it would have had to have been one or the other.

Daremo walked across the Seine, the river that frowned across the city—a narrow blue lip stitched together by little brown bridges that weren't more than four hundred and forty yards apart. He was lucky to cross the Pont Neuf, the oldest bridge in the city, smiled upon by the statue of Henry IV on horseback, who promised a chicken in every pot long before any American did.

All about him was glorious seventeenth-century architecture, with its granite blockwork and alternately flat and steeply sloped roofs. Tiny cars and tiny trucks passed him, none longer and wider than a midsize American car.

Daremo could have taken a taxi or the Métro, he supposed, but why waste the remnants of this glorious day? The night gathered around the city, a reddish light playing on the edges of the clouds. He was in the city's twilight—

after citizens reached home from work, but before they went out for dinner. He was almost alone on the narrow sidewalks, on the increasingly smaller streets.

There were no blocks in Paris. Any pedestrian looking for easily understandable straight lines was in for a rude labyrinth. Crossing the city required an infallible sense of direction and the willingness to go wherever it led you. Thinking of angles was the best bet, as well as possessing a strong appreciation of versatility.

Daremo went up wide avenues with flower-covered medians down the center, curving streets with angry cars buzzing side by side, gently sloped thoroughfares with barely enough room for one pedestrian and one auto on its cobblestones, and seemingly deserted roads lined with two-and-a-half-story *maisons*.

He had passed into the first arrondissement once he had crossed the bridge, then moved through the third, and finally the eleventh, before he stepped into the twentieth. The arrondissements were set in a spiral, starting from the center of the city. Their organization would make sense only from a heavenly perspective. It was hardly surprising, however, in a city that worshiped the corkscrew.

Daremo could plainly see that the city thought of itself as a work of art. All of it had a baroque majesty, even though flecked with dirt. Trees were everywhere, lined prettily or clumped in exacting designs. Their leaves cleaned the gray air as best they could, while the green-and-yellow grass fought with cement, marble, and asphalt for ground space.

Spires pointed accusingly upward amid the gabled walls, with either tall white shutters or wrought-iron fences to enhance them. The shops were closing or closed, while the street artists and performers were moving underground. Only the stores and cafés glowed with reassuring warmth. The darkened restaurants still had a good hour before the rush. Things moved slower here, and later.

Daremo passed Indian-flavor kiosks, which were papered with advertisements. He passed the similar-looking beige street toilets, now all armed with automatic sanitizing equipment that hydraulically hissed into action whenever an occupant left. He passed police, now all decked out in the severe new uniforms that made them look more like U.S. highway patrolmen rather than friendly concierges.

But as he walked, the neatly manicured shrubs gave way to thickets, and the fancy stores gave way to tiny neighborhood shops.

He was in the northeast section of the city now, away from most historic sights, just west of the Bagnolet suburb. He was in the twentieth arrondissement, one of three that served as the Parisian version of slums. The faces changed here. The white gave way to brown, black, and yellow. The gazes weren't vacuous. They were untrusting and slightly hostile rather than slightly apathetic.

The walls had more cracks. Heads went down here from necessity rather than by choice. There were things to avoid here. There were things to step around. The smells changed. The chestnuts and lilacs changed to urine and smoke.

Daremo stopped at the corner of the Rue d'Simenon and bought some things before continuing down the dark, wet street. He stopped at number sixty-eight and pressed the gold button on the wall to the right of the door. He heard the click, then pressed the tarnished plate on the thick wooden door. It snapped open, and he walked into the gloomy lobby of the apartment house.

The only light came from the manager's office, where the residents could pick up their mail from tiny open boxes on the far wall. There was no manager on duty. He was sick on the top floor, with some sort of persistent flu. His simple wooden chair was empty, reeking of loneliness. The lobby reeked of rotting wood.

Daremo could see there were no messages for him, so he proceeded directly to the elevator door, pressing the single call button. The motor clacked on with a loud hum, and the tiny car started down slowly. It finally arrived, and Daremo pulled open the door with the frosted glass to reveal a space no bigger than a phone booth. He pressed the very bottom button and waited for the door to clank shut.

The room jumped and descended with an ominous creaking. It stopped at the very bottom of the shaft with another stomach-punching jump. Daremo pushed the elevator door open onto a long, dark hallway. There was one bulb in the ceiling, and only three other doors. One a quarter of the way down on the right wall, one three quarters of the way down on the left wall, and one all the way down—a mirror of the elevator door.

Daremo went to the nearest door and knocked seven times fast. Seven times: life insurance. He remembered the legend from his childhood. When afraid for yourself, knock seven times fast . . . on anything. When afraid for someone else, kiss them on the nose or forehead seven times fast. Seven times fast, life insurance.

He heard the click and waited. The door did not open. Seemingly it had been unlocked by the wind. He reached down with his free hand and turned the knob. The door swung in by itself. The building had settled some time in the nineteenth century and now listed off to starboard.

He heard a strange sizzling noise. He saw the small, round-edged TV flickering when he walked in. It, and a small light over the sink, provided the only illumination.

The sink was to the right, along the wall with the small stove and half-pint refrigerator. The TV was on a small table in front of the far wall, near the left wall and the entrance to the minuscule bathroom.

The bed was to the left of the door, in the corner. A table was between him and it. A sofa was to the right of the door, also along the wall. Daremo stepped in and closed the door behind him, locking it.

"Food," he said, nodding at the bag he held while walking to the sink. "Good French fare. Boudin blood sausage. Goat cheese. Poilane bread. And a bottle of Côtes du Rhone."

His only answer was the sizzling noise.

"Hungry?" he asked, reaching down to open the fridge. The wine would need chilling.

"Television here stinks," came the answer.

"Why do you think everyone goes out at night?" he replied, straightening. The light from the fridge outlined her.

The tall form. The sleek shape. The angry, oddly cut black hair. The formfitting clothes. The padding at her arms and legs. The never still hands. The buzzing creatures that whirled around her fingers, darning in the air.

"The lavs are tiny, the kitchens are tiny, and the TV stinks," he continued, folding his arms, crossing his ankles, and leaning against the sink. "So people go out to dinner or a show or a movie. It makes the city work."

She said nothing for a while, just kept the sizzling things swirling around her hands and staring at the terrible reception on the small black-and-white set.

"Close the fridge door," she finally told him.

"I like looking at you," he answered with a smile.

"Use your X-ray vision, Superman," she suggested, turning her head slightly. The smooth, tight skin. The high cheekbones. The long, curving lips. The almond-shaped eyes.

He grunted and reached down to swing the refrigerator door shut. He did it slowly, purposefully. He carefully placed his face away from her. He put his back to her. The only sound was the crackling TV and the sizzling.

He returned to his previous position at the sink. The light behind his head made his copper hair glow with a borealis.

"When will we go out?" she asked innocently.

"You'll kill something," Daremo said.

"I'll kill you," said Rhea, turning.

She came at him like a panther: unafraid, unashamed, unflinching, unhidden. She took him straight on, choosing not to attack when his back was turned. The Hanzo Razors in her hands seemed alive. She did not seem to be twirling them. They seemed to fly around her fingers of their own will, like deadly pets.

She went for his face and throat with them.

He seemed to melt, going back and beneath her attack before taking form again to her right, facing her, still moving back. Her right leg swung around to catch him at the side of the head. His right arm came up to block it. He caught it, grabbed at the high-impact aerobic sneaker, then pushed it away.

She twisted all the way around, her back to him, her right leg landing on the floor, her left leg coming up to smash into his stomach. He let it come, pivoted, and swung his left arm around to knock it by.

He hopped back onto the sofa. Her right arm went forward, the Hanzo Razor suddenly gripped tightly in her fist, its two-edged blade between her third and fourth fingers, the spikes coming out from her thumb and pinkie sides.

He clenched his right fist twice. The sword blades placed side by side, back to back, surged from his sleeve and over his knuckles. He pushed his arm forward.

The blades seemed destined to meet, then Daremo's body melted again. His blades ducked under hers and shot down to bite at the Hanzo Razor in her left hand. The double-sided arm blades caught the swirling weapon, bit, and sent it into the wall beside the sink.

The Hanzo Razor in her right hand slammed into the wall over the couch, just over his face. Daremo's right arm swung around as his shoulder jerked forward. He knocked her back like a football player.

When she regained her balance, her hands were empty. The second Hanzo Razor was still in the wall, held there by Daremo's arm sword. He had stapled it there with his sword.

Rhea stood, her fists clenching and unclenching. Daremo's eyes had fully adjusted to the dark, so he finally saw her clearly.

Her porcelain-colored skin was flushed, almost green in the gloom. Her hair, once long and lustrous, was now hacked off, creating a punk look. Across her body was the dark red, high-necked, sleeveless leotard, and Spandex bicycle pants that ended just above her knees. Strapped to her lower arms and legs was dark blue sports padding. She also wore dark blue elbow and kneepads. On her feet were the black, high-topped running shoes.

Daremo pulled the Hanzo Razor from the wall with his own swords. She tensed, waiting for him to throw it, but he merely dropped it on the ground.

He bit back any words as she came at him again.

She threw herself through the air, letting loose an explosive exhalation of air. He dodged her flying kick, pivoting to the right, then brought his arms up as she pummeled at him with karate blows, thrown right and left as if her torso were a piston-driven machine.

He wanted to instruct her, say "Don't tense," but he knew that would infuriate her even more. Just dropping the Hanzo Razor was instruction enough. He dropped it because he was concerned her tensed body would not dodge his speed and accuracy.

She dived at him, anyway. She had to beat him. And the only way to defeat him was to keep testing. Both his limits and hers. So she hit. And when he blocked, she swung. He ducked. She brought the other fist up. He pushed it away. She brought both fists tight against her waist and kicked, her shoe points seeking his knees, balls, stomach, neck, and chin. Her ankles and shins sought his ribs. Her knees followed, seeking some of the same targets.

He would block and dodge until she felt the fury rising up her throat, blinding her. Then the arms would swing wide, and her lips would stretch off her teeth, and her mouth would open.

Only then would he stop retreating. He would block and strike.

His fist came down, his knuckles hitting her ear. She would be deafened, her head wobbling on her neck, but she would keep coming. She would keep swinging and kicking.

He would block, and block again, knocking her arms wide. Then he would strike again, his fists sinking into her stomach. She would be driven back, doubling over, groaning, and then his foot would swing. Her legs would be swept out from under her.

This time Rhea landed on the sofa, on her back.

Flashing through her mind as her body adjusted to the shock were images of the other times. She smashed into the wall, face first, arms and legs cushioning the blows. She slammed to the floor between the table and bed. She was swept over the table and into the wall on her side. She twirled through the air, spinning three complete times before hitting the rug.

Each time the dust would rise and settle. And like a mist that swept the nightmare away to leave reality, he would be there. Not angry, not threatening, not murderous, and not insane. He was like a man she was in love with, and she was like a woman in love.

Then they would eat. And sleep in the same bed, like strangers, not touching each other.

Rhea cut off a piece of sausage and a piece of cheese before pulling off a hunk of the bread. She squeezed the meat and cheese into the dough before taking a bite. After several dozen chews and a swallow, she washed it down with the wine in an Asterix mug.

Daremo had bought the entire collection of French cartoon mugs to serve as their only cups. He drank his wine from a Tintin container.

"What now?" she asked.

"Now," he said, "we relax."

"What?" she retorted sarcastically. "No countries to save? No populations to slaughter? No captives to torture?"

Daremo had his own acid flashback: to a raven-haired woman hung upside down in a closet. To a raven-haired woman tied to a Japanese chamber's uprights by her wrists and hair. He remembered cutting the woman down. He remembered the strands of black hair fluttering to the teak floor like night's scars.

Her images reflected into each other for eternity.

What had he done to her? What had others done?

"No," said Daremo, unfazed. "Just thinking. All I have to do now is think."

"And train me," Rhea reminded him, cutting off another piece of sausage with the angry flick of a kitchen knife.

"And train you," he agreed.

"I will beat you," she said flatly, pouring more wine. He said nothing, just looked at her, his lips stretching. "What are you smiling at?" she wondered.

"I was thinking," he replied. "Just thinking." He stayed silent for a few moments more. She stared back, the hate and love she felt for him fighting across her seemingly placid features.

"It's nice," he finally said with honest relief, "that you're the only one trying to kill me right now."

6

They could look directly at him and not know who he was. Of this he was certain. They would see a man in a long coat. They would see an oblong face with a slightly hooked nose and thin lips. They would see weathered, wrinkled skin. They would see hair that mixed light and dark in a window's peak. If they looked closer, they might see the thick, button-down, cotton shirt under the scarf. They might see the cuffed wool pants and the wingtip shoes.

But that was all they would see. They would not know him. They would not recognize the features. Oh, they might think he was a mature man, a friendly man, the kind they saw every day on the streets and in the supermarkets. No tie or suit jacket, so he was probably an artisan or a restaurateur.

Perhaps then they would take note of his hands. Such long, strong fingers. Such wrinkled palms. Certainly an artist, then. Perhaps a sculptor.

Yes, he was an artist. He did create breathtaking art with those very hands. He shaped the very fiber of life with those fingers. He was the ultimate artist. An artist in life and death.

He was a man standing on the corner of the Avénue Emile Zola in the fifteenth arrondissement, just a twenty-minute walk from Le Tour Eiffel, to the west. If he walked just a few more minutes south, he would be in the suburb of Issy-les. He stood and let the shoppers pass. They were just so much more wind to him, the wind that caressed his skin and ruffled his black scarf.

He let the pedestrians look at him. They did not know who he was. They did not recognize him. Would the cowl and scythe have helped? Would they recognize him then?

No, he doubted it. No one recognized him until he came for them. Le Moissonner. Who would he come for today?

He stood on one corner of five, where the many streets met to whisk the tiny cars and scooters to the restaurants or nightclubs. The night wind was turning brisk as the sun completely submerged. The last, fat afternoon raindrops slapped the gray pavement, and the clouds parted, searching for the moon.

The colors became so much more intense at this time of day. He could see the browns and blacks and mauves mixed with the grays of the sidewalk and the building walls. He could see the sharper greens of the leaves and the different brown-gray of the tree bark. The blues, reds, oranges, and purples of the sky seemed to separate from their rainbow blush to turn into streaked, individual lines. The heavens' watercolors were removed for the sharper evening oils.

Le Moissonner stood on the street corner. *Who called me today?* he asked silently. He looked from street to street. On these five corners alone there were two glassed-in bistros; two pastry shops; two pharmacies, their doorways marked with the identifying green neon cross; two huge magazine stalls complete with postcards, pens, and hardcover comic books; two supermarkets; a cheese shop; and a minuscule movie complex housing three screens.

All manner of persons walked past him, not seeing who he was. He waited patiently, as death does, to see who would call to him. Whether they spoke or not, he would hear the call . . . as he had heard all the other times.

He knew the area well. He had been called to it many times in the last fortnight. He stayed in his haunt until he heard the call, then followed the echo wherever it took him. If he did not find the caller then, he haunted the same area every day, waiting for the second, confirming cry inside his mind.

He was never bored. There was much to prepare. He had to make his caller's way through the nine levels of life.

Trapped in this flesh, he had to plan carefully his own entrance, as well as his exit. To recognize him was to call him, you see. If he was truly seen, that had to mean that the witness was marked by a higher force. Only the dead saw death.

Le Moissonner stood without moving his head. He didn't have to. He knew this corner very well. He had stood here often. The time for watching and listening has past. He didn't have to turn his head to know that the off-duty policeman would come for his nightly copy of *Le Monde* in six minutes. He didn't have to strain his ears to hear the on-duty policeman start his rounds in seven minutes.

The cops might meet at the ED market behind him, to his left. That was the food store that sold only generic brands. It was cheaper, so that was where the off-duty cop bought his nightly four pack of Orangelia and bottle of wine. That would be of no concern to Le Moissonner... unless they had been marked for removal.

He heard her call just as the on-duty and off-duty policemen met. The cops talked behind him as she called him forward. The cops did not even note his movement. He took a step away, then crossed the nearest street.

She was in the cheese shop. It was not so much a shop as an open-air space on the first floor of a building. There was no door or window. The proprieter merely unlocked a metal grate and pushed it up like a garage door.

Le Moissonner could imagine it would be like being hit by a wall of invisible *fromage* every morning. The tiny space, just enough for one auto if it had been a garage, was crammed with goods. The store itself seemed to consist of a cheese wall and ceiling. It was like a pocket of cheese, just off the street.

There was more to it than that, of course. There were bins of dried fruit, bottles of myriad condiments, tubs of wrinkled sausage, and a small barrel of freshly baked bread (bought from the major supermart across the way, no doubt). This was the Parisian version of a convenience store.

She was there, buying one can of a favorite spread. It must have been the one luxury she bought outside ED and the

supermart. She couldn't handle these tiny shop prices otherwise—
not on her fixed income. She pecked the few coins out of
her little purse, then carefully leaned over the counter to
deposit them firmly in the proprietor's hand.

"Anything else today, dear?" asked the proprietor, dropping the can into a small plastic bag.

"Oh, no," she said quietly, already clicking the purse
shut and beginning to turn.

Le Moissonner was there, behind her and to the side. He
had picked up another can and was fingering it idly.

She was calling him, so it was time to prepare. He let the
can drop from his fingers. It hit the stone floor with a clack,
and then a clatter as it skittered away.

"Here!" said the proprietor, pointing. "You've bought
that now!"

But the woman between the two hardly started at the
noise or the shopkeeper's angry reaction. Le Moissonner
smiled as he bent down to retrieve the can. His caller was
used to the sudden noises of the city. Nothing surprised her
anymore.

As he moved around to pay for the damaged goods, his
caller placed her can in her shopping cart and started sliding
her feet back toward the street. Le Moissonner saw her
stooped back pass him and smelled her aroma as she left.

Musty clothes, aging skin. The only perfume coming
from white, stringy, dry, washed hair. He paid the proprietor
and gripped the bent can. He walked out onto the street after
his caller.

She had turned left and walked down the street, away
from Le Tour Eiffel and the majority of the traffic. The
street became almost instantaneously narrower and quieter.
The asphalt changed into cobblestones, and the storefronts
became quainter.

The sky had turned dark blue, with that strange red piping
still along the edges of the clouds. High over his head, some
stars started to twinkle. He smiled. There was still some
minutes before the streetlights would flicker on.

He walked some fifteen yards behind her, feeling as if he
were walking through her life. He saw her ahead, moving

slowly, but as fast as she could. He felt her aura as he moved steadily along, having to pause and window-shop so as not to overtake her.

She was an old woman, but he saw a young woman in his mind. A fresh, lively young woman in 1918, her eyes wide and wondering at the results of World War I. Then he saw the young lady, curious and vibrant in the most glorious years Paris had ever experienced, drinking in the high life, which was everywhere in the twenties. He saw her first love, and then her second, and then the lovers who followed—all making lies of what true love meant. There would be no knight in shining armor for her.

He saw her husband, the man who ultimately had betrayed her. Not because he worked every day to support them, not because he shared his life with her, but because he died without giving her children. Because he left her alone. Because she had no friends who did not die, and because she couldn't speak to the young girls who had replaced her. And they could not or would not speak to her. Because they knew they would become her in just a few short years.

Le Moissonner drifted by the charcuterie, his nostrils filling with the smell of the spicy cooked sausages, the ones with the skin that cracked during cooking and were served with the meaty innards puffed out. Then came dessert as he passed the *confiserie,* where the smell of chocolate and sugared fruits wafted.

She walked and he followed. She took a right turn down an even narrower road, where the buildings loomed on either side and the aromas were even more powerful. He passed the *maroquinerie* and smelled the raw leather. He passed the shoemaker's and smelled the shoe polish. Finally he got to another *pâtisserie* and cleaned his nostrils with the smell of freshly baked pastry.

He kept the smile on his face as he passed the other pedestrians, who gave the old woman room and didn't even notice him.

" ' 'Tis the wink of an eye,' " he said quietly, " ' 'Tis the draft of a breath. From the blossom of health to the paleness of death.' " William Knox had written that.

Le Moissonner passed the pedestrians, who didn't listen. They never listened. And it was now just him and the old woman on the street. Her neighbors did what they did every day. The street was as empty as it had been when he passed here every day before.

All the good people were inside, taking off their shoes, reading the paper, preparing the supper, or napping. Only she was out shopping, because her weakened muscles could not haul a week's groceries up the stairs—and there was no one there to help her.

He stopped in front of a closed *librairie* and noted which new books had come out that week. A new Dick Francis. A new Waverly Root. When he turned back, she had already found her key and the lock. She had gone inside the one thing her late husband had left her, the tiny house at the end of the street. Le Moissonner walked carefully down the road and slipped into the first alley between buildings.

The old woman looked up at the stairs before her. No way out. The old fool had scraped his money together and bought them a home that went straight up. There was no parlor or hall behind the front door. Only a way to the cellar, a coat and hat rack, and stairs. A dozen stairs to the living room and kitchen. Another dozen to the bedroom and bath. The old fool.

The woman rationalized the trek the way she did every time. She was elderly. She needed the exercise. It was good for her. No sense sitting in your room, rocking your life away. Get out. Walk around. Breathe the fresh air. Even though you got slower every day and the looks others gave you became increasingly impatient and angry.

Here, she had to admit, the air was thick with dust and decay. His death still lingered in here, and sometimes, late at night, she imagined she could see his soul coiling in the moonlight at the top of the stairs. Those twenty-four damn stairs he had bought her.

Her arthritis-twisted fingers gripped the shopping cart handle tighter, and she lifted her leg to place her flat shoe on the worn paisley carpet. It was warm in here, she told herself, and friendly. This building loved her. The thick air and dark walls embraced her. They said, "Good to see you again . . . you can do it. Walk. Feel that pain? That's life. As long as you feel that, you're alive."

Is it better? she heard herself ask way in the back of her mind.

It's better, she heard her late husband's soul say from the top of the stairs.

She made it to the third stair, and the shopping cart's wheels clacked up the first step. That was a good sign. She was still strong enough to haul this. It drove her on, step after step, each movement an eternity.

It is only with age that the true miracle of life becomes clear, she realized. Everything the young took for granted was shrieking inside her now. Only with age did the network of nerves have any reality.

Clack, clack, clack. Up each step she went. Thank the Lord the kitchen was not on the top floor. She kept herself going by thinking of the little snack she would make. The tea and the cakes and the crusts of toast upon which she would spread the pâté.

That would hurt too. Spoons she could handle easily. They just had to sit in the crook of her fingers as she stirred. Knives were harder. She had to really grip them.

But it would be worth it. She could taste it now. She raised her feet. She heard the shopping cart clack. It was more than a noise; it was a reverberation inside her brain.

She did not hear the scratch at the back window. If she had, she might have thought it a cat and ignored it. Or she might have thought it a branch moved by the wind and gone on, oblivious. Either way it would hold no fear for her. What was there for an old lady to fear . . . except the Reaper?

" 'There is a reaper whose name is death,' " he sang to himself as he used the glass cutter. " 'And with his sickle keen, he reaps the bearded grain at a breath, and the flowers that grow between.' " Henry Longfellow had written that, he recalled. *The Reaper and the Flowers*, stanza one.

Look how the tiny implement cut, he thought, marveling. All those ground diamonds and sharpened steel on that tiny

wheel. He reached into his pocket and brought out the
suction cup he had taken from a toy gun set. He stuck the
orange plastic against the pane and pulled the tiny square
out. He placed it carefully upon the ground and reached
around to undo the window lock.

The old woman went through the swinging door into the
parlor. She felt safe here. The old wallpaper, worn rug,
hanging pictures with the dust-encrusted frames and dirty
glass, as well as the cracked ceiling, were comfortably
familiar.

And there was her old chair and the tiny television set.
There was the heat stove and the mantelpiece. There was the
kitchen door to the left. She pulled her groceries after her as
she went toward it.

Le Moissonner was in the cellar. He had slid through the
window like a serpent and landed lightly upon his feet. He
stood there now, in the darkness, feeling at home. He was at
home everywhere. Every home welcomed him sooner or
later.

" 'In the day, in the night, to all, to each, sooner or later,
delicate death.' " So said Walt Whitman.

Le Moissonner reached into his pockets and pulled out his
gloves. He pulled them on and then whirled back the way he
had come.

He reached through the opening and retrieved the glass by
holding the suction cup. He smudged the window lock with
his gloved hand, effectively cleaning it. He held the glass
aloft and flicked it off the suction. It fell to the cellar floor
and broke with a tinkle.

The old woman put the can of pâté down on the kitchen
counter with a solid clank and opened the cabinets. She put
the milk away before placing the pudding and vegetables in
the refrigerator. She put the pot on to boil some water, then
eagerly set about arranging the cakes and making the toast.

Only when everything else was ready did she concentrate
on opening the pâté can. Thank heaven for appliances. Even
so, putting the tin under the metal lip of the electric opener
was a trial, especially since the can was made for manual

peeling. The machine whirred, filling her ears with buzzing for what seemed like a minute.

Finally everything was ready. The old woman looked at her repast with glee, practically eating it with her eyes. This was a worthy reward for her trying day among the young. After this she could sleep.

She filled her old hands with the steaming cup and delicate china plate and turned back to the parlor. Her eyes were fixed on her chair and the small table beside it. She walked directly toward it.

She did not see Le Moissonner standing inside the parlor, to the left of the kitchen door.

She never saw him.

She felt instead. She felt his hand gripping her hair. She felt herself pulled back. She was never aware of the china leaving her hands, or of her tea spilling. Her senses were overwhelmed by the pain in her scalp.

This pain was even more powerful than the sudden, searing heat at her throat. It was only when his hand left her hair and she regained her balance that she felt the strip of heat, like a string of fire, along her neck.

Then she started to drown.

She felt as if her head had been thrust under water. She couldn't breathe. Her hands went to her throat and felt the moisture there. She was going mad, she thought. She had slipped into insanity in the space of a second. She thoroughly would have believed that if not for the pain.

She fell forward. There was nowhere else to go. She dropped heavily, unable to feel the further pain of her jarred bones. As she fell, Le Moissonner was revealed. He stood where he had been before, his hands by his side. His gloves were still on and were empty.

If it was not for the tiny metal tongue coming from under his coat sleeve, just beside his left wrist, there would not be a clue as to how he attacked.

The tiny, pointed tongue dripped red.

The ocean was a roar in the old woman's head now, and she wasn't aware of her fingers clawing or her feet kicking. She wasn't aware of her mouth gasping or her unseeing eyes widening. Her mind was filling with death as the blood poured out of her severed neck.

Le Moissonner, the Reaper, calmly waited for her to die.

"Death comes to set thee free," he recited quietly. "Oh, meet him cheerily, as thy true friend. And thy fears shall cease, and in eternal peace thy penance end." A fitting epitaph, he thought. From a Frenchman: Baron de la Motte Fouque.

The old woman stopped moving. The Reaper was glad. He got no pleasure from this. He wasn't one of those psycho killers who got off on killing. To him it was a science, a challenge. It kept his skills sharp. Sharp as the blade under his left arm. It was important his skills not lay dormant. That was what he was told, and he agreed. But if he had to kill, best he kill those closest to death. It was only logical.

The Reaper found a paper napkin in the kitchen. With it he cleaned her blood from his arm knife, then clicked it back into its metal scabbard with his free hand. He carefully walked around her widening pool of blood and tossed the crimson napkin into the heater. Then he waited, staring down. He waited until her scarlet pool joined with the few drops that had come off his killing blade. They mingled and sank into the wood and throw rugs, turning brown.

Only then did he go back downstairs and leave the way he had come. Relocking the window, he stood, rummaging in his pocket. From it emerged the dented pâté can he had bought. Examining it carefully, the Reaper raised it, then hurled it triumphantly at the remaining glass.

A perfect throw. It broke the pane, obscuring his perfect cut lines, and smashed down where he had broken the other glass. This would slightly obscure the expertise of his stalking and execution.

The Reaper looked around quickly, making sure no one else called to him. He had been called many times in the past two years by many elderly people. He had to take them closer to their maker. But that was no excuse for carelessness. If he was to continue doing his work, care and planning was everything.

Nothing moved. No gaze was returned. It was a quiet

residential street, like all the others. He wondered how long it would be before this one was discovered.

" 'Come to the sunset tree,' " he said to the quiet, shuttered, curtained windows around him. " 'The day is past and gone. The woodsman's ax lies free, and the reaper's work is done.' "

The Reaper moved into the alley quickly, his hands back in his pockets. He smiled appreciatively, remembering where he had heard that Felicia Hemans poem.

Napoleon had told him that one.

7

It took an enormous amount of research, understanding, and control. It was extremely hard to estimate which of those three things was the most important. It would be fair to say that each was equally important in staying on top and unsuspected.

The man only a few knew as Napoleon stood beside his desk, looking out at the street of floating cars. It was a tiny side street near the main shopping area off the Opéra Métro station. Like many of the Métro stops in Paris, the station was at the center of a star-shaped intersection, with boulevards stretching out in all directions.

Down one road was a mass of movie theaters and restaurants, each one sandwiching the other. There would be a glass wall, within which sat masticating people, then a giant billboard with a painted actor's face. It made a macabre *Gulliver's Travels* sort of image to anyone who cared to look at it that way. Little people eating while giants stared with expressions of either love or horror.

Down another road was the city's largest department store, the Galeries Lafayette, housed in two gigantic buildings, taking up two complete city blocks. Down yet another

road was a series of smaller shops, decked out like pearls on
a string. Down the fourth road were banks and necessity
stores, all housed in the gray stone buildings so prominent
here.

Finally there was the Opéra itself, the same Opéra the
infamous phantom haunted in story, film, and song. The
Opéra, in which the phantom dropped the huge chandelier
on the audience when his desire for his protégée had been
frustrated.

The image of that massive, illuminated, upside down
crystal Christmas tree fascinated the man Le Moissonner,
and Le Tenter, called Napoleon. The moving picture of it
crushing the handsome men in their tuxedos and the beautiful women in their gowns often flickered through his mind.
He had to admit that it had become a self-conscious obses-
sion with him.

The chandelier . . . the weight of it . . . the sound of the
phantom's saw mingling with the arias . . . the noise it made
when it dropped through the air . . . the slow motion image
of it . . . the cresendo as it landed in layers . . . the screams
of the terrified joining with the sopranos . . . the ensuing
chaos . . . the echoes of the destruction like piano keys . . . the
cries . . . the tinkling glass . . . the dripping blood . . .

And the images. The Munch-like faces swirling in horror.
The glazed, open eyes of the dead. The tears of the
wounded . . . the twisted flesh of the pinned . . .

"What a lovely view."

Napoleon looked away from the images of the floating
cars. He turned his head to gaze at a well-sustained beauty
of some thirty-eight years. Her hair was between white and
blond; she wore a tight gray suit, and red, round glasses
were perched on her nose. She held a tapered flute in her
hand, as did most of the people at this cocktail party.

"The entire street is lovely," she continued. "In the
center of things, yet so secluded."

"Yes," he agreed slowly. It was a veritable Shangri-la, a
business zone amid all the shopping, useless to anyone
except its workers. Given the way Paris was landscaped,
any pedestrian would come to this street by accident. It did

not link any establishments of interest; it merely got in the way.

It was a short block that emptied onto a circle, with uniform buildings no higher than five stories. It was a handsome, wide street, ending with slightly wider buildings decked out with Romanesque columns.

This building was in mid-block, and his office was on the third, and tallest, level. His windows were long, dirty, and hemmed in by little grates, as well as a crossbar just outside so children wouldn't topple to the street.

"The automobiles give it the final touch," he suggested. "Just that correct degree of implausibility."

The woman laughed.

The first Comité Royale was right outside his window, hovering over the cobblestone boulevard. That company, the Comité Royale, had paid astronomical sums to design and erect a unique advertisement for their classic car business.

Instead of a showroom or billboard, two wires were run across the street at varying points, from building to building, upon which the replica of a car could be hung.

There were eight antique cars, "driving" four stories across the air, four heading west and four heading east— their wheels just missing the gas street lamps.

It was fitting he worked here, Napoleon thought. He could imagine gravity taking over, and those cars crashing down . . .

"It suits your establishment," the woman said, taking up the conversation. "Very impressive." She looked around, and Napoleon followed her gaze. They saw the large desk, upon which the goblets and crystal punch bowl was set. They saw the opposite walls with the gorgeous oak bookcases. They saw the inordinately plush, ornate Oriental rugs on the teakwood floors. They saw the sections of marble. They saw the metal ceiling with the incongruous pipes in the corners.

"You like it?" he murmured, taking another sip of his drink.

"Of course. Very conducive to work. An oasis amid an oasis. Do you always keep the lights so low?"

Napoleon glanced at the reading lamps on the desk, as well as the ones beside the red leather chairs near the library shelves. ''Helps me concentrate.''

He watched the other guests sitting in those seats and milling around. They had several things in common. They talked calmly, at a low volume. They were extremely well dressed. They were healthy, and the median age was fifty.

Research, he thought. He had to know everything he could. That ranged from spending all his office hours reading, and all his free time talking. He read about almost anything that concerned him. He had to know about Paris, he had to know about the world, and he had to know about his namesake.

Napoleon, born August 15, 1769, on the island of Corsica. Son of Carlo Bonaparte, lawyer, and wife Letizia Ramolino. Genes incorporated strength, wisdom, will, and imagination. Learned skills of negotiation and conquest. Shared neither tradition nor prejudices of the French. Could view the country and the people as an outsider—a Corsican.

The modern namesake inhaled deeply, his chest swelling, his head rising. He did not share many physical attributes with the original. His hair was gray and thick upon a regal, chiseled head. His features were not European. His nose was straight, his lips thin. His jaw was clean-shaven and strong. His eyes were dark blue. But it was his height that truly set him apart from the original. This Napoleon was a full six feet five inches.

Where they were similar was in their intense ambition, their willingness to take decisive action when the opportunity offered itself, and their vision. Napoleon Bonaparte also saw the crashing down of cities, of countries, of entire hemispheres. He also chose the riskier path if it offered the greater opportunity for advancement and power. He was always willing to risk more than he could afford to lose.

It was that Napoleon who had fought on both sides of the French Revolution. It was that Napoleon who had commanded the troops who fired upon the counterrevolutionaries marching against the National Convention in 1795. And it was that Napoleon who had rolled over the Austrian and Sardinian

armies, then masterminded a French coup d'état. He knew
when to be the diplomat and when to be the warrior. He
was, above all, a man of conquest.

This Napoleon envied him. That Napoleon did not fear
discovery. That Napoleon did not have to be consummately
self-controlled. This Napoleon looked out upon the tiny
street near the Boulevard Haussman and the Rue Lafayette
and thought about what Paris had become.

It was a memory. Where once there were teeming armies
of soldiers and artists, there were now second-class citizens
just trying to survive. Where once there was a center of
accomplishment and creativity, now there were second-
stringers, hangers-on, and followers.

The city was a husk, buoyed by what the centuries had
wrought. Paris's glorious skin hid cancerous organs. The
cracks in its walls were growing. The city's name should be
changed to Très Fatigué.

This Napoleon smiled. The smile accentuated the wrin-
kles at the corners of his eyes and mouth. It made him look
stronger and wiser. It displayed his experience and rough-
hewn good looks.

"A franc for your thoughts," said the woman, submerging
her grin on the lip of her glass.

He returned his attention to her. "You'll have to pay more
than that," he replied.

She laughed again, as studiously as the first time. It was a
controlled laugh but not forced. It had a pleasingly husky
timbre.

"Who are you with?" he asked.

"You're very direct," she returned. "But I'm not surprised." She pointed with the hand holding the glass,
revealing a short, perfectly manicured, red-painted finger-
nail. "Admiral Seaworth." He was a short man in white
naval uniform, his balding fringe and beard pure white.

Understanding. He could not have chosen a better place
for their headquarters. Once he had gathered the facts, he
needed the insight to use them. All his free time he spent in
gatherings like these—in embassies, military posts, offices,

restaurants, and private clubs. He talked and he listened. He gathered. He reaped and he sowed.

"Interesting, isn't it?" the woman said. "How names can direct lives."

Napoleon nodded. "With a name like that, it was natural that he joined the navy."

"And rose quickly through the ranks," she added. "Like a calling. Take me."

Napoleon looked down at her pleasant face and smiled knowingly.

"You resisted the natural joke," she said. "Good for you." She put out her hand. "My name is Jennifer Hemphill."

He took it. "Similar to 'helpful.' Personal assistant to Admiral Seaworth?"

"Office manager," she replied, enjoying his warmth and strength.

Napoleon took the information and stored it. Control. Not only the desire to reply in kind with his own name but the urge to display the power and superiority he felt. The inclination to showcase his research and understanding. The ego-gratifying whim to brag. His strength lay in his control. In projecting the image of the calm, intelligent, trustworthy man.

"How good to meet you," he said, shaking her hand. "I'm so glad you could come."

"Do you have these"—she looked for the correct word, and it wasn't exactly *party*—gatherings often?"

He shook his head in the negative, taking another sip of his drink and surveying the crowd. "Not really. But every once in a while I like to touch base with my contemporaries."

"You work with these people?"

"Once. I'm retired now."

"Oh?" she pressed, her face showing gathering interest. "Writing your memoirs?"

He looked over her head at the small, round object stuck high up the wall near the entry door. To all other eyes it would appear to be a smoke alarm. So the little red light flashing on and off occasionally would raise no interest.

Three repeating lights. The Reaper was back without incident.

"Consulting," he told her.

"Hello, T. H.," said a soft voice beside him.

"Hello, Paul," Napoleon said without turning. He felt a strong hand on his shoulder.

"You've met our Mr. Cerveau, have you?" the new person said to the woman. He was about six feet tall, with a wide face, a permanent grin, and black hair.

"Cerveau," she echoed. "I wouldn't have guessed you were French," she said to her host.

"Little interoffice joke," Napoleon said diffidently.

"Oh, I see," she took up. "Cerveau. French for brain."

"Yes," said the newcomer. "In Germany he was Herr Gehirn. In Central America, Señor Cerebro. In the Middle East, Mr. Markh. I'm Paul Lansing, by the way."

He put out his other hand, and she took it. She did not bother with a "Pleased to meet you."

"And the T. H.?" she said instead.

Napoleon rolled his eyes as Lansing spoke. "Can't you guess? I'll give you a hint. He had three surnames."

She was quick. "Thomas Hubert Edward?"

"Or Theodore Harold Edwin," Lansing immediately retorted. "Or Thaddeus Henry Earl. Or Terence Herman Eugene. Anything with a T. H. E."

"How clever," she said dryly. "I gather you are with intelligence?"

"How did you know?" he asked, eyebrows rising.

"Your apparent lack of it." She put her drink down and turned to her host. "It was a pleasure meeting you. If you'll excuse me. . . ." She walked away, toward her admiral.

Lansing blinked. "Is it my breath?"

"Might as well be," Napoleon said casually, looking back toward the street. The other man kept his eyes on the woman's retreating figure, the image of her moving hips under the tight skirt pleasing to him.

"How are things in the COP?" Napoleon asked lightly. Corridors of Power. They used to have a dictionary of initials.

But Lansing didn't want to talk about that yet. "I don't get it. We can't all be tall, dark, and handsome."

"IIT," said Napoleon.

"Yes, yes, I know," said Lansing, sighing. "Intelligence. Insight. Test. What did I do?"

"Obvious," said Napoleon. "Too obvious. Don't your mistresses satisfy you?"

"You can't bring your mistress to one of these," Lansing muttered, finishing off his tall glass of Scotch. "Everything's fine, considering," he continued, putting the glass down on the desk.

Napoleon said nothing, letting his silence draw Lansing in.

"Tell me what you think," the intelligence operative continued. "Maybe you can make some sense of this. After years of spreading out in a sunbeam pattern, the bear is suddenly doing a pinball pattern on us. You know, bouncing all over the place."

"How big is the board?"

"Good point," Lansing acknowledged. "That's another funny thing. It's national. Just within their own borders."

"Really?" His tone was lightly doubtful.

"You don't miss a trick, do you? It's only recently turned inward. The last six months or so. But before then, the only deviations from normal activity were sudden, short, wild-card trips to NPPs." Non-pressure points.

Napoleon kept staring at the floating car wheel outside his window. "Quite a puzzle. Just a 'toy,' probably."

"You think so?"

No, of course he didn't think so. "Certainly. What else could it be?" Toy was their nickname for NAM, Non-aggressive Movement. The military and government liked stretching words out. Ballistically induced aperture in the subcutaneous environment meant bullet hole. But the intelligence division liked contractions and abbreviations. To them, bullet hole translated as NDA. Nondamaging attack.

Paul Lansing looked wistfully toward Jennifer Hemphill, who was in conversation with the admiral and some six-hundred-dollar-suited honcho from the English consulate.

"You got me," he said. "But I certainly wish you were back with us, T. H. No one's been sure of anything since you left."

"I made decisions," Napoleon agreed lightly.

"But you were certain of them," Lansing stressed. "Both attributes are hard to come by."

"I'm not a gambling man by nature," Napoleon said, putting down his own glass. "Not at those odds. My luck would have run out sooner or later. Better I get out unsmirched." He smiled knowingly. "My government pension is better that way."

"You're a consultant," Lansing countered, facing him. "So consult. I can assure you your fee would be very impressive. And this is not a personal request, mind you. Although I hasten to add that it is not a personal request with which I am greatly in agreement."

Napoleon shook his head. Doublespeak was becoming as complex and subtle as Japanese. "We both know the answer to that," he said.

"Yes, yes," Lansing said with disappointment. "No-go."

"No-goi," Napoleon said correcting him. Nongovernmental Interests. "I handle No-goi accounts exclusively."

"T. H.," Lansing said, shifting to look away. "Would it make any difference if this request had a bearing on my own position in the COP?"

Napoleon resisted the urge to sigh. First the man from the CIA had extended an invitation to return to the espionage community in an advisory capacity, then he'd said he would support Monsieur Cerveau personally, then he'd revealed that he had staked his own reputation on the appointment. Lansing *was* a fool . . . but that was not unusual in modern times.

"Get another drink, Paul," said Napoleon. "It looks like you need it."

"Good idea," Lansing said immediately. "At least I can always count on you for good Scotch."

And bitters, Napoleon thought as Lansing walked away. The man was a sore loser and a lousy actor.

So, Napoleon considered, the Russians are growling away,

are they? He let the information move through his mind, seeing if it caught on any outcropping. Would it have any effect on him? Could it conceivably cause his own house of cards to come crashing down?

"It looks like you're reliving the destruction of the *Hindenburg*," said Jennifer Hemphill. "Or at least the sinking of the *Lusitania*."

Napoleon looked down at the handsome woman who had approached him again. She was perceptive. He would have to be more aware of her. "Interesting," he told her. "I *was* thinking about collapse. The very nature of it."

"Really?"

"It's a natural result of intelligence work," he explained. "We don't create anything. We merely seek to prevent its collapse."

"And the military," she reminded him. "That's their situation as well."

"Indeed," he agreed. "So it is natural that we concentrate on the central aspect of the work."

"The weakest point in the network," she interpreted. "The point most likely to give way, bringing the whole thing down."

"Yes," he said.

She found herself getting excited that his eyes had begun to lighten, his skin darken, and his expression open up.

"The greatest moments in history are those when a single individual, or a small group of dedicated individuals, brought something down," he continued. "Not blew it up. That takes no real ability. Bring it down. That's personal. That's monumental. With your own two hands, bring something mighty and massive down."

"David," she said.

He looked at her.

"With Goliath," she explained. " 'A small leak will sink a great ship.' "

"Thomas Fuller," he identified, smiling with more honesty than ever. " 'An ant hole may collapse an embankment.' "

"What is that?" she asked.

"A Japanese proverb," he explained. "No one is sure

who said it, but studies have shown that the phrase came into use in the mid-1600s.''

''The feudal period.''

''Yes.'' He nodded. It was obvious that she was pleased they were interacting, that she had gotten him to respond. But he would continue to hold back. He would keep her guessing and working by dealing with her only on an intellectual level. He would continue to seemingly ignore the swell of her chest and the roundness of her hips.

''Yes,'' he repeated, ''the police state.'' When she looked perplexed, he went on. ''Ninety-seven percent of the population controlled by three percent. The most successful police state in modern times. Four hundred years.''

''Up until the early 1900s,'' she said, elaborating. ''The entry of Admiral Perry brought the samurai class down. And with them the Shogun.''

''No,'' Napoleon countered. ''No, it wasn't Admiral Perry, even though it appears to be. Perry was only the last stone in the slingshot that had already weakened the foundation of their system to the point of collapse.''

He had surprised her. Against her better judgment she had gotten involved with his driving interest. What had started as an innocent flirtation and might result in a pleasant night was rapidly evolving into a meeting of minds. He had piqued her interest physically. He was now involving her intellectually.

''What was it, then?''

''No,'' he repeated. ''It wasn't Perry.'' He looked at her, well aware that he was encroaching upon her loyalty to the naval view of history. He studied her carefully, wondering how she would react to this new threat on her desires. Would she relegate him to the same place in her mind where she sent Paul Lansing? Would she fight her disbelief and disappointment to continue the assault on his libido? Or would she simply laugh at him?

Any way it worked out would be fine with him. Either he will have created a new contact or eliminated a minor distraction.

''Tell me,'' he said, ''have you ever heard of the ninja?''

8

The ninja were dead.

There were no ninja.

Long live the *hakujin*.

The *eta* ninja sat inside the clear walls of the Menilmontant sidewalk café and read the comic book.

If you want to know the true feelings and worth of any country, seek out their junk culture. Don't go to the museums or the theaters. That is a city's skin, a superficial restoration to fool you into thinking they're better than they are. That is entertainment, but it isn't true. It is makeup. Beneath that is the truth. See their blemishes, see their pimples, see their freckles and their pores.

See it in their movie theaters and bookstores. Watch it on their television. Beside the white ninja was a pile of magazines and newspapers. On the tiny square table was another pile, of large-size hardcover comics that looked like a child's second-grade reader. The trash ninja read the trash.

In his hands was something called *LeFlic (The Private Eye)*. Lying beside his small glass, and bottle of Red Saumer-Champigny, were volumes marked *Les Aventeurs des Fanni Hall, Metal Hurlant, Moebius,* and *La Marque Jaune.* At his feet were the four daily newspapers, a fashion magazine, a movie magazine, two television guides, and a *Lui* magazine.

"The pigeon stew?" asked the bald waiter in the nasal tone of this arrondissement. He held a chipped ceramic bowl by its thick, lacquered handle.

"Here," said Daremo, moving the book aside so the man could put the bowl and tablespoon down.

The twentieth arrondissement, known as Menilmontant, had a different, improved attitude in the daylight. The distrusting looks were replaced by the deadened sort of enjoyment all Parisians mastered, as well as a stubbornness missing from the apathetic upper class. Even this waiter gave the impression that a truck couldn't move him if he decided to take a stand.

Daremo took the moment to notice that the rest of the patrons inside the awning-covered, glass-enclosed bistro had their noses in books. Most were schoolbooks, and most of the diners were students. It made sense: Menilmontant was for the genteel impoverished. And who were more chicly impoverished than struggling university students? It was one of the last places that could claim any hope for producing talent near the level of Paris's glorious past.

Nearby, in the Père Lachaise Cemetery, Chopin, Balzac, Bizet, Sarah Bernhardt, and Isadora Duncan were decomposing. Here, many toiled to be worthy of their memory. Maybe someone in this very place would be responsible for leading Paris back to artistic glory. All their other great white hopes had moved to the countryside.

Daremo took another swig of the wine and set in on the stew. It had loads of stringy pigeon meat; small, round potatoes; squares of carrot; and tiny peas—all set in a rich, light brown gravy. That and the wine should keep him going for the next twenty-four hours. By then Cristobal might have something to show or tell him.

The going, not surprisingly, had been rough. Each tentative step in no-man's-land revealed more obstacles. Getting around one wall often revealed two more. Getting over one bridge only meant building another one . . . sometimes in several directions. Daremo let the Peruvian do it while keeping a sardonic distance.

He remembered Cristobal's concentrating, sweating face. He had never seen it look so alive. It gave truth to Daremo's theory that Cristobal had forgotten, or lost, his roots. A few decades in Paris could do that to a person. But Cristobal was reveling in his natural habitat now. He was back in the trenches, doing what he was famous for, and showing all the doubters why.

Daremo let him play. They had found a natural use for all the Hong Kong dollars smuggled in as filling for "down"-insulated winter coats. The transfer of clothing from Asia to France was now commonplace. Where once Paris had been the center of fashion, it was now just a stage—as the Schubert in New Haven had been a step on the road to Broadway. Paris was now but a step toward the true centers of Milan and Tokyo.

Where once clothes were made and exported from the City of Light, they were now made in Taiwan, Korea, and China, then imported here. What better way to launder HK dollars than to create yet another import clothing business? The bank managers hardly blinked when they received new masses of Asian money. They took it and ran, giving Cristobal thousands of francs in the process.

He then funneled this new money into the project, which he had nicknamed Pipeline. Gathering the necessary goods was not the major problem. He could get his hands on everything from toilet paper to Mercedes with relative ease. The problem was instituting a series of fail-safe methods to get them over boundary lines.

For each one created, he needed a backup. And for each backup an escape hatch. And for each escape hatch a safety valve. And so on. Then, once one system of interlocking channels of transport were set up, he'd set to work on another, in case the first had to be abandoned because of some border guard's conscience or a too attentive police officer.

All this took money. It was just like building a legitimate road. Once all the initial costs were estimated, hidden payoff and graft costs had to be wedged in. Customs people, law-enforcement officials, and simple folk who knew a little too much had to be greased.

Daremo let Cristobal do what he did best, all while maintaining an I-know-something-you-don't position and attitude. He let Cristobal slave, trying to keep the bottom line somewhere in the black, even if by a fraction. That was the only way the black marketeer would feel triumphant. Daremo would sit, drinking, eating, and reading in the cafés until the last possible second.

Only then, if and when all looked lost, would he come forward and tell Cristobal a little secret.

It didn't matter. Let the setup costs overrun. This was to be a onetime incursion. If Cristobal could erect something he could maintain after Daremo was gone, all the better. But for now Daremo didn't care if it was held together with spit and Scotch tape. As long as it held together until he was finished.

Daremo glanced over at the flashing machine in the corner of the café. Almost all the cafés he had seen had one of these things. He recognized them from his youth. It was pinball. Daremo smiled, knowing that the Pipeline Project was like a pinball machine. There was no real gambling involved. The player was throwing his money away just to play the game. There was no return on the investment.

Daremo chuckled and returned to his meal. It was such a pleasure to leave the gin behind for a while. The Tanqueray, imported from England, called to him, and he knew the call would grow more insistent with time, but for now he quieted his crying maw by pouring wine down it. On Cristobal's suggestion he stayed with the vintages during and before 1983, promising he would drink every bottle of the finer harvests in the city priced under fifteen dollars. There was a certain budget he had to adhere to before he heard from Hama.

Cristobal had laughed at the suggestion, while Daremo had simply smiled and kept drinking. Most people preferred the whites, so he went hog-wild for the reds and burgundies. He now brought two bottles home after a hard day of reconnaissance. A bottle of wine for him, and a bottle of Badoit or Contrex water for Rhea.

By the end of the first week after he had met Cristobal, she had hurled one of these wine bottles at him. She had slid it across the table so that it practically had burned through the air at his head.

He had caught it in one hand, his palm placed up against his face, then, miraculously, held his glass at arm's length to catch the spurt that had spilled.

He'd placed the bottle back on the table and drank the excess in one movement.

Rhea had started to stand, going at him with a table knife, but his feet had moved at the same moment. They stretched under the table, straight out, one foot going into her stomach, then pressing down on a thigh. The other went into her knee.

He sat her down. She landed hard on her rear and blinked. He placed his glass down on the side of her knife, pinning it to the tabletop.

"Don't like the vintage?" he had inquired.

"Wine!" she had spat. "I don't want to drink wine. I'm not a drunk like you!"

So he'd brought her water. He'd spent all day outside, and she'd spent all day inside, doing what he did, only on paper. While he looked, she read. He saw the actual buildings. She saw pictures of them, even after he decided it was safe enough for her to come out. There were enough tall Asians with American-style bodies here so she would not receive undue attention. But she refused.

She liked the hole she was in, as if leaving it would dissipate the heat that was building inside her. Daremo pictured her moving in the cellar apartment like a caged panther. He imagined her literally climbing the walls, using first her fingers and feet, then her legs, to propel her to a forty-five-degree angle with the floor.

She would run up the wall, somersault backward, and land on her feet. She would spin and kick. Even when she fell, she would do it soundlessly so the neighbors wouldn't complain. She would do it all day until she mastered the move, until her body was limber and fluid. Until she could do it with power and strength. Until she could mingle the speed and silence of the somersault with an equally savage, powerful kick.

She would practice until she could strike before her and behind. Up the wall to confuse an attacker, landing behind him. Kicking him down, then swinging the leg back or around to sweep a second attacker. And then still being serene and balanced enough to continue running or fighting.

During rests she would eat just enough to power her muscles, and read to power her mind. By the time she was through, she would know the city like a cabdriver. Daremo would amend the maps when he got home, so she would not be confused by a printer's mistake or a compiler's oversight. He was a finer cartographer than they.

And then they would sleep, side by side. She would lie on the bed as if he weren't there. But sometimes, in her sleep, she would reach for him and hold him. She would trust him in her unconscious and subconscious. When she woke, she would simply rise, neither continuing or commenting. Sometime during the day she would attack.

She sat in the cellar now, burning with a loving hatred.

No one who had ever loved her did not use her. She was their weapon. Daremo understood she was now trying to become her own.

He chuckled again, pouring the last of the wine. It was like a vicious satire of women's liberation.

Daremo brought the glass up to his lips. He looked beyond the bottom of the cup. He looked through the café's glass wall. He looked into the windows of the tiny cars moving by.

There is a theory that people who make trouble find trouble. That they serve as magnets for it. Daremo didn't believe that. He believed that the gods gathered, every moment of every day, and sought to entertain themselves. That they implanted obsessions and desires in different people and sent them hurtling toward each other just to see what would happen when they collided. Life as part of a gigantic, heavenly train set. He was just another toy soldier in the lords' army.

He saw a teenage girl and a teenage boy in a car. It wasn't so much an auto, really, but a yellow gumdrop on four play-wagon wheels. It moved around the corner and down the street among all the other bumper cars, its right side just in front of the bistro wall.

The boy was thin, with high cheekbones and sunken cheeks over narrow eyes, and a mop of black hair. His fingers gripped the steering wheel with white knuckles. His shoulders were hunched, and he sat heavily, his face in a stubborn, frowning rictus.

The girl wasn't giving him a chance to talk. Her rich lips were moving incessantly, set in a wide, lush face crowned by lustrous hair held in a thick ponytail by a rubber band. She wore a black beret.

In one hand she held a batonlike pipe. She pointed, jabbing, with the other hand. She was pointing at the sidewalk. Then she pointed to where the sidewalk turned at the corner of the street, emptying onto the black asphalt.

Daremo's gaze flitted longingly over the empty bowl and glass. He looked quickly around for any other way out. There wasn't enough time to get into the kitchen, and there might not be a door there. He was trapped. Now it was just a matter of reducing the odds, knowing that any decision he made had an equal chance of not working out.

He stood quickly, his hand in his pocket. He dumped money on the table, not wanting any waiter to interfere. He started toward the glass wall, keeping his eyes focused on the road beyond.

The girl wasn't giving the driver any choice. She twisted the screwlike cap on one end of the pipe. Daremo knew that it would break the thin metal disk inside the tube, allowing the corrosives to mingle.

There was no more time. He had to make an immediate choice.

He saw her hit the back of the driver's seat with an open palm. He saw her slide over to the right window. He saw her mouth open. He heard the word in his mind.

"*Allez!*" The French word for *go*. "*Vite!*" she cried, bringing up the pipe. *Quick.*

The café started to freeze as Daremo surged forward. It was not so much a run but a sudden explosion of energy, blasting his body toward the street. The waiter's arm was up, his mouth opening. The people at the table in front of him started to recoil, thinking he was attacking them. Heads started to turn, catching the blur in the corner of their eyes.

The little auto's wheels jumped the curb. The boy sent it speeding down the sidewalk. The girl leaned out the window, her arm up. She threw the pipe like it was a knife for a circus act. It spun in a long, lazy arc through the air, heading directly at Daremo's face.

There was no wall of glass in Daremo's mind. It was just more of the atmosphere to him. There was no gravity. His feet walked on air, the way they would on earth. He went over the table like a cannonball.

The diners fell back as the glass wall broke outward, spinning away from the man in gray and black. The pure force of his dive slapped them to the floor, the strength and speed of his movement making a silent thunderclap that knocked them down.

His feet were already moving toward a clear section of sidewalk. His right hand was already up. He caught the pipe on the other screwlike end. His fingertips felt the metal beginning to rend, like one of those cooked spicy sausages. Only this meat would be acid and belching flame.

His left foot landed on the concrete. His right leg stepped forward. He brought his arm down like a spearthrower, already twisting his body away as the glass fell around him in a crystal rain shower.

The pipe hurled back at the tiny car as if reflected there.

The girl's face was flushed with excitement and accomplishment. She pounded the back of the driver's seat with her open hands. They had done it. She hadn't felt like this since her time under the city streets when she had experienced *le grand jeté*.

She watched the road loom directly ahead of them. She didn't care now if any pedestrian appeared from around the corner. She would run him down and they would escape. They would spin onto the street and course down the avenue, away from the destruction. The sound of the breaking glass just thrilled her more. She waited for the orgasm of the explosion to fill her.

She did not hear the rear window of the car breaking at first. Instead she felt something at her sleeve, as if someone had swung at her and just missed. Then she felt the driver's seat jerk, as if someone had punched it. But finally she felt the insectlike bites on the back of her neck and heard the tinkle of the falling glass.

Then the bottom of the car opened up like the jaws of Satan, and the fires of hell swallowed her up.

Her scream mingled with the roar as the pipe bomb detonated. The little car jumped in place, the concussion pushing against the acceleration. The explosion nailed the undercarriage to the sidewalk for a second, bursting two tires. Then the vehicle husk hurtled forward, slashing across the road.

All four windows had blown outward, the glass carried by tongues of flame.

Daremo had just gotten to the opposite corner, his body twisting away from the splashing acids, when the Devil smiled across his side.

He hissed between suddenly clenched teeth. He slammed his back against the wall. He grabbed at the bottom of his jacket. He felt sweat beading on his face. He looked down.

The coat was ripped. His shirt was sliced. Under both, on his right side, from beneath his shoulder blade to just above his spleen, was the thin, red, wet grin of the demon.

Daremo's head went back, and he heard himself moan. It was a disembodied voice, coming from somewhere else. Then he felt the pain. His brain was faster than he was. It panicked before signaling him. He immediately let his jacket slip from his shoulders and across his arms. He grabbed it just before it fell to the sidewalk and pressed it against his right side.

He looked as he did it. Big mistake. He saw the Devil's smile widen, and the horrible teeth appear. He looked away quickly before the awful image could take hold. Before the orange haze filled his eyes, he saw the big piece of triangular glass on the sidewalk, one side of the pyramid coated in red.

The boomerang bomb. It came back and back and back again. A shard of glass from the car had spun right at him. It had done something no shuriken, ninja throwing star, had ever done. It had bitten, and bitten deep. He felt his head smack up against the wall. He felt his legs start to buckle.

The second explosion snapped him aware. He turned to look back around the corner. He saw the yellow gumdrop across the intersection, melting against a tree. It had smashed into the wooden trunk and set the branches alight. The entire thing was now a torch—its own funeral pyre.

Daremo thought he saw the balking, burning heads of the auto's occupants. The hair was the first to go. He thought he saw their flesh bubbling and melting. He thought he saw their skulls. He thought he saw their jaws open to laugh.

They were dead, so they knew the joke was on him.

Daremo started to turn away and collapse when an image froze in his mind's eye. It was the image of a man. A good-looking man in an expensive suit. He stood on a corner several streets away from the "accident." He looked at the devastation just like everyone else on the block.

But his face was different. He wasn't horrified and fascinated. His face was angry. His expression was hard and set. He was frustrated and infuriated. He was surprised.

Shit, Daremo thought, forcing his legs straight, trying to ignore the horrible twisting sensation inside him. He couldn't stay there. He couldn't slide to the street and wait for the ambulances. He couldn't sink into the ranks of the other wounded and marvel at their miraculous rescue.

That man had seen. The angry man in the fine suit knew. That man was not going to reward him.

Daremo let the rare sensations flow over him for a few seconds. It felt as if his mind were trying to escape through the top of his head. His brain was inflating. He felt the hands of the demons sinking deep into his internal organs and pulling. They held on, tugging, their feet kicking. He felt pins being pushed through every one of his pores from the inside.

How interesting, he told himself. He held his jacket tightly against his torso and took his first tentative step away.

9

Le Tenter's head spun around. He looked from the accident to the corner where the man had stumbled. The flames from the car wreck made it seem his hair was on fire. Yellow and white light flickered around his skull, giving him a glowing halo.

His face, however, was demonic. Memories of the girl's flesh made his fingers itch and twist. He could imagine her disintegrating under him now. He knew his dreams would be filled with that decaying imagery for weeks.

He was the only one in the growing crowd who looked away from the devastation. Only he looked at the entire picture. The man who had caught the pipe bomb, threw it back with a savage perfection, and ran, had not achieved very much.

Following in the explosion's wake were almost a dozen more accidents, as cars swerved to avoid the wreck and crashed into each other instead. One auto jumped the opposite sidewalk and hit a pedestrian. Another pedestrian had a heart attack.

The force of the detonation blew out the windows of several stores, slashing those inside. The other glass wall of the café was also knocked in by the bomb's force. Several diners were hurled down by the concussion, and others were hurt diving to the floor for protection.

Le Tenter made a quick survey. Almost everyone in the café was bruised or cut. People were sitting or lying on the floor of the stores, their faces bloody. Drivers and passengers were groaning, their noses broken by steering wheels and dashboards. He saw one woman holding her side, gasping, her ribs broken.

The man . . . the man in gray and black who had run . . . Le Tenter suddenly realized he had only caught and hurled the bomb to save himself—and himself only.

Le Tenter strode across the street, through the smoke of the car wrecks, toward the corner at the right of the café. He stopped just before it and took a last look back. The yellow car was unrecognizable. It was now just a smoking husk, the hungry flames eating out the last of its guts. The corpses lay across the seats in charred twists of burned bone.

Le Tenter slipped his hand into his jacket pocket. Slipping into his fingers was the Walther TPH. Its barrel length was only two inches, and it weighed only fourteen ounces without rounds. He kept only one .22-caliber long rifle bullet in the chamber. He clicked the safety off the small automatic's rear section and gripped it tightly.

His other hand went into his other jacket pocket where the small, rectangular clip was—filled with five other rounds. He put his front to the wall, brought both out, and slipped the magazine load into the belly of the small weapon. His large palm and long fingers hid the gun from view. He put his arms by his sides and stepped around the corner.

The only thing there was a tiny, almost negligible dot of splashed red.

His cuff, Le Tenter thought. The blood must have seeped through his pants. Only when he moved to escape did one tiny fleck come off his cuff.

Le Tenter glanced to the street. The triangular piece of glass with the red-splashed edge was now shattered. Le Tenter imagined the escaping man stepping down on it in some kind of mock vengeance, like a nonsmoker crushing a still lit cigarette as he passed.

Le Tenter looked down the street. He spotted the escaping man immediately. Try as he might to look casual amid the other pedestrians, his shoulders were hunched, his step was uneven, and he held his jacket to his side. To cap it off, he was the only one who didn't seem to care about the chaos around the corner.

Le Tenter grinned humorlessly, slipped the gun back into

his pocket, and walked quickly down the street after the man who had killed his latest lover.

The people who passed the hunched man pressing his jacket against his side mostly ignored his mutterings. One or two girls who were stuck by his tight, handsome face and steely eyes paused after he had passed to wonder whether he was in shock or something.

As he went farther down the street more and more people made way for him, thinking he was some sort of strange beggar. Pedestrians the world over had learned to ignore studiously the ravings of muttering street people. No one understood the intense man or the strained, quiet words he was babbling.

He was speaking in Japanese.

"In this book of fire," Daremo was reciting intently to himself, "I describe fighting as fire." They were the words of Miyamoto Musashi. It was the *Book of Five Rings*.

It was the thing that kept Daremo going. If he could concentrate on the words, maybe he could understand their hidden meanings. Maybe he could finally see beyond the letters to the truth. Maybe he could ignore the demons taking huge hunks of his insides and stuffing them between their shark teeth.

"Let the contest be decided as with the folding fan."

Where was he? Menilmontant. Twentieth arrondissement. Many kilometers northeast of the Seine.

"Learn such trifles as hand and leg movements."

Where could he go? Home. Just a few kilometers away. Into the pit, where he could rest . . . or die.

"The training for killing is by way of many contests."

How could he get there? Walk. Stumble. Crawl, if he had to.

"Fighting for survival, discovering the meaning of life and death."

Don't die here. Mustn't die here. Must reach nothingness. Must reach his Rhea: his own personal void. He couldn't die without her knowing. He couldn't cheat her of that.

"The way of strategy is the sure method to win when fighting for your life . . ."

Let him die in front of her, with her. Let her take what solace she could. Let her go on.

"... against one man or one thousand...."

The man. The man who had seen him. The man who supervised the terrorist attack on the café. He would be coming after him. Daremo's lips quivered. Let him come, his mind thought. Let him see what he could do against the woman.

No.

He was a professional. He would follow Daremo, kill him if death didn't claim the ninja master first, then report to his associates. They would watch Rhea for weeks. They might kill her in such a way that she could not fight back. A bomb in a restaurant, a theater, a store, a plane, or the apartment building itself.

"One man can beat ten, a thousand men can beat ten thousand."

Lose this guy. Dump him. Get rid of him. Die in Rhea's arms. Let her puncture her hated loved with the Hanzo Razors. Let her perforate him. Let his blackened soul escape through hundreds of holes.

Daremo stopped. Le Tenter was surprised, stopping in mid-step some thirty feet behind him. Daremo stood straight.

Hsing-I. He had been studying it for years while Hama and then Yasuru had been searching for him. His expression was one of distaste, his lips curling. His head was forward on a straight neck and back. His muscles were tensed. He still held his jacket tightly against his right side, but his left arm was moving.

His left fingers were curled, except for the forefinger, which was straight up, every joint slightly twisted. Le Tenter watched, fascinated, as the arm made smooth, complex patterns in the air. For a moment it seemed the escaping man was trying to maintain balance, but then Le Tenter saw that his feet were planted like lead weights.

Breathe, Daremo told himself. Not just breathe. Push the air into every part of the body. Fill the body with power. Become the air itself. Become part of the atmosphere. Take life from the environment.

Use the force, Luke.

China had the secret centuries before *Star Wars*. It was their internal kung fu systems. T'ai chi ch'uan had been turned into a harmless morning ritual, but Pa Kua and Hsing-I were still esoteric, obscure, and powerful.

"Become free of self," Musashi had said, "and realize extraordinary ability. Come to possess miraculous power."

Le Tenter watched in amazement as the escaping man reached out with his left hand, grabbed a curtain bunched on a shop window, and pulled it off with a tug. He snapped it out, letting the dust fly off. He then threw it over his shoulder.

He let his right hand drop. Le Tenter saw the long, bleeding wound, like a coat of red paint, being poured over his side. The escaping man ripped his shirt off with his left hand. He pushed it against his side and wrapped the curtain around it. Then he put his jacket back on and started walking again.

Le Tenter was impressed. The shopowner didn't even know of the vandalism. The escaping man hadn't wasted a movement. It was tight, purposeful, and direct. What had this last lovely terrorist revealed to her Tempter?

Much of the man's hate left his mind, replaced instead with a certain thrill. It was the excitement of a consummate artist discovering another worthy of his talent. It was the inspiration of a bored master leaving behind the mediocre opposition for a possible equal. Le Tenter continued the chase.

Daremo walked forward, keeping his legs moving steadily and evenly so his body would not rise and fall with each step. He felt his top lip stuck to the top of his teeth. He felt his teeth clenched.

He felt his mind flying back through history. He was a Chinese warlord. He was a Chinese demigod of the Peking Opera who would push his own intestines back into his sliced body, tie them in, and fight on for hours more.

He buttoned his jacket closed with his left hand, keeping his right flat on his side, putting as much pressure as he could on the wound. He imagined he looked jaunty now, in a sick sort of way.

The man was following him. He could feel it. What would Musashi have him do?

"If the enemy can be seen, keep the fire behind you."

Fine. The fire was behind him.

"You must look down on the enemy."

Fine. Who'd you steal that suit from? Where did you get that crummy haircut? What book you learn to tail from? *How to Pick Up Girls*?

"Chase him toward awkward places. Try to keep him with his back to awkward places."

Now you're talking. Daremo kept up the feverish pace until he saw the green metal archway and railings of the Menilmontant Métro station. He moved across the street and to the steps, where his body balked. No way he was going to get down those stairs without his pancreas and kidneys falling out.

Daremo placed his buttocks on the center banister of the steep stairway and raised his feet. He slid down the stairwell with the left side of his body and landed on his left leg. He kept walking quickly to cushion the shock of landing. He allowed himself to slow naturally so he could come to a comfortable stop before the glassed-in cashier in the little room recessed into the left wall.

The money was in his right pocket. The cashier couldn't understand why the man with the tight smile started sweating, his skin turning white when he reached into his pocket. But he gave her the coins. She handed him the ticket and he walked stiffly on. The cashier checked the cash carefully.

Daremo had felt his skin tear. He had felt his organs stretch. Little red pin bursts obscured his vision. He found his left shoulder sliding along the tile walls toward the platform entrances. He straightened in time to slip his ticket into the turnstile and walk through, picking up the ticket when it stuck out the other side of the machine like a little yellow tongue.

Le Tenter already had a weekly ticket and closed much of the gap between them at the turnstiles. He was curious which entrance the escaping man would take. Daremo turned down the northbound corridor. Le Tenter followed dutifully, both men emerging in a hangarlike room.

There were two platforms, one on each side of the space. Down the middle were two subway tracks. The station walls were covered in beige tiles and coated with huge billboard advertisements for department store sales and movies coming soon. It was light, spacious, and clean.

Men in suits, women in dresses, students in jeans, and children in down outfits were milling around in groups. A large, glassed-in room was at the very end of the platform, where men in uniform shirts and ties labored over schedules, lighted wall maps, and microphones.

Daremo ran into a trash can. He held on to the robot-size refuse receptacle with both hands. It bothered him. He hadn't seen it. He was becoming faint or going blind. He felt his side covered in his own body fluid. He felt it coating his belt and pants. He imagined it darkening his jacket. He dared not look down.

But now, relatively still, he heard the sodden noises with every slight move. He felt the blood at his wrists where his gloves ended. He felt how wet his right sock was. People weren't staring at him, so he hoped the stains made his dark pants look fashionably two-toned, like denims that were a purposeful combination of gray and black.

Le Tenter stood near the entrance to the platform. He looked around. No one was paying the escaping man any notice. The man was standing against a garbage can, his back to him, so no one might see Le Tenter walk toward the escaping man. He could use the escaping man's own body to block anyone else's view as he pumped two bullets into the back of the man's skull.

Some might hear the pop of the .22 automatic, but when they turned around, all they'd see is the falling man. They couldn't help noticing his wound, so by the time the police arrived, most would have chalked the popping sounds up to natural station noises.No doubt they'd let the overwhelming visual evidence say he was knifed.

Once the bullet wounds were discovered, it would be too late to retrace the investigation.

It would work. Le Tenter had no doubt of it. Maybe then the dead girl would not scream at him in his dreams. Maybe she would come to him and murmur thanks, swirling against his mind with love. She would rest in peace, knowing that what she did was a strike for equality.

Le Tenter took a last look around and put his hand in his right pocket. He wrapped his fingers around the trustworthy TPH. He walked forward. The escaping man's back grew larger and larger in his vision. He heard a train coming in on this side, and an announcement over loudspeakers that there was no need to crowd—another train would be in momentarily.

Perfect. The noise would even cover the automatic's pops. He had done this sort of thing before. He could strike and walk away. Even if someone looked directly at him, he would be safe. Eyewitness descriptions were rarely good enough, and most everyone stared at the victim, not the assassin.

Le Tenter closed in, the gun coming out of his pocket. He was ten feet away. Then seven. At five the gun would be out. At three he would point. At two he would fire.

He was staggered when the escaping man turned and started walking at four.

The gun was out, but Daremo ignored it. He had turned toward the opposite end of the platform, at a thirty-degree angle from the gunman, and walked past him. He looked at Le Tenter as he went by, his face expressionless.

To all the world he seemed like a man without a care. He walked to the center of the wall opposite the glassed-in station office and put his back against it. He looked passively at the gunman.

Le Tenter slipped the gun back into his jacket pocket, stunned. The escaping man was daring him to kill, wound and all. He was challenging Le Tenter to a duel of nerve. Could he shoot him face-to-face? Would he take the risk of being seen?

The escaping man was some distance from anyone else. Le Tenter's back would be to the others if he shot him that way. Then all he'd have to do was walk to the stairs a few feet away. Up and out, as simple as that. And he'd have the satisfaction of seeing the escaping man's expression.

A clean, wide, metal Métro train on thick plastic wheels came into the station on the southbound side.

Le Tenter took a step toward the escaping man.

Daremo's right fist clenched twice in rapid succession. The swords shot out from his sleeve, the click of them locking in place over his knuckles drowned by the braking train.

Le Tenter stiffened. He would not be able to get within five feet of the escaping man without being gored.

His right hand almost came out of his jacket. He almost decided to shoot him from there.

Daremo smiled. Then he walked to his left, just as the northbound train appeared.

Le Tenter watched, stunned, at the escaping man's perfect timing and bravado. He reached the station platform lip just as the northbound train stopped. The escaping man kneeled down and slipped off the platform behind the last car.

Le Tenter looked behind him, at the glassed-in office. The Métro officials were studying their maps and charts. No one looked at the end of the train. Le Tenter looked back. The escaping man was gone.

Daremo nearly collapsed when his feet hit the tracks, jarring his body. He could have landed as lightly as he wanted, and it would have made no difference. His organs jumped, and the wound yawned wider. He felt himself hit the back of the train. The metal was harder than flesh-covered bone, making no sound.

"Look down on your enemy!" Musashi shouted. "Keep his back to awkward places!"

That, and his use of the advice, woke Daremo up. He wouldn't want to die just yet. What, and miss all the juicy irony? Thankfully his feet kept moving without the help of his conscious mind.

Le Tenter moved quickly to where the escaping man had jumped. He saw the escaping man going past the stopped northbound train to the front of the southbound train on the other side. His hand almost came out of his pocket again, but then the escaping man moved his left leg out, and stepped into the mouth of the tunnel.

He was gone. If The Tempter wanted to kill him now, he'd have to climb down onto the tracks himself. He looked toward the office. A Métro official was staring directly back at him.

Le Tenter swallowed and looked at the track again. What could he do? Call the official? Stop the trains? What good would that do? The escaping man would still elude him.

Le Tenter looked up helplessly, into the escaping man's reappearing face. He had leaned back out of the tunnel. He looked directly at the Tempter. He smiled wider.

Both trains started moving. When they had left the station, Le Tenter waited until the disembarking passengers had gone up the stairs and he was alone on the platform. He walked slowly toward the glassed-in office where the same official was still watching him curiously.

Three quarters of the way down the platform, Le Tenter stopped, turned, and looked. From this angle he could see the tunnel entrance as if it were a whale's mouth.

Jonah was gone. Swallowed up by the beast. Le Tenter smiled grimly. There was only one thing to take solace in. Grabbing on to the front of that southbound train must have cost him dearly.

10

I

Paul Lansing was greatly impressed and flattered when T. H. Cerveau came to his office. That was not to say it wasn't a lovely office. A trifle cramped, of course, but with plenty of head room. And what the office itself lacked, the building and area more than made up for.

True, his dirty office window displayed nothing but the

gray stone wall of the building next door, but the windows in the main halls were something else again. The building was nestled in the corner between the Esplanade des Invalides and the Palais-Bourbon, near the Ministrie des Affairs Etrangères.

The location would take anyone's breath away. The Invalides, a gigantic high-art compound, was built to welcome and house the wounded, back from the Louis XIV wars in 1676. The Palais-Bourbon was Paris's Senate, while the Ministrie was the Foreign Affairs Department.

There was more sculpture, magnificent architecture, landed gentry, and politicians that you could shake a crutch at. It was the center for all espionage activity in the City of Light. Every fifth person was probably a spy.

Napoleon hardly seemed impressed, however. No sooner had he appeared in the doorway than he spoke. "Let's take a walk."

That was fine with Lansing. The area was gorgeous. They were near the Quai d'Orsay, where barges and pleasure boats drifted by all day and all night. In front of every building was a park and statues. On every building were sculptures, columns, gables, and intricate wrought iron. Behind every building was a courtyard. In every courtyard was a garden.

And around it all were shops stuffed with riches. Lansing was always pleased to explore the neighborhood and look at the women. The most beautiful women in Paris were here, attracted, like all women, to money and power.

Like all men as well, as a matter of fact.

"Ms. Hemphill asks after you," said Napoleon.

"Who?" Lansing turned back to his associate, letting the round blonde go by.

"The woman you chased at the party."

"Chased away. Too obvious, remember?" Lansing's head swiveled after a redhead. "Probably not natural," he said, sniffing. "Asked about me, did she. What did she ask? Whether I had AIDS?"

Napoleon grinned and shook his head. "Where has the

language gone? Asked after you, Paul. Not about you. It means she inquired as to your health.''

"See?" Lansing retorted. "AIDS again. I'm fine. Don't I look it?"

They walked by the Alexander III bridge, with its astonishingly ornate lamps and overstuffed sculptures of chubby naked men and women preparing to jump into the Seine.

"You look . . . forlorn," Napoleon responded.

Lansing inhaled with a snort. "You'd look forlorn, too, if you had my job. Reduced to little better than a paperboy." He put his arms out. "But what a route, eh?"

"'Into their gray the subtle spies of color creep,'" Napoleon quoted. "John Freeman," he explained to the startled CIA man.

"You make me sick," said Lansing.

"That's why I get the big bucks," said Napoleon, walking ahead. "Maybe some of them can come from you."

Lansing caught up quickly. "I was hoping that was it. No wonder you didn't call me to your place."

Napoleon held up a finger. "It's not a fait accompli yet."

"I was afraid of that. What do you want?"

Napoleon acted innocent, his hands up. "What else? A sign of faith."

"Oh," Lansing said knowingly. "So that's what this is all about. How much do you need, what kind, and in what denominations?"

"Not money."

"Not money?" Lansing echoed incredulously. "You don't need women. What, then?"

"I told you. A show of faith. I don't want to wind up in an office pushing classified papers around, spending all my time getting permission to see FYEO." For Your Eyes Only. "I want to know I will have access to the information I'll need to make comprehensive decisions."

"What can I say?" asked his confused companion. "What will satisfy you? A letter? A-Level clearance?"

"Just talk to me, Paul. Tell me a secret. . . ."

II

Le Tenter had stalked into Napoleon's office by one of the three secret routes. They couldn't have the nest of Paris spies taking pictures of all who entered, now could they? The photos might be fed into their overstuffed computers, and some very disturbing conclusions might come vomiting out.

The route Le Tenter had taken started across the street. He went down stairs to a courtyard, which emptied into the cellar of an office building. Only by walking through certain disused rooms beneath the street could he emerge in the basement of Napoleon's building. Then he took the back stairs to the third floor and entered the office complex through a side door.

He had signaled Napoleon as to his arrival with the beeper on his belt. He had placed the Walther TPH in a small basket on an otherwise empty desk. He knew it would be thoroughly cleaned by the time he returned, fingerprints and all. The barrel might be replaced or rebored. He never saw the people who did it, and they never saw him. It was safer that way.

Napoleon had closed the shutters and pulled the drapes in the meantime. He turned to his desk the moment Le Tenter entered, who was already angrily reporting. Napoleon sat and listened wordlessly until the facts ended and the opinions started.

"It is infuriating," Le Tenter said, seething. "There were weeks more use to be made of this one. Maybe months. She was beautiful yet innocuous. She could go anywhere. She would be looked at longingly as she passed, then forgotten. And if not forgotten, no one would ever tell the authorities about her. They would remember her with pleasure and stay silent—"

"As, perhaps, you should do," Napoleon said, interrupting with quiet strength.

Le Tenter looked at him from a red leather chair. His fingers gripped the arm tighter for just a second, then he leaned back and relaxed.

"Of course," he said with humor. "You are right. But it was good this time. Better than ever. A real connection. Rare."

"No," Napoleon disagreed. "Not rare. Not anymore. She was not special. You are. She is just another French girl. Empty, waiting to be filled in body and mind. It is you who are rare. It is you who is special. You are . . . becoming" —Le Tenter laughed with pleasure—"ever more proficient at the task assigned you," Napoleon maintained. "You are doing well and getting better."

"But there was something . . ." Le Tenter complained wistfully.

"Her body was better," Napoleon interjected. "She responded more. But that was in response to your sharpening skills. Certainly you will miss her. You were looking forward to her warmth and firmness. You are disappointed. But do not confuse that with her limited use. Warmth and firmness are out there in abundance. You are simply loath to seek it out so quickly."

Le Tenter immediately saw the truth in his statements. "I will not settle," he concurred. "Each reconnaissance must be done with consummate skill. It cannot be rushed. It cannot be forced."

"He stole a masterpiece of your work from you," Napoleon explained. "Not irreplaceable, but the arduous process must start again. He threw off your forward progress."

"He stopped it!"

"Not stopped," Napoleon countered. "Never stopped." But then the man at the desk became philosophic. "The young man—that driver—would have had to be eliminated, at any rate. He would have complicated the situation no matter what had happened."

"Yes," Le Tenter agreed, contemplative. "And there is no true way of gauging her reaction to his death. I could have controlled her, certainly."

"Certainly."

"But . . ." Le Tenter segued back to his anger. "Now we will never know *how* she would have reacted!"

Napoleon nodded. "A necessary test canceled."

"I want him!" Le Tenter snapped, leaning forward. "I want the one responsible!"

"So do I," Napoleon replied, rubbing his chin thoughtfully. "So do I."

III

Paul Lansing grinned, stopping on the sidewalk. "What do you need to know?" He liked this. It gave him a feeling of power over his envied associate.

"Tell me what you think," Napoleon countered, using Lansing's own words from the party. "Maybe you can make some sense of this. There seems to be a wild card in the deck." He started walking again, and Lansing kept up with him.

"Where?"

"Here."

"More."

Napoleon told him. He described a man of great observational and physical skills. A man of impressive intestinal fortitude as well. A man with tremendous command of strategy, even under the most trying of circumstances. A man of cunning, daring, and wit.

"James Bond," said Lansing.

"He has scriptwriters," Napoleon retorted without pause.

"Not very good ones anymore," Lansing muttered. "Can you be more specific?"

"There was an accident in town yesterday," Napoleon said carefully.

Lansing straightened. "Yes?"

"What do you know about it?"

"What do you?"

"The man was there."

Lansing started to smile. "Oh, yeah?"

"Yes."

"You wouldn't happen to have a description of this . . . man, would you?"

Napoleon thought carefully. He considered all the ramifications of revealing more. But Lansing's tone seemed sarcastic, almost goading. It wasn't like him. It wasn't like him at all.

Napoleon capsulized Le Tenter's description. "About six feet. Slim. Tightly muscled. Copper-colored hair in a crew cut. Steel-gray eyes."

Paul Lansing stopped dead in his tracks. He stared at Napoleon with wide eyes and slack jaw. Napoleon saw an ominous cloud pass over his features, but then the man started laughing. He turned and walked away, waving his arms.

"That's great! That's rich! You really suckered me in on that one. Where are we eating? You owe me a lunch."

Napoleon strode after him and took him by the arm. He turned Lansing to face him. "What is the joke?"

Lansing looked at him and his laughter died. A smile stayed on his face, however, as he carefully removed his arm from Napoleon's hand. "Enough," he said. "The joke is on me. I'll tell you, I never expected such reverse subtlety from you. You're the last person I would have expected this from." He looked around. "Is there a good restaurant here?"

"Paul," Napoleon said seriously, "I promise you, I'm confused. I don't understand what you're telling me."

Lansing looked at him carefully. Then the light went on over his head, his eyes widened, and his teeth showed. "That's it, then. They got *you*! The great T. H. E. Cerveau is sucked in by the oldest one in the book!"

"What are you talking about?" Napoleon asked, mesmerized.

"Who told you this?"

"What?"

Lansing stretched out each word, as if talking to a toddler. "Where did you get your description?"

Napoleon rolled over his own pause. "A trusted contact."

"Yeah, right," said Lansing. "Well, stop trusting him. He has just described to you the greatest operative in the world."

"Who?" Napoleon almost shouted.

"Moe Dare," said Paul Lansing.

"Who?" It was a question this time.

Paul Lansing started walking down the street. "The greatest espionage operative ever known. The finest mind, the toughest body, the most amazing fighter, the most brilliant strategist, and the most accomplished assassin in the world." He finished with a satire of Sean Connery. "His name is Dare. Moe Dare."

"Who is he?" Napoleon demanded.

Lansing was more than happy to oblige, rolling each word off his tongue individually. "No one."

"I beg your pardon?"

"He doesn't exist!" Lansing trumpeted. "I don't know who started it, but I'm pretty sure it came from the central agency in Washington—D.C., that is."

"It?"

"It. You know. You ever have one of those assignments where everything goes right and you don't know why? You think you've just stuck your face into the world's deepest shithole and you come out smelling like roses?" Napoleon nodded. "Well, they've come up with a reason. Moe Dare is watching you."

"Moe Dare . . ."

"The man who can do no wrong," Lansing said, hooting. "The undefeated, unstoppable, unbelievable, nonexistent Moe Dare." He looked upon his associate with pity. "It's been an in-house joke for months now. It's the biggest thing since pet rocks and Irangate. Things go wrong and you can't explain it? Blame gremlins. Things go right and you can't explain it? Blame Moe Dare." Lansing looked up at his comrade sympathetically and patted him on the arm. "You've been right and truly screwed, old son. Somebody's been pulling your leg, your nose, your ass, and your dick, pal. Now, where do we eat?"

IV

Napoleon walked slowly back to his office, a distance of nearly two kilometers. He passed the magnificent Tuileries, the huge courtyard with the sculpted, interlocking lawns dotted with flower beds and Maillol statues. He passed the Musée du Jeu de Paume and the Place Vendôme. He hardly noticed them. Lansing's words kept echoing in his ears.

"Get off it, friend. There's a major explosion on a Paris street. Okay, could be a terrorist attack gone crazy. Could be a sniper bullet hitting a gas tank, accidentally or no. Could be the hand o' God itself smashing down two naughty nasties. It makes no difference! Any way you look at it, nobody knows squat about the thing.

"So along comes your buddy, all slick and aiming to please, who feeds you this line about Superman descending from the skies and saving the day. Maybe he was kidding, I don't know. Maybe he thinks you know the joke and will guffaw along with him. But you go off and start investigating the whereabouts of Clark Kent. I'm telling you, T. H., it's Moe Dare!''

So Napoleon laughed, made light of himself, and let Lansing take potshots at him all during lunch. So now the CIA man had a new story deflating the great Cerveau for the next coffee break, and Napoleon had all the information he could scrape from the annoying loser between insults.

"I told you before," he had said. "I don't know where it started. It's like the man who never was, all right? All I know, and I'm not sure about this, is that it started in the U.S. Probably in Washington."

"How would I know who used it first? Some guy with something to hide. Some guy who wanted to prove how humble he was. Some guy who was working when he should have been screwing his best friend's wife. How should I know? Who am I? The Amazing Kreskin?"

Napoleon let it be. He marched into his building and up the stairs. Le Moissonner was waiting for him. He was sitting at the desk, spreading pâté from a can onto crackers.

"Where did you get that?" Napoleon asked.

"Brought it with me," said the Reaper, popping one in his mouth. "Wanted to know what the attraction was."

"Find out?" Napoleon came around the desk, waving him away.

Le Moissonner gathered up his lunch and moved to the red leather chair the Tempter had sat in. "Nope. Tasty, though. You look like you just ate a bad oyster. Coffee making you irritable, bunky?"

Napoleon looked across the desk at his most trusted associate. Scratch that. He looked at the man he had the most faith in. He trusted no one. "I've always believed that all legend has its basis in fact," he said.

"Wow," said the Reaper. "That's a surprise."

Napoleon couldn't help but smile and bite. "What?" he prompted.

"I never thought you believed anything. Just didn't disbelieve." He ate another cracker.

"Just goes to show you can always learn."

"That's the other thing you've always believed," Le Moissonner reminded him. "Learn or die."

Napoleon nodded, considering it. "What are you doing here?" he asked suddenly.

"Basking in your glory," the Reaper answered without a blink. "You think I like hanging around in dives? 'Ill company is like a dog, who dirts those most whom he loves best.'"

"Jonathan Swift," Napoleon identified. "'Learning makes a man fit company for himself.'"

"Who?" the Reaper asked quickly.

"Thomas Fuller."

The Reaper slapped himself on the forehead. "Of course!"

"How did it go?"

The Reaper smiled widely. "'Drawing near her death, she sent most pious thoughts as harbingers to heaven; and her soul saw a glimpse of happiness through the chinks of her sickness-broken body.'"

Napoleon's smile matched his associate's. "Thomas Fuller," he said.

"Bingo," said the Reaper.

Hard to believe, Napoleon thought. Quotes aside, they had created the greatest espionage unit in modern times. Yes, Lansing or any of his spook buddies would get quite a shock if they had the ability to effectively stake out this location. Their bugs and cameras would record dozens of visitors. And if their computers could strip off the disguises and hear through the building's audio mufflers and masks, they'd realize that every visitor was a "retired" secret agent.

Somewhere in their files was Napoleon's case history. More than twenty years of exceptional service. Instrumental in the Camelot administration. Shamed by the right-wing coup d'état in the early sixties. Resurrected to power through Watergate manipulations. Helpful in the "Mod-Con" government takeover. "Retired" after arguing vehemently against Irangate. Not doing it—but how it was done. As "pasteurized" as a well-known, well-liked expert on strategy.

The Reaper was his right-hand man. Already an Olympic marksman, he came under Napoleon's supervision after rejecting the "Grassy Knoll" assignment. When the smoke cleared after the ramifications thereof, he was still standing while everyone else involved was six feet under.

Spent the next decade lying low while his history was being erased. Only came out a few times as a "Loose Ender." He cleaned up the messes zealots made, making sure there was nothing left for the public to know. He emerged from the underground as a "Nowhere Man." A thorough search of secret files would now uncover nothing.

"I think I've become the doctor," the Reaper told his superior. Doctor meant DR, which signified the Law of Diminishing Returns. "I'm on the line, boss." That was the assembly line. He had gone to the edge of the envelope.

Napoleon smiled at him knowingly. "There is something to be said for even that, my friend. Perhaps we'll see how long you can stay on the line without a diminishing of quality."

"Indefinitely," the Reaper promised casually. "Though we may run out of product." Their extraordinary indifference to human life was compelling. Any visitor would have thought they were talking about stereos. "Or quotes," the Reaper finished.

He could always get Napoleon to laugh. "You're right, of course," he said afterward. "Use your own discretion." He knew he could trust the man with such power. The Reaper, like all the others, was a person of infinite control and no human perversions.

"As the muse strikes me, eh?" the Reaper responded, eating the last of the pâté. He placed the remaining crackers in a perfect pile on the nearby table by putting them carefully on top of one another. "What's the matter, bunky? Can't think of a topper?"

"Of course I can!" Napoleon snapped. "It's not that. It's just . . ."

"Yes?"

"What's the point?" Napoleon finally answered.

The Reaper looked around. "Is there an echo in here? Where have I heard that before? Oh, wow, déjà vu."

Napoleon laughed again. "Stop. All right, I admit it. It's the same old song."

"But with a different meaning now that you've been gone," finished the Reaper.

"Surprisingly, yes," Napoleon told him. "I've proven my point several times over. A red lightning bolt with the letters CCCP could strike the Washington Monument tomorrow, and it would be like nothing happened the day after."

"Yes, yes, yes," the Reaper chided in a singsong voice. "I know the tune. Espionage isn't espionage anymore. The game for adults has become a child's game."

"And what's the difference?" Napoleon asked, testing him.

"No stakes," the assassin said immediately. "A child's game has no stakes."

"We used to struggle for peace," Napoleon mused. "We have peace. So no struggle."

"The Palestinians will be happy to hear that," the Reaper wisecracked.

"You know what I mean," Napoleon countered. "Today there is only existence or total destruction. Whatever anyone does will not change that. I—we—have proven it time and time again."

He . . . they . . . had destroyed things. Huge things. Civilian things. They did it in a way that it would seem like an accident. They did it in a way that the word *sabotage* was never even breathed in the media. They did it in a way that the government had to scramble to keep the public from knowing the truth.

"Oh, I get it," said the Reaper, standing. "More existential angst, is it?" He walked over to the desk, pointing down at his mentor. "That's your problem, you know that? Everything has to have a purpose for you. Things just can't *be*."

Napoleon smiled up at him. "I imagine they have this same argument in heaven."

The Reaper turned in disgust. "I imagine there is no heaven. No gods arguing. Just a freak accident of biology and then nothing."

"We are given rational thought," said Napoleon, "so we seek to give purpose to existence."

"Not we," said the Reaper, turning back. "*You*."

Napoleon leaned back, his hands behind his head. "That's why I get the big bucks."

"Okay, okay," said the Reaper, putting up his hands and returning to his seat. "I give up. What's on your mind, o vaulted one?"

Napoleon leaned forward and mingled his fingers on the desktop. "I have something new planned," he assured his associate. "Nothing quite as grand as our previous exercises, but this one has a new wrinkle."

"Oh, goody," said the Reaper. "What is it?"

"A deadline."

The Reaper whistled. "They're not going to like that." These people were used to plying their trade with no time-clock.

"Tough bushwah," said Napoleon. "They have achieved the ultimate several times over. They are becoming jaded. They need a new challenge."

The Reaper considered it. "All right. I'll buy that for a dollar. What's the deal?"

"Oh, no," said Napoleon, "not yet. There's another factor."

"Which is?"

"A legend," said the man behind the desk. "The world's greatest assassin."

The Reaper's eyes narrowed. "*I'm* the world's greatest assassin."

"Perhaps. That is, if this legend doesn't exist."

The bastard, the Reaper thought. He's enjoying this magic-mirror-on-the-wall routine.

"Come on," the Reaper demanded. "Cough it up."

"The Tempter saw him."

"That psycho?" the Reaper muttered.

"The pot calling the kettle," Napoleon said mildly. "Psycho or no, he doesn't hallucinate. The legend is in this city. . . and he's wounded."

The Reaper thought about it, frowned, then twisted his lips up into a wide smile. "Sounds good. Better than singing to old ladies."

Napoleon had a quick look of distaste. "You find him, *ma moissonner*. You put him to ground. Then we shall know who's the fairest of them all."

The Reaper stood. " 'The lion is not so fierce as painted,' " he quoted from Thomas Fuller.

"Prove it," said Napoleon. He told the assassin all he knew and sent him on his way. He had other things to do. He picked up the phone and put a call into Admiral Seaworth's office.

His people had proven his point several times over. While he waited for the Paris phone lines to wheeze into action, he fingered the embossed design on his stationery. It was a silver lighting bolt in the shape of an uncurled *S*. But only the sharpest eye could see the two thin lines of gold dissecting it. It turned the lightning bolt into three lightning bolts, side by side by side.

It made the design into three striking *S*'s.

The Secret Secret Service.

"Jennifer Hemphill, please." He was put on hold.

Anyone clever enough to look *and* see would realize that all his contacts were retired espionage operatives who shared one thing. They were sickened by the state of the industry. They spent all their agency time on political infighting.

And what for? It all came down to whether the button was pushed or not. And if it was, who would be left to care? It rendered the entire process into a tired, stupid joke.

And Napoleon had proven it to the selected few. They would play the game by the right rules, he promised. They were the elite. They should be treated as such.

"Hello?"

Napoleon spoke to the admiral's office manager. He invited her to dinner, which she graciously accepted, knowing she would have to break another date. But she was certain it would be worth it.

They decided the time and place and went back to work.

If espionage was a game, it should be played as such. Only the pawns would be real. Napoleon had put meaning back into his employees' lives. They were the finest agents their countries had to offer. They were united in their own excellence. They lived by their own unique code of honor. Secret honor.

There had been only one other group of people as dedicated and as expert.

Napoleon looked forward to his dinner with Ms. Hemphill. He wanted to talk more about the ninja.

11

I

Daremo was astonished when he woke up. There was the split second of horror when he saw the concrete an inch from his eyes, but he realized that coffins and morgue walls weren't made of cement—even in Paris.

The second shock came when he tried to move. He felt glued down. That wasn't the shock. The shock was what he was glued down with. He rested in a dried pool of his own blood.

He didn't remember falling off the Métro train. He didn't remember moving to the wall on the other side of the tracks. He didn't remember lying down, wound side up, still holding the shirt tightly on the cut.

"The three methods to forestall the enemy," he said to himself, maybe just to prove he could still talk. He tried to bring his legs up.

"Ken No Sen; forestall him by attacking." Daremo had confronted the man in the Métro station. "Tai No Sen; forestall him as he attacks." Daremo laughed inside, remembering the man's face when Daremo's arm sword came shooting out. "Tai Tai No Sen; you and the enemy attack together."

Daremo's legs scraped the rock and refuse-covered dirt. His left hand clawed a the tile-and-dirt wall. He started to crawl up it. He concentrated all his energy into his fingers, knees, and feet. He pushed with one, pulled with the other. He was alone in the darkness.

He didn't know how long it took him, but no other Métro train passed as he toiled. When he could see clearly again, his left hand was sandwiched between the wall and his face. The fingertips were right in front of his eyes. The nails were cracked and bleeding.

Daremo tried to laugh. What was a little more blood between friends? At least he still had blood to bleed.

He needed a drink.

He turned so his left side was against he wall. He let his head fall back. There was a small circle of light somewhere above him.

Maybe he *was* dead. Maybe this was purgatory, and the white above was a crack in heaven. One way or another, he would have to find out. But he wasn't about to let his right hand off his side. If he *wasn't* dead, he didn't want to feel that pain again.

He started to put his left arm out, slowly. He reached for the light with his left hand. He didn't get it. His hand started shaking and fell against the wall. Instinctively the fingers clutched, and there was a thin bar in his grip.

Daremo lost consciousness again. When he became aware

once more, he was still standing. His left arm was still over his head. His fingers still clutched the large metal stair.

"Very funny," Daremo mouthed. There was no way any angel or devil was going to let him die easily. Not after the way he'd been acting. They didn't slice him open just to let him die. "Very, very funny."

He didn't think about it. There was nothing to consider. He was awake, so he wouldn't just remain there. Pain he had felt before. All they could do was turn up the volume.

Yeah, but wouldn't it be funny if he struggled so hard to climb the metal stairs stapled into the wall that he ripped himself in half and everything just spilled out? Wouldn't that be a riot?

Fuck him if he couldn't take a joke. Daremo let his left arm muscles contract. He let his left leg step onto the wall.

There was a step, like a stirrup, cut into the wall. Praise the heavens. He didn't have to just hang there, letting his side open more, as if it were caught in an invisible can opener.

Using just his left arm and leg, Daremo pulled and pushed himself up the wall. "You can win by quickly taking the lead," Musashi had said. "You must make the best of the situation." Daremo thought of this only. The pain had simply moved in and set up house. There was no use arguing with it. He concentrated on the words instead.

Halfway up, his brain started to thunder. A third of the way up, the walls started to shake. Three quarters of the way up, the cave started to fill with light.

"Either I *am* dying or a train is coming," said Daremo. The Métro cars started appearing from around the corner, the Cyclops eye of the headlight sweeping across him. "Lucky me."

Daremo kept going as the monstrosity roared past. He wasn't sure which was louder: it or his breathing. He kept going until his skull hit the light

"Ow," he said ludicrously. He twisted his head around and blinked into three little circles of light. "Great. I don't have enough problems." It was a manhole cover.

Daremo took another step up, leaning his head down. He

couldn't bend forward. His side couldn't take it. He placed the back of his head, the flat of his neck, and his shoulders against the cover. He kept climbing.

"It'll have to do," he said. "Stop me. Just try to stop me."

The sides of the thick iron circle scraped against the metal band holding it in the street. Daremo would not bend. He used his body like a pressurized ram. He just kept pushing. The manhole cover rasped out.

Daremo's head popped up. He took a step more. He was in the middle of a narrow, sloping side street. A tiny Citroen was rolling toward him. He just stared at it. The driver saw him at the last minute and wrenched the wheel. The car hopped the curb and smacked into a street lamp.

Daremo climbed out of the manhole, placing his left hand flat on the street. The stores on the left side were closed. The sky was a deep, dark blue. To the right was a sidewalk café and charcuteire. Everyone sitting in the seats and waiting on them were frozen, staring at him with their mouths open.

"I need a drink," Daremo said in something between a gasp and a growl. He stood unsteadily on the otherwise empty avenue, holding his side. "Give me a drink!"

He had taken two steps toward the café when the driver of the car came at him, babbling angrily. Daremo put his left elbow back. There was a nasty cracking sound, which Daremo fully felt on his right side, and the driver's head snapped back. The driver's feet went out from under him. He landed flat on his back, arms out, unmoving.

Daremo hissed, the wound grinding, then he continued to stumble toward the sidewalk.

"I said . . . I want . . . a drink!"

A few people shrieked and scattered as he fell perfectly onto a woven basket filled with loaves of bread, sausages, and wine bottles. Daremo shouted in pain, which gave him enough strength to stand again. He was holding a bottle by its base.

He smacked it against the wall as he lurched away, the

bottle neck breaking off. He kept shuffling down the sloping road and tipped the bottle over his face.

His head went back and the wine splashed into his mouth. It drooled down his front and shoulders. He screamed as it seeped through the jacket and reached the wound, setting it afire.

No one in the café moved.

Daremo weaved down the street, screaming.

Mustn't fall down the stairs, was the last thing he remembered thinking. *If I fall down the stairs, she'll find my top half at the bottom, and my bottom half at the top.*

II

The pain brought him back. It wasn't the same sort of pain as before. Before, it had been pain that filled his body like acid filing an empty vessel. It had been a grinding pain at the wound, and a horrid flame eating throughout his body. It had been a pain that sliced through his mind, like his swords slicing through an enemy.

This pain was different. This was a sharp, localized pain, like a long pin pushed into one specific area. It was a pain that pricked. It was a single lightning bolt, that struck and disappeared.

His eyes opened. He looked at the ceiling. It was cracked and dirty.

He was home.

He lay on the table. He was naked.

Rhea's head appeared in his vision to the right, like the moon rising, wisps of black clouds shimmering before it.

She was moonlight smiling down upon him, her almond eyes filled with swirling emotions. He could just imagine what she was thinking.

He started to laugh.

"My love," she whispered, her hand stopping just above his chest, "don't."

He lost consciousness again.

Her hand remained where it was, just above his chest. It

stayed there, as if anchored there for eternity. His chest rose and fell minutely, but her hand did not move.

The power there, she thought. Still. Anyone else would have died thrice. He lived. Just barely, but that was all that was required.

The strength inside. She could practically see it there, through the layers of skin. He was so beautiful. The muscles were so tight. The shape was so exquisite. He was perfect.

She raised the needle with which she had sewn him together. Difficult? Perhaps. Not at all impossible. She had gone to the corner where the green neon cross had shone.

She had known where the money was. She took it from the cushions of the couch. It was an old trick, fallen into disuse. No one would think of looking there or in mattresses anymore.

She had bought the needles and the sterile thread. She had used a candle to cauterize. She was *kunoichi*: female ninja. How many of her ancestors had to do the same thing, to save their lords and masters from the bite of samurai steel?

It was commonplace: the *jonin* and *chunin* would crawl back from their missions, hacked and sliced in many places. Were the women to wail as they watched them expire? Would they sit by and mouth philosophy to bridge their lovers to the void?

Rhea had left Daremo on the table and gone to buy a needle and thread.

Rhea pressed the sterile padding against the wound she taped it there with the medical adhesive from the white metal spools. She loosened the bandages and placed them beside her hated lover.

So perfect, she thought. Even torturing her, he was perfect. He cared as he had tied her. The last thing she saw before he sealed her lips and eyes, before filling her ears, was his concerned, loving face.

He left her without food or water, left her to soil herself, as she listened to his instructions on the endless tape. Out of the box, she saw his face above her as he had sex. Not they.

He. She was still immobilized. She was just the object of his will.

Soon she felt what he wanted her to feel. She thought what he wanted her to think. She did as he wanted her to do.

She understood. There would be a time when she would be told to kill him. There would have to be. It was her birthright. It had been and would be again. The first time she had been told, she tired and failed. The second, he had forced her to see *yes* as *no*. To tell her to kill him was to tell her not to kill him. He had seen to that.

But not before she was tortured again. Not by him. But he allowed it, so he could kill another with whom he was evenly matched. She was his weapon. She was also his enemy's weapon.

She was Rhea: nothing.

So perfect, she thought. So perfect. She held the needle in one hand and the bandages in the other. She looked from one to the next.

How easy it would be, she thought. Just slip the thin pin of steel under his skin, under his sternum, into his heart. How simple, how elegant, how right. It would be the ultimate show of her love. Stop his suffering forever.

She smiled down at her hated lover.

"No way, Jose," she said. "You're not getting off so easy."

She plunged the needle into the table up to its eye.

III

The pain didn't bring him back. It was something else this time. Daremo felt it in his mind even before he awoke.

The angels were stroking his brain.

He had never felt anything like it. It was pain and pleasure mingled exquisitely. He ached all over but he rested. He felt himself massaged but with heavenly hands. His pleasure centers were being pressed repeatedly.

He tried to move, but a lancing pain came each time. He

tired to comprehend what was happening but could not without regaining consciousness.

He swam up through a sea of oil and vinegar until his head broke the surface.

His eyes opened and he felt. He groaned. The sensations did not stop. He tried to move away, but his body wouldn't respond. It was paralyzed from the neck down with exhaustion.

So he used what muscles were available to him. He raised his head.

His brain was nailed to his skull with six-inch spikes by that act. Creatures of impossible description swam in his sight. Cosmic secrets were revealed, only to be swept away on tides of agony.

Finally he was able to see through the mist. He saw his body. He saw the very edge of the sterile padding and tape that covered the wound. He saw Rhea leaning over him.

Her head was between his legs.

His voice was a distant, hollow, hoarse whisper. ''You bitch.''

He didn't see her smile. He *felt* it.

His head sank, its neck muscles spent. He had to lay back and attempt not to move. He had to try to control his deadened body with his tormented mind while her expert mouth and tongue caressed him.

Her skill was incredible. Images of a woman in a ceramic Noh mask lying with him in Chiba prefecture swam through his brain. But mostly he ''saw'' the sensations. Again and again she sent him flying to the edge of the cliff, but she never let him fall over.

Each time she would fly faster and faster, but each time he would land just on the lip of the chasm. Then she would hurl him back, higher and higher—only to fall to the edge of the abyss once more.

Finally he could go no higher. He could fly no faster. He was thrown to the cliff. He was falling over.

His wings disappeared. He felt her arm under him. He was sitting up before he could feel the pain.

She quickly wrapped the bandages around his torso while he was still stunned. The really amazing pain started just as she pulled it tight and clipped it in place. He didn't remember being laid back down. He only gasped and lost consciousness once more.

IV

When the security guard first saw the hunched figure by the cabinet, he was certain it was another drug addict.

It had been happening everywhere for years. The pathetic wretches couldn't even rob old ladies anymore. Their shakes were getting so bad, all they could think of doing was raiding the local hospital.

No big surprise that they would lose their way after sneaking in. Any hospital was confusing, but especially to an addict going cold turkey. They couldn't see, they couldn't think, all they could do was search wildly for some relief.

Only this person wasn't shaking. This person seemed to be moving quickly and methodically through the refrigerated cabinet.

Well, that really wasn't much of a surprise either. They say insanity can make a person stronger, and any far-gone addict was certifiably insane. No surprise, therefore, that the security guard called in two of his fellow guards and three burly orderlies.

The guards had short clubs. That was permitted. One orderly had a sedative in a syringe, another had some restraints, and the third had a straitjacket, just in case.

"Mon ami," said the guard. That was funny. The other guards and two of the orderlies chuckled. Imagine calling this guy "my friend." Look at that long coat. Look at that punk haircut.

The figure didn't reply. The figure didn't even seem aware of their presence. If anything, the figure's arms moved even faster. The guard was surprised when the hunched figure slipped one of the plastic pouches from the cabinet into a coat pocket.

"Vous!" he barked, pointing his nightstick.

The figure put another pouch in the coat's pocket.

The guard was really angry by this time. He stepped

forward, his stick leading. "Hey, those aren't drugs," he said. "That's bloo—!"

He had jabbed the end of his stick into the figure's hunched shoulder.

The figure whirled around faster than any of them thought possible. The light from the hall illuminated the small storeroom and the figure's face.

Asian. Female. Beautiful. Angry.

For a second they were all stunned still. She wore dark red Spandex under the coat. It was skintight, ending at her neck on one end and her lower thighs at the other. Her shins and knees were padded. High-topped, black, high-impact running shoes were on her feet.

When she had swept around, she had grabbed his night-stick with her leading, gloved hand, pulling it wide. She planted her other gloved fist into his face like a piston driver.

He went down hard on his back. The stick remained in her hand. The second guard came at her, swinging his stick. She hit his right arm with her club, blocking the strike, and hit him in the face with her fist. He went down.

An orderly jabbed at her side with the syringe. She swung the club onto it. The needle sunk all the way through the wood. She twisted his arm down while kicking him in the throat with the point of her sneaker. His hand spasmed, the sedative squirting onto the floor.

The third guard stepped forward, into the puddle, and slipped. He dropped onto his back, howling. Rhea laughed and put the back of her fist into the side of the sedative orderly's face. He let go of the syringe and dropped.

Rhea pivoted and hit the restraint-holding orderly in the arm with the club and the needlepoint. He dropped the leather cuffs and hopped away, yelling.

The last orderly jumped forward, trying to use the straightjacket like a net. Rhea went to one knee under it and hit him between the legs. He stiffened and bent. She spun around in a crouch, her right leg wide. She knocked his legs out from under him.

It looked like he had stepped on two banana peels, one for each foot. He slammed down on the back of his neck.

She was up already, sliding her feet across the floor toward the door. The third guard, who had slipped, tried to get up. She stepped hard on his solar plexus in passing, as if crushing an inordinately large cockroach. He whoofed, contracted into a ball, and stayed down.

She stopped at the door and looked at the restraint orderly, who was backed into a corner, rubbing his needle-punctured arm.

"What do I look like?" she asked him tellingly in French.

His arms were up, his hands waving pleadingly. "*Rien, rien,*" he begged. Nothing.

"Perfect," she said.

V

Rhea stood by the table, watching the plasma drip out of the plastic pouch and seep into Daremo's arm. She had rigged the necessary stand out of a hat rack. If necessary, she would have dragged the table to the wall and nailed the bottle there.

Why still the table? She didn't dare move him to the bed. And she didn't put him on the bed in the first place because the mattress and sheets would have gotten in the way of sewing.

He was ninja-trained. He was used to hard places.

He was babbling in his sleep now. Rhea didn't even try to make out the words. Something about "seeing what he had made." Something about knowing "what pain was." She doubted they would make any real sense. He had too many nightmares to choose from. She just nursed him through the transfusion.

"Who has done this to you, my love?" she said softly, leaning over the table, hands on the edge. "Who?"

Who could? Only a master. Rhea snorted with mirth. She hadn't been able to do it. Hama hadn't even been able to defeat Daremo's student. Daremo's student now had only one arm. Everyone else who had been better than the white-trash ninja was dead.

Save one. But that one would not slice him open. That one would only touch him once and let her venom rip him apart like a cooked spicy sausage. And then, only if there was no other way to escape. Otherwise that one would plan an ironic, agonizing, karmic death for him. As she was no doubt doing this very moment.

Rhea knew that one very well. From the inside. Rhea had come from that one.

That one had tried to drive Daremo from Rhea's mind. That had not been possible.

Hari. The Needle. Was she here?

No, Rhea decided. If she was, Daremo would be dead. Rhea would be dead. No one and nothing would be joined in darkness.

So, if not Hari, how bad could it be?

"Don't worry," Rhea said, caressing her hated lover's brow. "Do not worry, dear one. I shall find out. I shall discover the one truth. Rest well. Rest easy. Mother is going hunting."

Buban Ni

"ISHIS"

"Ye are spies: to see the nakedness of
the land ye are come."

—Genesis 42:9

"Sweet is revenge—especially to women."

—Lord Byron

12

I

There was something about her. Georgetown was full of attractive women, but there was something about this blue-eyed blonde. She wasn't the tallest; hardly five-seven in her cream-colored pumps. She wasn't the shapliest; there wasn't the aggressive ratio of chest to waist to hips that many of the man killers either enhanced or bought. She wasn't even the most overt; her outfit wasn't eye-bulgingly tight or revealing.

That isn't to say she wasn't selling something. The silk shirt was V- necked. The beige sport jacket was tailor-made. The off-white skirt had Lycra in the cotton, which outlined her legs as they swept under its miniskirted hem. Her stockings glittered. They were held up by a garter belt, not attached to panty hose. She collected stares wherever she went on the wide, clean walks, but it was not just because she was sexy.

Maybe it was because her clear blue eyes weren't hidden behind sunglasses. They were cool and intelligent. Maybe it was because her hair wasn't sprayed into a plastic paralysis. The gold, yellow, and platinum strands bounced around her head, caressed her shoulders, and curtained her face as she walked confidently and purposefully down the street.

Maybe it was her perfection. She didn't ladle on makeup to create her beauty. She didn't enhance the shape of her face or body with surgery. She wasn't an Amazon or a China doll. She wasn't a bombshell or a kitten. She was not an exaggeration or a satire of a beautiful woman. She was, simply, a beautiful woman.

She was Cynthia Gamble, companion to an up-and-coming congressman.

Some of the street recognized her, elbowing their friends or mates before whispering the latest gossip in their ears. It wasn't unusual. Georgetown, that exclusive suburb cuddled into Washington D.C., was innuendo central. Shopkeepers and restaurateurs prided themselves on knowing the latest dirt, as well as spreading it around.

Was Jason Walker up-and-coming because of his charisma and intelligence, or because he had to be charismatic and intelligent to land her? Cynthia Gamble was not hired help—paid to be on his arm so he could look good for the cameras. She was a literate and eloquent young lady. The best and the brightest had made propositions to her, only to be shot down. Therefore Walker *had* to have something on the ball.

Cynthia knew the routine well. She had heard the whispers in ladies' rooms, in cocktail party chatter, and around Senate corners. Which came first, the chicken or the egg? Did Gamble want him because he had it, or did he have it because she wanted him? Cynthia ignored the catcalls. She knew what she was doing.

Her serene perfection was marred momentarily as her lips curled up in slight disgust. It was a bad habit, which she was fighting. It looked as if she were about to spit, or at least had a bad case of Elvisitis—the disease that made your lip curl. She maintained her brisk pace and tried to pull her frown out.

She couldn't help it. Every time she thought of him, she got that taste in her mouth. It was his taste. The taste of flesh, hair, sweat, and dirt. It mingled until the aroma became a stench in her nostrils—and then her entire head.

And yet she still fed on him. She let him paw her. She let him suffocate her in the deep recesses of the soft bed.

There were times she thought she would scream with claustrophobia. There were times she did cry out, clutching and pulling at him, but she was able to let the moans rattle at the last moment, disguising them as passion. There were times she was certain she would lose her sanity. There were times she was just as certain she already had.

She let none of her paranoia show now. She was away from him. He did not own her when they were apart. She could breathe and live again while he was filibustering. It was only late in the afternoon when she had to perform: by his side, on his arm, on her knees, under him.

Her lip curled again. The bile rose in her throat. Think about other things, she told herself. It was impossible. His cancerous presence had invaded every nook of her life. Even today, even now, she wasn't shopping for herself. She was shopping for him. She was buying a new outfit for a new party. A party he was invited to because she was with him.

His work on the Farming Subcommittee was coming to a close. He was thinking of quitting the Famine Relief Fact-finding Commission.

"Bigger and better things, baby," he would say, leering at her. "It's time I think about moving up to bigger and better things."

They were not his words. He was just repeating what Congressman John Tyler had told him. The senior Tyler had more than enough ambition for all of them.

This party was the first toe in the waters of greater power and prestige. The uppity-ups had to check the new boy out for the right stuff. So he wanted his companion to give off just the right combination of class and sex appeal. He had opened the bank for her. He had given her his gold card and instructed her to buy the best. So she had parked the beamer (BMW) and was walking to Raub's.

It was the new chi-chi boy on the block, opened by the wife of a publishing magnate. Georgetown real estate was hard to come by, but Laurie Raub had somehow found a

swash of square footing and got the very best architects and
decorators to fill it. Cynthia went directly to the thick white
door with the gold fittings. She put her small hand, with its
perfect, red-painted fingernails, around the shined brass
door handle and pulled.

The door swung open reluctantly, with the weight of a
vault. The allusion was not inaccurate. Inside was a wide,
plush embarrassment of riches. The thick carpet was a light
gray, the walls were papered in silver and red, and narrow
Roman columns went from floor to ceiling. On Louis XVI
chairs lay lovely gowns of gold lamé and black velvet.

Laurie Raub approached her personally. "Ms. Gamble?
Your four-fifteen appointment?" After Cynthia nodded, Laurie
led her to the back of the shop and immediately got under
way. This store waited for no woman. "You're very lucky
we could squeeze you in, but with your figure I don't see
any problem." She laughed at her own joke—a high-pitched
giggle that probably had poodles cringing for blocks around.

The proprietress had put her design staff on Cynthia's
situation, and they already had a variety of possible creations
prepared in her size. "Models?" Laurie asked.

"I'll be wearing them," said Cynthia, "not the models.
So I think it's best if I try them on."

"Very wise," Raub agreed immediately, as she would
have no matter what Gamble had said. Laurie turned and
signaled the staff to start bringing over the dresses. Cynthia
finally chose a classic gown of dark blue, with silver
swashes and highlights. It combined formfitting fabrics with
a draping effect, so gave the impression of sexy elegance. It
had spaghetti straps and a deep-plunging neckline. It had a
long skirt that hugged her thighs but ended in a gently
pleated hem, which gave her shoes room to appear. She
took it over her arm and went to the private dressing room.

Unlike other stores, this changing area lived up to its
name. Rather than a closet with a mirror on one side, this
was more a room. Small but comfortable, with a lounge
chair, a reclining sofa, and a series of full-length mirrors—
one on legs, one attached to the wall—with wings, so the
patron could see every side.

Cynthia watched herself change clothes. She slipped off the jacket and unbuttoned the silk shirt. She dropped both on the pink fabric of the couch. When she pushed the skirt down and stepped out of it, she viewed what Jason Walker saw in her.

Her perfectly proportioned breasts held in the lacy bra; she didn't need underwires. They were as strong and buoyant now as they had been when she was sixteen. Her waist was not an example of anorexia. It was curved and gentle and sloped, covered by just enough flesh and muscle, and yes, fat. Sculpted adipose that made her soft but not heavy.

The perfectly shaped legs encased in sparkling satin. The small feet pushed up on her painted toes by the high-heeled pumps. And in the center of this star, beneath a tiny triangle of silk, lay what it all led to . . . where it all connected. The secret that Walker and all his contemporaries craved.

She understood its perfection as well. Its perfectly grown and groomed cover of blond hair. The muscles within Akuma Kiro had so carefully trained. The places he had touched and manipulated and stimulated. The place from which he traveled throughout her body. The place where he had started her enslavement, until she could no longer claim control of her own mind.

The place in which she ached for him now. The place Jason Walker invaded with his clumsy, selfish stupidity. She almost laughed giddily at the idea that he had any place in her heart. He remembered the look of conquest he always gave her no matter what he had her do. It was that retarded expression of triumph, as if he knew all.

He knew nothing. If Akuma Kiro had not instructed her to be Walker's, she would have laughed at him. No, worse. She would have ignored him. No, spit on him. He would have made some disgusting, pathetic proposal, and she would have dumped her drink into his lap, smashed the glass into his face, ground it into his flesh, and then spit on him while he writhed on the floor. She would have kicked him in the stomach, then in the balls, with the hard, pointy toe of her high heel, before walking out with her head held high and back straight.

Then she would have heard that he was in the hospital, in terrible pain. That the doctors couldn't get all the glass shards out of his face, and at least one of his testicles was crushed, never to drop down again. They would tell her he could never have children and she would laugh. She would throw back her head and laugh

"Good!" she would say. "Good! A man like that should not procreate or recreate! Let him be the last of his line. The world will profit by it!"

She gasped at the pain in her scalp. For a second she was afraid that Akuma Kiro was still there, stamping on her mind in anger for any thought of betrayal. But then her back arched and she was pulled back, her right hand reaching for her hairline.

There were fingers in her hair, she realized. They gripped and pulled. She saw the walls and then the ceiling. For a moment she saw the angry face of a god, staring down at her from a tight, yellow face with almond-shaped eyes.

Then the thunderbolt struck. The thunderbolt came down from the sky so fast that it was a blur in her peripheral vision. It smashed down between her breasts and nailed her to the floor. She fell flat to her back on the plush carpet, her legs straight out. She was blinded by the shock.

When her vision cleared, the god was right side up, still staring down at her. She was about to call it by name when his right hand appeared. It reached for her, then disappeared under her chin.

"I wasn't going to scream," she tried to say before the hand clenched her throat and tightened. Then all that was left were the tears and trying to breathe.

She wrapped her own hands around the wrist of the yellow god, but they had as much effect as they would on a cement post erected there. Her body quaked, shaking on the carpet as she struggled.

"You will be quiet," he said. Then he pulled. He lifted her off the floor by her throat with one hand. He held her at arm's length. Her wide, wet eyes looked directly at him. Her numbed mind realized they were the same height.

He watched her writhe in his grip. Her hands clutched his

wrist, her arms trying to pull his fingers from her neck. Her teeth clenched, then opened, as she tried to breathe. Her red lips worked. Her eyes opened and shut, tears squeezed out and falling onto his wrist. Her body twisted, her high heels digging into the carpet as she tried to wrench her body away. She made gasping sounds.

He reached down to grab her shirt from the sofa. He pushed it at her with his other hand. With his fingers and thumb he began to jam it into her mouth.

Cynthia's eyes widened and her body froze. As he forced the silk between her lips and teeth, her body started to vibrate uncontrollably. She tried even harder to pull away, but it was as if his palm were glued to her neck. Suddenly he took three steps toward her, and she was jammed against the wall—between the mirrors.

It was a horrid fun house. Her predicament was reflected over and over again in the corners of her eyes. It was as if her attack were being played back on a never-ending loop of videotape.

Between his choking hand and the shirt being pushed deeper and deeper into her mouth, she couldn't make a sound. She felt and saw her cheeks puffing as the cloth filled them. She saw her arms moving feebly, her fingers still clutching his arm. She saw one leg straight, and the other leg bent, trying to kick out. But she was too weak, and getting weaker.

By the time she thought of reaching for the cloth stuffed in her mouth, his hands moved. The choking hand moved up slightly, the thumb and forefinger pressed under her jaw and chin. The other hand went down, to grab her left wrist. The elbow on that same arm pressed down on her right wrist. He surged forward, pushing his body between her legs. He sandwiched her against the wall. She had no choice but to keep a wide stance.

She thought about kicking. She thought about falling. Then his fingers squeezed her throat tighter.

It was as if he had found her off button. It was as if he had pulled her plug. She simply lost power for a second.

When she came to, the memory made her shake with terrible fear. He turned her off a second time.

When she came to this time, her own belt was wrapped around her elbows, holding them together behind her. Otherwise she still stood in her high heels, her legs planted wide, her shirt in her mouth.

The man was still there, his hand on her throat. She could now see that he was just a man: a small Asian with short black hair; pointed chin; and wide, high cheekbones. A ferret, she thought instantly. A horrid little gook who wanted to attack a white woman.

But how did he get in here? What was he going to do?

His free hand was below her sight as he held her jaw up. She tried to reach for it, but the belt cinching her elbows wouldn't let her hands reach all the way in front. He pulled back the elastic top of her underwear and slipped his fingers inside.

Oh, no, she thought, screaming inside her head. Oh, no.

But they did not molest. The did not rummage around, seeking any sort of angry satisfaction. They went directly to her sensitivity and pressed. Pressed and pressed again. Repeatedly, in a slow, purposeful rhythm.

Her on switch. She felt it first as electricity—shocking—but then powering her. She felt it first as an assault but then as a signal.

"Akuma Kiro," she tried to say through the gag. It came out as a moan. She didn't even feel the stretching pain in her shoulders anymore.

The man kept up his steady stimulation as Cynthia Gamble stood against the wall, pressed there by his body, her head beginning to loll on her shoulders. Her eyes opened and closed as before, but not with the same panic and urgency. Every time her vision and thinking processes cleared, she would feel the horror, but then the sensations would envelop her, washing over her like a sedative.

This was not Akuma Kiro. But he would have to do.

The man smiled, maintaining the process. He knew that if he released her, she would start to fight. She was a hungry woman who was so starved for any true caress that she would even accept it like this. He brought his face close to hers and spoke.

"I am not Kohga," he told her softly, in lightly accented English. "Kohga is *of* me. He did not send me. I sent him." There was no way of knowing whether she truly understood. The man did not care. It made no difference. He kept her riding on the waves of pleasure.

They were both moving now. The man's arm and hand, Cynthia Gamble's entire body. Never let this end, she begged silently. Take her away. Do not send her back to that monster. Comparing this attack to Walker's lovemaking was like comparing sculpture to demolition.

"This is your time, *mei li*," whispered the man. "Your moment. You have been prepared for this precise instant in history." Cynthia Gamble moaned, her eyes closed. "Do as I say. Make him feel the way you feel."

Her eyes snapped open. She stared at the yellow man, the waves slapping her face as if she were staked under the rising tide. She shook her head and started writhing. She said the word over and over again under the silk shirt filling her mouth.

"No. No. No, no, no, no, no, no, no, no . . ."

But then there was nothing left but the groans and weakness. She slumped on him, her weight resting on his hands. He drove her on until the collapse was complete. He drowned her in her own sensuality, pouring more crystalline, sparkling water into the pit she lay at the bottom of.

When she awoke, he was gone. She was on the floor in her underwear. The shirt and belt were back on the couch with her skirt. Only the moisture in the silk and the marks near her elbows gave evidence to her ordeal.

Gamble scrambled off the floor, grabbing the dress she had come in to try on. She ran out, holding it to her. She stopped on the showroom floor, Laurie Raub and her staff turning to stare at her in surprise. There were only a few other people in the shop, and they hadn't noticed her yet. Outside the windows were a few pedestrians looking in or going by. None were Asian.

"Ms. Gamble . . . ?" Laurie Raub had approached and

was looking at Cynthia anxiously. Cynthia kept looking for any sign of her attacker.

"Where is he?"

"Where is who?"

"Didn't you see him?" Gamble asked, despair sapping her panic.

"See who?"

Of course she hadn't seen him. Of course not. He would not have allowed her to see him. After meeting Akuma Kiro at that party she had bumped into people who had been there. In idle conversation she had learned repeatedly that they could not describe him. Most hadn't even seen him. He was seen only by those he wanted to see him.

Still, she had to try. "The little man. The yellow man. Didn't you see him?"

"Here?" Laurie Raub asked, looking around her own store. "A chink? Where? Now?"

Cynthia felt like crying. She felt like grabbing the proprietress by the hair and shaking her, screaming, "Yes, now! The little man who came into the dressing room and raped me!" But that would be impossible. She had been loved by Akuma Kiro. She lived for him. She would do as he asked.

But that *wasn't* Akuma. The skin was yellow but the face was different. The eyes were different. They did not come from the same place. What did the man say? "I am not Kohga, but he is *of* me?" What did *that* mean?

"Do you want the dress?" she heard a tiny, tentative voice ask.

Fuck the dress, she thought. Who can think about a dress at a time like . . . ! But then she wouldn't have anything to wear to this important dinner, and Jason would be hurt and confused, and then he'd get that stupid stubborn expression like a petulant six-year-old everyone hated and plotted against, and it would all come out later that night when he'd get that sick look of triumph and make her crawl across the floor to him . . .

"Oh, God, yes! I've got to have the dress!"

II

"Don't move, lady."

Cynthia almost screamed as the hand pushed her against the wall. Not again, she said to herself, hoping her legs didn't buckle. Not again, she thought, keeping her hysteria capped.

But then the hand was pushing up her arms and tapping her sides. She heard a scrape, and then a slight tickling between her legs. Before she realized what had happened, it was over. She had been professionally and completely searched.

"All right," she heard. She turned and faced the man who had sneaked up behind her.

She didn't recognize him for a second. His face was dirty and long but strong. His clothes were tattered and stank, but they hung on a wide-shouldered frame. He was the bum she had passed in the doorway.

Incredibly, Gamble blushed, looking down. She had driven all the way across town, parked near the church across the street, and prayed that the office was still open, even though it was after five. She wouldn't be able to hang around this sort of neighborhood long otherwise.

But once she had reached the staircase going down in the old, mildewing building, the bum, who had been stretched out on the sidewalk, had come after her on silent feet.

"Go on," he said. "You're clean."

I wish, she thought as he trudged back toward the front door. She watched as his shoulders hunched and his back bent. By the time he reached the entrance, he was the wretched derelict once again. For the first time in a year she felt the memory of hope fluttering in the back of her mind—like a captured butterfly escaping its pins.

Cynthia went down the dark, curving, wooden stairway carefully, her white high heels clacking. She made it to the basement, only to be faced by a large metal door. But as she was deciding whether to knock or try pushing, she heard locks give way. The door swung in before her.

Cynthia Gamble stepped into the offices of the city's only

counterculture political gossip newspaper, *The Washington Ragg*.

"This way," said a nice-looking middle-aged man with thinning brown hair who appeared from the other side of the metal door. He was slightly stooped, like many reporters, but well dressed in dark slacks, a button-down blue shirt, and school tie.

He was not what she expected, but the others were. As she went by the rows of desks in the cavernous room surrounded by the printing and reproducing equipment, she saw the young people in their jeans and sweaters, wearing their sullen, distrusting looks.

Cynthia liked it. For the first time since she'd grown tits and her braces had come off, she felt she was being looked upon as a human being, not just a beautiful girl. They couldn't care less about her miniskirt and high heels and still moist silk shirt. What else did she have to offer them?

That brought her back to reality. At least there weren't any yellow men here. Here she wouldn't be captured. Here she could turn and run, if need be. The older man in the shirt and tie brought her to the one private office in the place; to a door set in a wall that covered the entire back of the basement.

"Here we are," he said, turning the knob, and pushing it open for her. "Good luck."

Then he walked back the way they had come. "Thanks," she said after him, then turned to the open door. This gave her one last chance to consider fleeing. She started to run but then thought about what she was turning to. The image of his pig eyes, hairy nose, and thick lips filled her vision. She felt the bile in her throat and her lips twisting. She stepped into the office.

Nothing much had changed in the many months since a reporter named Larry Tanada had walked through those same doors. The room was still long and high. It was gloomy, lit only by a few standing lamps. The walls were still covered by charts and bulletin boards. Clippings were still on those boards, still placed so that they would appear to be the most artful mosaic, but now the clippings were faded, yellowing, and chipped.

Cynthia thought of Venice. The image of empty gondolas floating on a city that was being swept away flitted through her mind. She turned left and saw the big desk, covered with piles of curling, brittle, dusty paper. To the right of that was the long table built into the wall, upon which sat a few computers. Beyond that was the long, low sofa. Beyond that was the conference table.

Seated there, her back to Cynthia, was a woman with red hair.

Red hair . . . ? Another memory flashed through Gamble's brain. The image of auburn hair floating in the water. Under the water . . . a denizen of Atlantis? A beautiful woman drowned? what was it . . . ?''

"My sister," Cynthia breathed, for reasons she couldn't understand. She put her hand out and stepped forward. She moved toward the figure in the chair like a sleepwalker. "Sister . . ."

She reached the table. She went around it. Her own hand loomed large at the bottom of her vision, coming upon the figure in the chair.

Hair the color of fire. She held the image of that mane in her mind as if it were her own. This was a woman like her. A child . . . a lover . . . a prisoner of Kohga.

She touched the hair. The chair turned around. Cynthia Gamble stared down the barrel of a satin-finish nickel-plated Taurus Model 85 snub-nosed revolver.

The redhead stood up smoothly, keeping the short barrel of the gun aimed directly between Cynthia's eyes. It wasn't so much the gun that shocked Cynthia, but the woman's unbelievably placid countenance. A countenance Cynthia now realized stirred no memories for her. This was not her Kohga sister. This woman did not know Akuma Kiro. She was too self-aware and assured to be his captive.

She glided to the side, and out of the shadows came her mate. He could be no other. Cynthia felt a pang of remorse and envy as they neared each other. Both had their undivided attention on the blonde, but she knew that they were just two parts of a single entity. They lived, and no doubt would die, for each other. They were the perfect specimens mad scientists in movies were always striving to create.

No, wait. Scratch that. Nearly perfect. Cynthia could see there was something slightly wrong with the nice-looking young man. It was in the way he held himself, favoring his left arm. It was in the way it rested stiffly against his side. It was in the way his fingers were unnaturally still, the flesh waxy and plastic. Close but no cigar. The mad scientist would attempt to destroy him. And the two would eradicate the scientist and all his kind as a result.

She was right to come here, she realized.

"Ms. Gamble. . . ."

The voice was behind her. It was not so much a voice but an electronic garble. The words were not so much said as played, as if on a synthesizer. She turned to see a man coming out of the shadows there. Shorter, wider, squatter, older. The light lifted across his features like a rising guillotine blade. He was bald. He had a scar between his brows. His skin was deep, dark yellow. His eyes were almond-shaped.

All her strength, all her conviction, and all her hope dissipated, as if burned out of her. She had come here to confess. She could think of no other place to go. She had tried calling the CIA, but they had played games with her. She couldn't trust them. They would not connect her with the man she was told she could trust. Her only option then was *The Ragg*, for which that young reporter had worked.

He had followed her. She recognized him from other D.C. events. She had called someone someplace and told them about it. The young man had stopped following her.

So now she had a choice. She could do what she was told, or she could tell what she could do.

She loved Akuma Kiro. He was her life. She could not live without him. But he was not here. The only one who was here was Jason Walker. There was only his face.

She tasted the bile before fainting.

13

The man who had created Moe Dare stood before the picture window in the Marriott Inn and thought about his life.

It was his birthday. He looked at his reflection and the way the image was superimposed on the small city of some eighty thousand. Look at that: a fat little man casting his shadow on a bunch of rubes who wouldn't know international espionage from a beef brisket.

There was the smell of sheep dip in the air. It was the Sioux Falls perfume, signifying success in the meat market. It was the stench of money for the tristate area. Sheep, cattle, wood, and metal made in Minnesota, Iowa, and South Dakota what they were. Top it all off with the fine stink of plastics, and the financial status of the Midwest was secure.

Is this all it meant, then? he asked himself. All the years of slaving, committing himself to the greater good of law enforcement, only to end up in the middle of America, doing the same work he'd been doing twenty years ago? It wasn't because he hadn't risen through the ranks, God knows. It was just because there was no one else to do it.

For some reason he thought his promotions would mean more command, not just more responsibility and a bigger pay packet.

"Now, Joe," he was told, "you know I'd love to get you more people, but things are tight just now. What with the Russkies using advanced psychology and our own administration depending more and more on electronics, we're up to our armpits in assholes. You know that.

"Why screw up a good thing? You've been doing great so

far. Just keep on keeping on, if you know what I mean. Recruit and train your own people, like you've always done. Everything's going smoothly, correct? You're on the tail of the tiger, aren't you? What's the matter? Your classification's high enough, isn't it? You're already top-class in the expense department. Look, I'll even try to get you to first-class. No higher than that, is there?"

But it wasn't the money and perks Agent Anthony was after. He was tired of moving through the maze. He wanted to solve the puzzle. He wanted to find the end. And to do that he needed more people to go down the twists and turns. He didn't have time to do his job and say "Uncle Sam wants you" as well. He wanted to draw the map, not explore the whole damn thing himself.

Look at that, he thought. Look at the tired old man. Look at that paunch. Look at that double chin. Look at those bloodshot eyes. Look at that wrinkled suit. Look at the wide-open spaces on every side of him.

Anthony chuckled self-consciously. Why did he have to feel sorry for himself? He had made the decision back on the SFPD to forgo husband and parenthood, hadn't he? Besides, he wasn't truly alone. He had Moe Dare to take care of him.

Moe Dare . . . the first name Anthony could come up with when the heat from above became too much. It wasn't enough for some that he was succeeding. They wanted to know why. It became an agency in-joke. When he wanted someone to trust him, or when the stakes were getting a little too high, all he had to say was, "Moe Dare sent me."

"A little Moe Dare told me."

"Chalk it up to Moe Dare."

"Because Moe Dare said so, that's why."

Why was Anthony beginning to think that this deity, his own personal fairy godfather, didn't know any more than anyone else did? Maybe because now, more than ever, he seemed to be walking a trail that never ended. Maybe because he finally was suspecting that Moe Dare had given him a problem with no solution.

"People died in North Africa," Moe Dare had whispered to him.

"People die all the time," Anthony had said. But then the kidnapped girl with hair the color of fire had begun to spit out Russian names. And men with yellow skin and slanted eyes had come to New York State to take her.

Anthony remembered his associates' report. Mary Ann Huntington had clinical amnesia. She was not aware of what she was saying or its significance. All she had in her subconscious were the names, as if overheard while asleep. She had regurgitated them when emerging from a state of deep shock.

Subsequent questioning under hypnosis and drugs had revealed her to be the victim of an extraordinary form of brainwashing that could not be fully understood. Much of the process—or ritual, if you prefer—was deeply buried in her subconscious.

"Perhaps wisely," the report had said. "Much like a bullet lodged near the heart or spine. Surgical removal might eliminate the danger . . . or cause the round to move, killing the patient." Anthony recognized the sensitivity of Dr. Jane Phillips in that paragraph. But Phillips was distracted by the presence of the remarkable child, the goddaughter of the bullet-shaped Japanese man.

Thank heaven for Bernstein, Anthony thought. His clinical point of view balanced the woman's emotionalism. Unlike the CIA physicians in the movies, he was completely uninterested in creating mutated human psychic weapons for the U.S.A. Even if he believed various Carries and Firestarters existed, he knew they would be too unstable for government work. He kept Phillips distracted long enough for Hama and the child to exit Upstate New York gracefully.

Which left Anthony exactly where? He snorted, turning away from the window. Bernstein and Phillips were like the intersexual Odd Couple—the Bickersons in lab coats. God, he missed them. Ah, he heard in his mind. That's what this is really all about, isn't it? Ah, look at all the lonely people. That lyric from the Beatles song, "Eleanor Rigby."

He smiled again. He was reminded why he was in Sioux

Falls to begin with. There was a double purpose. Although the Asian assassins who had attacked the sanitarium in Upstate New York had been eradicated, they probably had leaders who were alarmed when they did not report or return. The security of the Lowy Hospital had been breached. The girl under their protection, the girl Moe Dare had given them, had to be moved.

Anthony was left with the decision: where to move her and how. He didn't need an extra baby-sitting job, and he didn't want Hama to look after another child. Even though Huntington was in her late teens, her ordeal had rendered her vulnerable. Although her body was lush, her mind was pubescent. And there were her kidnappers to consider. According to her, they were a mass of Orientals, like the ones who were exterminated at the sanitarium. Anthony had to make the correct choice for her best protection.

Hama had left the New York State clinic with the child. Anthony had left the following morning with a brunette and his young associate, Stevens. Bernstein stayed behind. The redhead stayed in her room, surrounded by guards.

The brunette, of course, was Huntington. He took her to the CIA safe house in Washington, D.C., personally, advising her to keep the brown wig on. The redhead was the still comatose Lynn McDonald, with her own wig.

Once the various witnesses and victims were in place, Anthony had other things to occupy his mind. He never discovered the identity of the woman who had called HQ asking for him, but there were enough other questions he could answer. The mystery was how North Africa, Russia, the Orient, and Sioux Falls, South Dakota, all fit in. He had traveled to the latter to find out.

That was the second purpose of his trip: to meet the one operative who had performed above and beyond the call of duty throughout Operation LCD (Lowest Common Denominator). The agent whose code name was 1 After 909.

"Move over once," he heard. It made perfect sense to use the lyrics to that Beatles song as passwords. He turned completely away from the window to look into the palest blue eyes he had ever seen. They seemed to be opal windows straight through to the speaker's mind. They were set in a wide, fleshy face with high cheekbones, surrounded by the limpest blond hair Anthony could remember, cut in a pageboy.

"Move over twice," said Anthony as he looked at the person who was professing to be 1 After 909. She stood before him, the open-air lobby of the Marriott stretching behind her, complete with piano, bar, plush seats, little tables, escalators, and a mid-lobby fountain. She wore a starched white shirt, black pants, and a black, insulated jacket.

"Come on, baby, don't be cold as ice," she said softly, smiling.

"You got me traveling on the one after-nine-oh," he said quickly. This was not part of the code, but he thought he should at least finish the chorus to show his good faith.

"You got me traveling on the one after-nine-oh," she echoed.

"You got me traveling on the one after nine-oh-nine," he finished. They both laughed.

"Imagine, another one who knows Beatles tunes," she said as he motioned her to the nearest seat, away from the rest of the lobby. She chose to shake her head from side to side and stand by the seat.

"I'm not that old," he replied, moving around the seat to the one opposite it, where the heavy metal case he had brought sat.

"We've got some driving to do," she said, her voice husky but still feminine. "Best to talk in the truck."

Sure enough, a Dodge Ram waited for them in the parking lot. It hardly stood out among the other trucks, vans, and four-wheel-drive vehicles in the huge area. South Dakota's idea of a small family car was a station wagon. Anthony looked down at his suit and lined trench coat and felt slightly out of place. 1 After 909 unlocked the passenger door, pulled herself up, and slipped behind the steering wheel.

Anthony took a last look at the gently rolling green hills

upon which a variety of hotels were nestled before pulling himself up after the agent and settling in.

"Weren't expecting a woman, were you?" she asked, beating him to the question as they took Colfax Avenue out of town. He glanced over to see her smiling. He couldn't help but look her over again. She was a solid woman with reddish-white skin. He also couldn't help wondering what nationality she was, as well as her sexual preferences.

"Makes no difference to me," Anthony said, "as long as the job gets done. And you were doing just fine. But I can't call you one after nine-oh-nine all the time. All right if I call you nine-oh?"

She laughed. "Rhymes with Joe," she said. "Naw, too confusing." She put out her hand. "Try this on for size. My real name is Moser Grzyzga." It was pronounced Moe-zer Griz-ga.

That explained the nationality and her wide, ever so slightly mottled face. She was Polish. He took her hand and they shook on it. A firm handshake, another good sign. "Moser is fine," he said. "Sounds like someone else I know, in fact. Where are we going?"

"To my surveillance spot across from the Huntington Industries factory," she explained. "I felt pretty bad leaving it for any time at all."

"Anything happening?"

"Nothing really new since my last report, just more of it. They're getting even busier, if that's possible. But you never know when something new is going to start. I get this image of everyone simply waiting for me to leave before the elves come out to make thermonuclear weapons."

It was Anthony's turn to laugh. "Yeah, I know the feeling." He was beginning to relax. It was nice to share his birthday with a woman—*any* woman—and he enjoyed her assured presence. "Don't worry, we're not looking for atom bombs."

"Mind if I ask what we *are* looking for?"

"Anything," Anthony replied without hesitation. "Anything at all."

They spent the rest of the trip debriefing each other, like

longtime associates reunited. He brought her up-to-date on the puzzle, and she informed him about Sioux Falls. They passed the nuclear power plant—the first commercial reactor of its kind ever put on-line.

"That's another thing," Moser said. "The Huntington Factory is cunningly placed to be left alone. Nuclear power is still not trusted, and the factory is set downwind of this place. Parents, teachers, and kids still stay away, unless it's on a dare. Afraid they'll grow a third eye or something."

Anthony looked over at the woman, judging her age to be somewhere between twenty-five and thirty. "You don't seem concerned."

She grinned. "Daddy wanted a boy. When he saw my neck and shoulders come out, he thought he had one. It wasn't until my hips cleared that the sky fell."

"Daddy?" Anthony replied, searching his memory. "Your father wouldn't be General Grzyzga, would he?"

"No," Moser said sarcastically. "My dad was Rear Leftenant Grzyzga. Of course I'm General Grzyzga's daughter! How many Grzyzgas do you know?"

"Sorry," Anthony said sheepishly, then repeated it with more feeling when he remembered where he'd last seen the name. "Sorry. I just read about your father's death."

Moser shrugged. "I'm a big girl. At least I knew him. Mom died trying to get me out."

"Jesus," Anthony breathed. "Maybe we should get off this subject."

"Don't worry," the driver said quickly. "I'm not handling this brilliantly, but believe it or not, all of it was a preface to saying that you don't have to worry about me. Covering your ass, I mean. I was dad's best soldier, believe me. If he was still around, he would've told you himself."

Anthony sized her up yet another time. No, she didn't seem to be a mass of psychological loose ends. She was saying all this flatly, as a statement of fact. He remembered meeting the bull-like general only once, but even then the man didn't have an ounce of bull in him. He was a direct, realistic man. Seemingly much like his daughter.

"I believe he would," Anthony finally said.

Grzyzga's face got slightly redder, but her head and eyes didn't move. She kept watching the road carefully. "Yeah. He often bragged that I could hit thirty different targets with one Uzi clip . . . on automatic."

"Impossible," Anthony said dryly.

"Try me," Moser Grzyzga said with a grin. "There it is," she announced, pointing. Anthony saw the squat, wide buildings in the distance.

"Might as well be on the dark side of the moon, huh?" he concluded.

"Spent a lot of money clearing out no-man's-land to build it," said the woman. "Wasn't financially feasible, but somebody wanted it away from prying eyes." She took a right onto a narrow dirt road and started a steady climb over rocks and branches. "Hold on. The ride's going to get a little bumpy until we reach our cruising altitude."

The truck finally pulled across a forest to stop a few yards in front of a tiny cabin set in the side of the hill. It was a small construct erected from red pine. White smoke was coming out a duct on the side, being dissipated by a built-in fan, which was whirring with a small hum. The six large windows were made of smoked glass, which was hard to see through.

"Where did you find this place?" Anthony wondered aloud, hopping out of the truck and pulling the case behind him. He stood in the small grassless yard, between a pile of split wood and a tree trunk that had an ax imbedded in it. The view was lovely in the late-afternoon sun.

"Dad's Fortress of Solitude," she said. "He wrote his memoirs here."

"Memoirs?" Anthony echoed. "I didn't see anything about his memoirs."

"Left them to me in his will," she said, heading for the door. "In case I needed any protection." There were two locks on the thick, windowless obstruction, both sophisticated, and both, no doubt, tied into some sort of alarm system. "Daddy liked isolation and security too," she said, tending to the keys. "He would've had a shit fit if they'd tried to build the factory while he was still here.'' She opened the door and they went in.

Anthony nodded in satisfaction as he set the case down and started taking off his jacket. It was essentially a one-and-a-half-room cabin, but the one room was very impressive, what with its vaulted, beamed ceiling, the skylight, the shiny wood floors, the animal rugs, the sumptuous padded wood furniture, and the smoky glass, which was crystal-clear, looking out. It was also toasty warm. Anthony imagined the place was very welcoming in the winter.

"Bedroom's over there.'' Moser pointed beyond the stove. "Bathroom's there, and kitchen's there.''

"Let's get this show on the road,'' Anthony suggested, and pulled the case over to the table where Moser's binoculars and telescope were set up next to the side window. "Night's coming on.'' Out of the padded case he pulled another telescope, but this one was shorter and wider than Moser's.

"The latest thing?'' she asked, unzipping her jacket and coming over.

"You bet,'' said Anthony, setting it up. "More powerful than ever, works on six levels of magnification and focus, better infrared capability, and an installed thirty-five-millimeter camera, with fifteen hundred ASA film.''

"Neat,'' she said, watching as he put it on its own tripod and set it before the window. "We're looking at the north and east sides of the factory,'' she informed him. "They built it on a diagonal from this vantage point, a mile and a half away. We get to see the loading docks as well as the dumpsters. Couldn't ask for a better vantage point unless we were inside.''

"Did you try to place an ear or eye there?'' Anthony asked, still fiddling with the equipment.

"Our nearest office is in Omaha, Nebraska,'' she said, shrugging. "They couldn't spare an operative, they said, and I thought it best not to compromise myself. No doubt they have cameras in their lobby.''

"Probably best,'' Anthony muttered, squeezing his eye

onto the black rubber cup over the tube. "Let's see what we have here . . . ."

His view came into focus as Moser grabbed her binoculars and joined him. They both saw the factory's smokestacks belching, and the loading docks busy with two tractor trailers.

"Hmm," Anthony mused, clicking the second lens into use. Nothing much to see in the dumpsters, so he refocused on the loading docks. "You identify anyone since the operation began?"

"Couldn't get close enough," Moser complained. "I've been bellyaching for something like your machine for months, but Omaha keeps taking the film I took through my telescope, saying they sent it on to you, then shutting up."

"Well," said Anthony, "today's your lucky day. . . ."

The third lens clicked into place. The woman had been right. No thermonuclear weapons. Just farm equipment. Anthony shook his head slightly. Yeah? So? Farm equipment. Why would anybody in North Africa, Russia, or the Orient kidnap a girl to get farm equipment? All they had there was sand, snow, and sweat. They weren't planning to march on the tristate area with tractors, were they?

The fourth lens clicked into place. Look at those workers go! It wasn't like any factory Anthony had seen for quite some time. All the bodies he saw there were moving quickly and professionally. No looking at the clock, no leaning toward the watercooler. They were packing and loading this stuff like their lives depended on it.

The fifth lens clicked into place. Anthony moved the telescope around slightly, trying to capture the workers in his eyes. He started taking pictures with the small syringe trigger attached to the rubber tube hanging off the scope. The lens flitted from the farm machinery to the packing machinery to the trucks.

"Just one more . . ." Anthony said quietly. The sixth lens clicked into place.

"Fuck," said Agent Anthony. Then he sat up and leaned back in the chair, his face showing chagrin and amazement.

"What is it?" Moser asked, putting down her binoculars

and leaning over the new scope. "Christ on the cross, those are . . . gooks." Sure enough, the faces she saw under the hard hats scurrying around the trucks were Asian.

"Japs," Anthony responded. "Chinks, Vietnamese, Koreans, Thai, Malaysians, Filipinos, Singaporeans, who knows? But yeah, instead of good farm boys, they've got Orientals. I was expecting something, but not this."

Moser looked at him. "What *were* you expecting?"

"Russians," he said. "That would make some sense. If they didn't open their mouths, you couldn't tell the difference between them and us. No surveillance pictures would reveal any secrets."

"My photos must've had smudges for faces," she said fretfully.

"True. Most surveillance photography is designed for the big picture, not details. But now we've got faces, and they're Orientals." Anthony remembered only one kind of Asian . . . the kind who came in the night to kill guards and abduct a sleeping young redhead.

"What's going on, Joe?" Moser wondered.

"Nothing good," Anthony replied, getting up quickly. "You take as many facial photos as you can. I'm going to call Omaha and get their butts in gear. I want those trucks followed. I want those shipments traced."

"Phone on the wall of the kitchen," she told him, already bending to the task. He moved around the sofa, beneath the dying rays of the setting sun from the skylight, and grabbed the red phone from the wall unit.

He put it to his ear. There was no dial tone.

He stood very still for a few seconds, the only sounds being the click of the telescope camera. Then he slowly and silently hung up the phone.

"Moser," he called quietly, "how often do you R.S.V.P.?" That was their cutesy code meaning "checking for reverse surveillance."

She stood up, the syringe camera plunger still in one hand. "Every day. Dad installed all sorts of bug busters in here, and I check them every morning and every night. I use the HQ-assigned stuff too. Why?"

"Nothing. Listen, we're going to take the film out of the scope, go to your truck, and drive to Omaha. All right?" He didn't turn around, but his eyes were looking everywhere.

She, too, became very still. "All right," she answered. Then they both started moving. She had seen enough of this sort of equipment to be able to remove the film. He picked up his coat and shrugged it on.

"Come on," he said, holding his arm out to her. "Omaha is about a hundred and seventy-five miles away. We can make that in about two and a half hours."

"Not the way I drive," she said tightly. "Two at the most. We'll be there before it gets dark."

They opened the door and stepped onto the narrow, roofed porch. The scene before them tested their sanity. There were three men between them and the truck. They wore black, loose-fitting clothes. Their skin was yellow. Their eyes were almond-shaped. Their hair was black. Two were clean-shaven. The one in the middle had a thick salt-and-pepper mustache.

One held a long, hard stick, its red painted tip pointed at the darkening sky. The other held a strange metal club, with a ball-like top and a spike at the tip. The one with the mustache had empty hands.

"Can I help you?" asked Moser as she and Anthony stood on the slightly raised porch.

The man with the mustache held out his hand. Even that movement had an elegant strength. His fingers were long. His palm was wide. They were the hands of a master. A master of something: art, music, or maybe death.

"Give me the film you are holding," he said, each word soft.

Moser was faster then Anthony. Her Heckler and Koch P7-M8 automatic was out before his Smith and Wesson Model 25 revolver. It was irrelevant. Both barrels were soon pointing at the Asian men before them.

"Clear out," said Grzyzga.

The man with the mustache just smiled, his hand still out. "Put down your weapons."

"Stand aside," Anthony growled.

The man with the mustache looked down and shook his head, still smiling. "You never learn, do you?"

"All I know is that you'll be dead before you come near," Anthony barked. "I said, stand aside!"

"We will not move."

Moser took a step forward. Anthony instantly held her back. "What's the matter?" she said, flaring. "This is a 9-mm. That's a .45. What are they going to do? Catch the slugs in their teeth?"

"We won't have to, my dear," said the man with the mustache.

Moser looked at him in amazement, then gasped. She stared at the gun in her hand. It had started to bite, then burn her. Anthony sucked in his breath as his gun seemed to heat up in his hand.

It was as if the guns had been set afire. Soon neither operative could hold them. Both dropped them, gasping, astonished, and stepped back. The guns hit the wooden porch, bounced, and lay still, seemingly unchanged. The agents' astonishment was magnified when two short blades erupted from between the porch slats and went through each weapon's trigger guard.

Moser tried to grab her gun, but Anthony pulled her back as both blades shot forward, across the porch, dragging the guns with them. The guns flew off the blades at the porch edge and fell into the dirt a few feet in front of the man with the mustache. The blades disappeared under the porch again.

"Step into the house," Moser hissed, holding on to Anthony.

"What?"

"Get . . . into . . . the . . . house!"

Moser stepped back through the door quickly, leaving Anthony teetering on the base of the frame. "What happened?" he shouted at the man with the mustache. "What did you do?"

The man simply smiled wider, and the area suddenly grew yellow men.

They stepped from behind trees. They jumped from the

branches. They crawled out from under the porch. They dropped from the roof. Eight in all. Some held short blades with lacquered handles. Some held short, hollow sticks dripping reddish powder.

"You had to come with new equipment, didn't you?" said the man with the mustache. "You couldn't leave well enough alone."

"Get inside," Moser whispered.

Anthony ignored her. "Who are you?" he demanded, sounding bolder than he felt. They had drizzled the powder on them from above. It burned their exposed skin. They had crawled under the porch and waited with their short knives. They were like the men who had infiltrated and attacked the sanitarium, only worse.

"That is not important," said the man with the mustache. "Our images are. Give me the film and we will go away."

"After what?" Anthony yelled, feeling fear for the first time in years. For the first time since leaving the SFPD, in fact.

The eyes of the man with the mustache narrowed in appreciation of Anthony's insight. "Do not give us the film and we will take it. In thirty seconds."

"The house has a concrete foundation," Moser hissed in Anthony's ear. "The porch does not. Get . . . in . . . now!" She yanked on his arm, and surprised by her strength, he stumbled back. But she did not close the door. Instead she filled it. She put her hands on the frame and yelled at them.

"We're not giving you squat! Come and get it, prickless wonder!"

The man with the mustache was unimpressed with her obscenity. He motioned four men forward—the ones who had been on the roof and under the porch.

They came faster than Moser had anticipated, but she only reacted more quickly. As Anthony watched, sprawled on the couch behind her, she stamped her right foot.

The floor slat she stamped on gave way. It went down, held by a pin support, like a seesaw. The other side came up, throwing something from under the house into her hands.

She had vaulted a mini-Uzi into her fingers.

How often had her father made her practice that trick? He was not a stupid man. He had the paranoia life in the military caused. He knew there'd be a time of social or economic chaos. He knew people would be coming to this door sooner or later.

Moser pulled the trigger and sprayed the front yard. The first three approaching couldn't get out of the way. The slugs jerked them around. The fourth was able to duck and get around the house. The others scattered.

Moser didn't stop. She slammed the front door closed and turned her back to the wall. "The walls are steel-reinforced. Only the windows . . . !"

The window from which they had been watching the factory exploded inward, as if blown by a wind machine in one mad, big-bad-wolf gust. A basketball-sized hole appeared in the center, then the rest shattered inward, spinning.

Moser Grzyzga stood her ground and fired, shouting at Anthony all the while. "Under the couch—9-mm!"

Anthony hit the floor, grabbed the sofa legs, and tipped it—partly for the gun taped there, partly for protection. The Uzi chattered, the glass splattered on the floor and furniture, and he came up with a Browning Hi-Power automatic.

The window on the other side of the room blew in. Moser screamed and turned in that direction. Anthony shot up on one knee, his automatic pointing at the first window.

The more experienced agent was right. They came in from the first window. The second was a diversion. He shot the man leaping in, through the top of his skull. He hit the floor dead, the bullet digging through is brain, his throat, and his upper chest.

The second man came behind him. As the first fell, he was exposed. Anthony shot him in the gut, and Moser perforated his top half. He jerked in place, his arms waving, metal spilling from them like molten blood, and then he fell back onto the window frame.

"Cover me!" Moser shouted, throwing away the spent Uzi and rolling toward the table where her binoculars were.

Anthony spun toward the second window, and everything started exploding.

The door was cracked and almost swung inward from the center. The front window near the stove exploded in. Anthony put two slugs into the heaving door before moving his arm toward the shattered window. Moser grabbed the table legs and pulled it over. She ripped the 9-mm Browning Hi-Power automatic from under there when a man came through the *unshattered* window, followed by a man leaping through the broken one.

Anthony blasted the man in the shattered window opening. He caught him in the side as he passed. The man slammed to the floor in front of the kneeling Moser. She came around as Anthony aimed the Browning at the fallen man's head.

Anthony was in the way. From her position she'd have to shoot *through* Anthony to get the one behind him.

"*Joe!*" she screamed in agony as he fired. The fallen man's head erupted. Anthony jerked in place, his head, shoulders, and elbows going back, as if he were fighting a massive yawn. His face was twisted in pain and surprise.

Moser Grzyzga stood up. She used the other man for target practice. As he ran to the back of the house she shot him once in the ribs, once in the chest, and once in the head. He jerked over, jerked up, then smashed his already rended skull against the wall.

The cabin was a smoking, arid, gore-drenched hellhole.

Grzyzga immediately grabbed the leg of the the table and yanked it upright. She scrambled under it, then slid it across the floor as she crawled toward Anthony.

He finished his unnatural yawn, and all his strength seemed to leave him. He fell to his elbows. Moser choked and held back tears. The agent's back was covered in steel shards.

Grzyzga pulled the table over the two of them, grabbing him by the arm. "Joe," she begged, shaking him. "Joe, don't leave me."

He looked up, his expression mingling surprise, pain, and a strange happiness. That alone unleashed Moser's tears.

She couldn't keep them from streaming down her face any longer.

His eyes focused on her, and he tried to smile. He knew he was dying. The blades were nothing. It was the poison rushing through his body that was ripping huge chunks out of his internal organs. The chemicals were burning through him from inside. He didn't have time to tell her what a happy birthday this had been. Or how good she had made him feel.

Because now he understood. Operation LCD was over. He knew how the Asians and North Africans fit in. He was only sorry he wouldn't be able to tell her about it.

But with her, and her skills, lay hope. She would either save his ass at the CIA, or join him in hell. Either way he won. And these bastards lost.

The ends of his lips twisted upward. "Find the Russian," he said.

"What?" she cried. Her tears had been deafened by the roar of the guns.

"Find the Russian," he told her, rubbing his face on her fine, limp hair. "Get him. For..."

Joe Anthony's face fell, slamming onto the floor. His nose was broken but he didn't feel it. His eyes were open but he saw only death.

II

Daremo's eyes opened. A tear was rolling across his cheek, toward his ear. It had woken him up. What had he done to deserve this?

"I'm sorry," he whispered to the ceiling.

Maybe that would appease whatever he had disturbed.

III

The skylight exploded inward. Moser Grzyzga grabbed the 9-mm automatic out of Anthony's limp hand, spun onto her back, and slammed both barrels to the tabletop.

She pulled both triggers repeatedly, blinking the tears out of her eyes.

The table danced on all four legs as the slugs tore through the top and into the ceiling. One man was hit in the foot and toppled backward off the roof. Another was struck in the hip and shoulder as he jumped through, the burning dust from a hollow tube spilling.

He slammed onto the tabletop, bouncing, the table legs bending and groaning. The powder slipped through the bullet holes, but Grzyzga rolled to the side, rose, and pointed the guns before her.

She pulled the triggers simultaneously but didn't watch the slugs staple the fallen man in the side. They slid him off the tabletop and knocked him to the floor, his ribs and hip shattered.

Grzyzga ran to the kitchen instead, emptying the rest of each gun's thirteen rounds into the back window. She threw the guns away and wrenched open the stove door. She pulled the Uzi from the top rack. She wrenched open the fridge door. She pulled the other Uzi from the bottom rack.

She turned and danced across the cabin floor, shooting.

"Never load a clip full if the gun's going to lay," she heard her father say. "A full clip'll bend the loading spring."

Thirty rounds in each Uzi, she thought. Dance, girl, dar.ce. Fire through the side windows, spin around, fire through the back window and skylight, reach the door. Keep going.

She had to keep them off her. She couldn't give them a chance to pop up, throw their metal shards, and duck. She went through the ruined door opening. She fired out at the trees, but when she stepped on the porch, she fired through the ceiling and into the floorboards.

She kept moving quickly, feeling the weapons emptying, seeing no one. She jumped off the porch, spinning, so she fired into the woods around her, then across the roof as she backed toward the truck.

Her back slammed into the vehicle's side as the guns clicked empty. *There, Dad*, she thought. *There. You'd be proud of me. I timed it perfectly.*

She let her legs go out from under her. Her back was against something solid so they couldn't get her from behind. They'd have to hit her from the top, sides, and front.

They heard the weapons empty as well. They started popping up like chipmunks in an arcade mallet-whacking game. One came over the lip of the roof. He was smiling. Grzyzga liked his smug expression. It said what she had hoped; they'd underestimated her. She was a hysterical woman. She would throw her tantrum, then they would get her.

He held up his hand. There was a knife in it. Grzyzga moved her body so it blocked his view of her hand going beneath the wheel housing. The man gloated a moment more. He threw the knife when Moser swung the Glock 17 automatic forward.

Boom. The first of the Austrian high-tech plastic 9-mm's seventeen rounds took the top of the man's head off. It was an Armageddon haircut. One minute his skull was there. The next, his scalp was flying behind him in every direction.

Grzyzga didn't savor the moment. She leaned forward, letting the knife slam into the side of the truck, inches behind her. Her arm went right and nailed a man coming from behind a tree, his powder tube swinging. Her second shot set him back into the trunk, the powder hurtling toward her like an air tsunami. She ducked and rolled under the vehicle.

She stopped halfway out the other side, on her back. The man who leapt from the truck bed, knife flashing, thought he would pounce on her as she got to her feet. She pointed the Glock straight up and blew out his chest cavity. Grzyzga rolled out from under the truck, her left hand holding the second Glock, which had been taped to the wheel housing there.

She stood, arms out, pulling both triggers. The guns blasted a small path to the driver's seat. She kept firing with her left hand as she opened the door, slid in, and dug for her keys.

Men came running at her from the right side, thinking she needed that arm for the ignition.

"Ha!" she screamed, hitting the engine button, set low on the dashboard, with her knee and bringing up the first Glock. She blasted out the right window as the truck roared to life. The earliest automobiles all had ignition buttons. General Grzyzga liked that idea—one never knew when one would need *both* hands.

The first man didn't react fast enough. The truck's right window blew out, and the slug caught him in the chest. He was thrown back into the cabin wall while the others dived. Moser rammed her foot on the accelerator, and the truck lurched forward. She slammed both guns to the steering wheel and spun the tires to the forest path.

"Now!" boomed the man with the mustache, waving the P7-M8 she had dropped. "Now!" They had not expected the woman to put up such a fight.

A man raced behind the truck, leaping onto the rear bumper. Two more men dropped from the trees. Grzyzga shot the one to her left on his way down. His feet hit the hood of the car, then he dived backward, splitting his head on a tree. The one on the right landed, grabbed the top of the cab, and held on. In his free hand was Anthony's revolver.

She was faster than him. She brought the other Glock up and fired through the windshield. The glass flew, spiderwebbing around a ragged hole. The 9-mm bullet caught the man directly in the wrist.

"Incredible," said Yung, the man with the mustache. "She doesn't register surprise or shock. She doesn't pause. She just keeps going." He slowly went to one knee, his eyes narrowing, watching the truck weave through the woods.

The man on the hood didn't scream. His right hand disappeared in an explosion of broken bones and blood. He fell, still holding on to the cab with his left hand. His head slammed into the windshield, cracking it. Still, he did not scream, and he didn't slide off.

Grzyzga threw the guns to the seat, needing both hands to

keep the truck from bouncing into a tree. She couldn't get stopped now, not after all this!

The man on the hood grimaced, raising his head to stare at her. He had to stay on. He had to distract her. If he could keep her attention the man behind her could sneak up with his knife. His vision was getting fuzzy, but he could see her hands, tight on the wheel. There was a roar in his head, but he could still hear her. What was she saying? Was she talking to him?

"Hey!" she was shouting over the truck's thunder. "Hey! I got something to say to you! Are you listening?"

He blinked, trying to concentrate over the pain. If only he could let go and get at his blade! Then he would show her. But no, all he could do now was hang on and distract her. His friend would get her. He would see to it. He stared at her, his lips coming off his teeth in an agonizing version of a smile.

"You listening?" Moser Grzyzga screamed, her hands fighting the wheel, her right foot tromped on the accelerator. "Good! Listen to this!" Her left foot suddenly went up and sneaked under the thick black wire that hung under the dashboard.

She stepped hard, pulling the wire down like it was an emergency brake. The two sawed-off shotguns screwed to the back wall of the engine block, their barrels pressed against the hood, fired.

Two big holes appeared in the hood, looking as if two invisible fists went through them. The shot spread, one hunk soaring into the trees, the other tearing out a fifth of the man's side. He jerked up, then down. Moser sneered at his expression—the one mixing shock and failure. The man then slid off the hood, as if the wind had taken him.

"Yeah!" shouted Moser. Let's hear it for paranoia. She never forgot her father's story of the time his truck had been stopped in the woods by the Klan. He had been helping the blacks in town, and the white-sheets didn't like it. They had climbed all over his rig with their ax handles, smashing the steel and glass, completely terrorizing her mother. He vowed that wasn't going to happen again.

"Never again!" his daughter shouted, reached back with her left hand, and grabbed the wire hanging off the rear cab wall, just beside the seat back.

The man in the truck bed put his hand on the ceiling of the cab. She yanked the cord. The shotguns mounted under the seat, pointing up, went off with a ripping boom.

Again, one hunk of shot punched through the thin sheet metal and went into the air harmlessly. Most of the other shot went right between the man's legs. That's what the general had designed it for.

The man slid back, feeling nothing at all for a second. He was just wondering why his knees were together, his legs bent, and his shoulders hunched. Then he felt everything.

Moser yanked the wheel to the left. The man slid all the way across the truck-bed floor and toppled head over heels out the side. He did a crazy cartwheel headfirst into a boulder.

Yung stayed on one knee as the truck roared down the hill, taking the second-to-last parallel path. She'd turn right once more, then a quick left onto the main road to escape. There were no other roadblocks, since no one thought this operation would be difficult.

If they were to stop her, they'd have to stop her now.

The man with the mustache had no doubt. Even though most of his men were dead or dying, he was enjoying this. He looked forward to making *her* death very slow and pleasurable . . . for him. There were legends that told of a *sifu* who ate his victims. He swore that their strength became his. In this case Yung would take of her flesh in another way. A woman of this skill could be rewarding in more ways than one.

The P7-M8 was in his hand, rock-steady. There were eight rounds. He would flatten all of the truck's tires and still have four bullets to "guide" her to him . . . or wound her, if it became necessary.

He waited until the truck went across his kneeling position. He would strike the left rear tire first, making the vehicle skid around, catching the back against a tree. He fired without blinking.

The truck kept going. The man with the mustache looked over the gun.

"It's not stopping!" said one of his men.

He didn't reply. He brought the gun to the left and fired again—directly into the left front tire. That didn't explode or deflate, either.

"Solid!" he suddenly realized. "They are solid rubber!"

Moser Grzyzga heard the shots over the throb of the engine. She "felt" the slugs hit. Her lips pulled back in a satisfied sneer. *Thank you, Daddy,* she told him. *Thank you for the fear, your paranoia, and all the extreme measures. You were right, Daddy. They really are after us.*

She'd take the time to be amazed and shocked later. They had murdered her CIA superior with burning powder and poisoned darts. They attacked like a horde of rats. They had nearly killed her a half dozen times, and still they came. Who *were* these guys?

Grzyzga leaned down to the right, getting her body out of sight. Her right hand went out and tapped the glove-compartment button. It fell open, but then she needed both her hands to make the last turn before the main road.

Yeah, maybe the steel walls of the truck, could take the bullets, but maybe not. Either way she couldn't chance it. Sooner or later the man with the mustache would peg her. This called for some apocalyptic strategy. She had no plans to come back here, anyway.

"I'm a big girl now, Daddy," she heard herself say. "Out into the world, like you always wanted. No more protection."

The man with the mustache brought the gun up. Six more rounds to pepper the cab with. He no longer cared whether she was captured dead or alive. Perhaps he'd even enjoy "taking" her while she was wounded. He *would* enjoy her screams of pain as her torn limbs were moved by his passion.

He aimed, and his finger tightened.

Moser Grzyzga pressed the button on the small box in the glove compartment. It looked like a garage-door opener. A little red light went on at the front of the gadget.

The cabin exploded.

The bombs the general had installed just before he wrote his memoirs detonated without a hitch. Better dying through science. The cabin walls were torn apart by the force of the shock wave. The ball of yellow-orange flame looked like a defiant fist punching through the ground.

The men went flying, knocked off the ground by swinging, invisible slaps. General Grzyzga himself came down on Yung's back with both feet, slamming the Asian's face into the ground.

His daughter swung the truck onto the open road while slipping one Glock into the shoulder holster under her jacket. Then she drove with one hand while holding the second Glock in her lap.

"That'll teach those gooks," she said, flooring the rended truck down the open road. 'You're in South Dakota now.''

14

"The spirit is to win in the depths of the enemy. . . ."

Daremo heard it as if from the end of a long hall. He knew then that he was dreaming.

"Ken No Sen," he correctly identified, his voice flat and quiet. He knew Musashi couldn't hear him. "Ken No Sen!" he called louder, but his voice was as flat as it had been the first time. He did not say it a third time. He wasn't that scared or stupid. A scream would accomplish nothing. Dreams worked by their own rules.

Where was he? Here. Where was here? In a cellar in Paris, France, yes, but that was not all. He was everywhere he had ever been. He was seeing everything he had ever seen.

He ignored the meaningless parts now—his birth, his happy childhood, the death of his brother, his education, his marriage, his business, the slaughter of his parents and his pregnant wife, even his subsequent revenge and initial ninja training. Thirty years . . . gone like that.

It was unimportant, he told himself. Sweep it away.

He hovered over the years since instead.

He watched himself making love to the woman Tagashi.

He watched the man Hama studying and meditating for hours.

He watched the man Yasuru take the golden needle meant for him.

He saw the insanity that gripped him as if it were a living thing. It became the fifth creature in his ryo. He watched as it sent him away.

He saw decapitated heads rolling down the Salvadorian mountainside, their skin covered with lotus petals.

He saw other men writhing, their bodies covered in stinging yellow-and-black insects.

He saw the two men fighting without words or weapons in the middle of the camp cut in the side of a mountain.

There was no noise, save their breaths, and the sound of arm striking arm, leg hitting leg. The men looked like they were dancing.

They danced from there to the desert, where he saw the man he was fighting was himself.

He saw that man marry a woman with auburn hair. He saw that man work with the spark of life itself. He saw that spark of life become a spark of death.

He saw a field filled with sparks, and the two people who lay in it. One was the man Yasuru. The other was the bride Shika.

They lay still, their eyes open, as the field of sparks spun slowly beneath him.

He flew away from there, deep into the desert. Below, groups of almond-eyed Asians looked up, shielding their faces from the sun.

As he flew farther there were more and more Asians. They stood in bigger and bigger groups until they became the land itself. Passing clouds obscured their millions.

He landed on a mountain where the clouds became a carpet stretching from horizon to horizon. On the peak sat a wizened, naked Chinaman, the sun making a spotlight and a halo behind him.

"They have all deserted you," he said, laughing. "Your army of dead is gone."

"I don't need them," Daremo told him.

"You lie," said the mystic. "You are alone."

"As you," Daremo countered. "As all."

"You are alone," said the oni, the demon who laughed at all that was human. "You cannot fly."

"Then I will fall," said Daremo.

He stepped through the clouds. He dropped into the blackness.

He fell and fell and fell until he could no longer tell whether he was falling or not. He was so deep in the darkness that he could no longer tell if his eyes were open or closed. Only then did vision return. He could just make out two points of light.

They flitted before him like fireflies. He could not judge their distance. They could be inches or miles away. They moved up and down slowly, weaving from side to side. As he watched, they started to sparkle. He could not tell whether they were living or inanimate.

It made no difference. They were all there was in this new world. They were beautiful but somehow threatening. He watched as they continued their hypnotic, rhythmic movement. Up and down, side to side...

The blackness began to fade. These two stars were beginning to create an environment. There were wet, soft walls with peeling wallpaper and water stains. There was a sagging ceiling with a single hanging clear light bulb. There was a sloping floor with cracked, warped tile. There were tightly closed, locked doors. There was a stairway going up into the darkness, its steps made of rotting wood.

The waving, weaving stars began to hum.

II

Finding this place had not been easy, but it had not been incredibly difficult, either. Le Moissonner had started at the

Menilmontant Métro Station and walked around. He walked in ever greater spirals, as the city itself had been designed. He walked through Saint-Maur and Père-Lachaise, where the cemetery tombs were covered with dead, potted, chrysanthemums, their stiff petals blowing across the coarsened grass. He walked past the wall where the last Commune, rebels were shot in 1871.

He walked through the Pigalle. He went past the porno shops with the most disgusting, degrading magazines. They were this city's pornography, since beautiful sexuality could be found in most magazines on any street corner. He passed the theaters showing the worst films the world had to offer—*Molested, Le Centaur Rouge Contre le Dragon Blanc*, and others. He passed the Moulin Rouge and other tourist traps. He passed the hard-faced prostitutes who still wore the desperate trappings of a bygone era—striped top, slit skirt, fishnet stockings, and a beret.

He walked and he watched. He walked and listened. He walked and talked. He asked directions . . . then other questions. He occasionally checked to see if any bodies were discovered in the subway tunnels. He stepped into local police stations to report his wallet stolen by a gray-eyed man with copper-colored hair.

"That's funny," said one gendarme. And then Le Moissonner heard about a café owner who had complained of a derelict with copper-colored hair. That man had accosted his customers and stolen some wine.

Le Moissonner sat at that café every night from then on. He chatted with the regulars. He walked through those neighborhoods every chance he could. He checked the local hospitals for any sign of his gray-eyed "cousin" with the copper-colored hair.

"He drinks too much and is not at all well. Try to find out where he's staying if you see him. . . ."

The Reaper looked around until someone called to him.

His head swiveled around when he heard the cry that night. There was no mistaking it: It was the cry of someone wishing death's embrace. It was the cry he hadn't heard for weeks. No, there was no doubt; it was the same cry he had heard intermittently over the past two years.

He had never failed to perform his duties then. He could not ignore them now. His head craned around to look over shoulders and between bodies. He had to pinpoint just who was silently calling death.

Too many people . . . there were people all over the street. The avenues were thick with students and neighbors and tourists in this, the last of the quaint inner-city villages.

It did not help that the roads were narrow and winding here, with suddenly sloping stairways nestled in corners. The walks were lined with little cottages and gardens. Tiny cars and mini-trucks clogged the cobblestones. Le Moissonner looked this way and that, unable to pinpoint his subject.

But just before the caller turned the far corner, the Reaper got just a glimpse of a dark raincoat.

He rose smoothly and dropped money on the tiny round table. He moved forward quickly and smoothly. He went past everyone else on the street, ignoring their faces. He knew what he had to do.

He followed the tall, hunched figure to the side street and the dark, run-down, three-story, building in mid-block. The figure descended the cellar stairs without pausing or looking back. Le Moissonner grinned, knowing the person had no idea death had heard the call. He went to the steps and looked down. It was a dark pit, with the stairs descending into darkness. Fitting.

Le Moissonner looked both ways. The street was slick with the afternoon's rain. Wisps of steam came from the pipes in the corner of each building. The only light came from streetlights around the corner and the moon. The place was colored blue with an off-white halo. The walks and avenue were deserted. It was as if Le Moissonner were alone in the world.

He took his first step down into the pit. He already knew this neighborhood. There would be no gendarme patrols here. There would be no laughing lovers skipping down the sidewalk at the wrong time. There would be no concerned neighbors running around to investigate strange bumps in the night.

Still, he hesitated. Should he go, or report this new subject to Napoleon? Why? He had never done so before. There was always time to inform his mentor. Besides, each reconnaissance started with a single step. He risked nothing by starting his intimate study of death's next subject.

He heard the hum halfway down the steps. It was interesting, his mind told him. It was a hum unlike any he had ever heard. It was not an engine or a furnace he recognized. Perhaps he should retreat, but he would never know what the hum was without investigation. Forewarned was forearmed. He took another silent step downward. He lowered his head so he could look down the long, gloomy hall.

III

Daremo wasn't there.

The sparkling stars had gotten so bright that he could see nothing but white. As he had been in blackness, he was now in white. It was white as far as he could see or sense.

He soared again, across the whiteness, his arms straight out. The exhilaration filled him. The cold stiffened his features and limbs. Smoke poured from his mouth, as if his torso housed a furnace.

It was not a fire inside him. His breath was condensing. It was freezing in the sky, and he soared over snow. He kept flying through the bitter cold until he could go no farther. He slowed, then stopped, then hung—the way falling water became an icicle. He scanned the horizon but saw nothing. He listened carefully but could only hear the breathing.

"What is that?" he asked. No answer.

He listened as the slow, steady breathing became louder. He listened until the sound of the breathing filled his head. He listened until the breathing became his own. He saw what the breather saw. He heard what the breather heard. He felt what the breather felt.

He recognized it all. He had been here before. He had been here recently. He knew whose mind he occupied, only the mind was not aware of him. Daremo watched through the boy's eyes and listened to the boy's thoughts.

"It's so cold. These gloves don't do anything—they're just the lousy dime-store kind, anyway, with plastic instead of leather and that fake fur-fuzz lining. Same with the shoes. Why did Dad have to be so cheap? At least I got the hat Grandma gave me. That holds in some heat and's got thick earflaps. Only, everybody in school thinks I look like a dork.

"Who cares what they think? I don't need them. They're not going anywhere. Just like me. What makes them so special? Why am I sitting here, anyway? Why don't I get up, go someplace? The snow's seeping through my pants.

"Yeah? Where would I go? Home? Forget it. Dad'll just look at me like he always does. God, I liked it better when he hit me. Now he gets mad and comes at me but gets that sick look on his face, like he's gonna puke or something. Then he backs off. He backs off! He thinks I'm the plague.

"He hates me.

"He doesn't do anything anymore. He just sits and drinks. Mom doesn't do shit, either. All she does is cry. All she ever did was cry.

"I don't get it. Everything was fine until Mr. Brett left."

Daremo woke up, but he was still asleep. He felt himself become aware, but the dream would not stop. He tried to sit up. He tried to open his eyes. He could do neither.

He had to lay there and feel Peter Sirmans dig around in his pocket until he felt the tiny things inside. He had to lay there and see Peter Sirmans's hand come up. He had to look through Peter Sirmans's eyes, down at the pills.

"A green, a red, a white," the junior high schooler said. He was still amazed that these things could do what they did. He was still amazed he could get them. But somehow there always seemed to be enough money for lunch, video, and drugs.

"Should've gotten a blue," he muttered. "Patriotic." He opened his mouth and threw all the pills in.

That'll warm me up, he thought. He folded his arms and snuggled closer against the tree in the school yard.

Maybe I'll just stay here until I go to sleep forever, he thought. *Nah, No such luck. I'll wake up and go home and hell will continue. Lucky me.*

He looked up to where the soft metal throwing star was still imbedded in the tree trunk.

It was the Brettree, named for the history teacher who had brought them just so far... and then dumped them.

Peter Sirmans felt the pills start to take effect.

"Let... me... out!" Daremo screamed, ripping through the boy's brain, then his skull, then his hair. He soared into the stratosphere, gasping.

I didn't want that to happen... I wanted the father to stop beating him... I wanted to teach the man the meaning of pain... I wanted him to think before striking the boy... I didn't want him to hate him...!

What do you care? he asked himself. *Who cares about the boy, or his father, or anyone? Remember what you are. Fallen angel, man. No one. Nobody. It doesn't make any difference what happens to them.*

Daremo sank. He floated down again. He moved through the small town. Past the junior high school, past the high school, past the agricultural college. Yes, good old Moscow, Idaho, home of tomorrow's farmers. It was the place that promised to turn deserts into paradise....

Daremo opened his eyes.

He lay on the bed in the Paris basement apartment.

CIA agent Joe Anthony was dead.

Peter Sirmans, one of the students he had taught in Moscow, Idaho, was taking drugs. His father, who had been taught the meaning of pain by the same teacher, had retreated into a world of self-pity and self-loathing.

The Russian had left Idaho. He had what he wanted.

Paradise...

Daremo knew these things as if he had experienced them himself. As if the Chinese mystic, Hui, the scientist-god Daremo had killed on the mountaintop, had whispered them in his ear.

They had taken Hui's brain machine and tried to drive him crazy. They had ripped open his mind instead. Hui had gone into his mind and tried to kill him but cured him instead. All that was left were the echoes.

These echoes.

His friend had died. His student was slowly killing himself. The Russian had paradise.

Only after he realized these things did he hear the muffled sound of humming coming from the other side of the wall.

IV

Le Moissonner stopped at the base of the stairs. He stared down the hall at the figure leaning against the right wall, playing. He was tempted to turn and leave, but the image was so fascinating, so striking, that he held his breath and his ground.

She leaned on the wall like the most casual of lovers. One foot was out on the floor, anchored, and the other was on the wall, her knee bent. Her back was flat against the wall as well. Her lips were shaped in a small smile, and she looked only at her hands—*not* at the things in her hands.

No, those things were not *in* her hands. They never rested in the fingers themselves. They flitted around the hands. They danced, they sang, they floated, they flew. He couldn't even tell their exact shape because of their speed and movement. He didn't know if they were some sort of bird, or made of some sort of flame.

He didn't know until she caught them. Her fingers and forearms stopped moving, and the Hanzo Razors were suddenly in her grip. She turned her head and looked at him from under her chopped bangs, still smiling.

"Are you a juggler?" he asked.

"I am nothing," she said mildly.

There was no mistake, he realized. This was the one who had called to him. This Asian vision in Spandex, sneakers, and raincoat. "We haven't met, have we? Do I know you?"

"No," she said. "But I know you." She pointed at him. "*You* are death."

He was stunned by hearing it. He had always known it,

but he had never heard it actually said by a subject. For a moment his brain burned as he considered every possibility.

She was an enemy agent. She had been tailing him. She was a test from Napoleon. She was the world's greatest assassin.

But these thoughts popped like a bubble when he looked at her again. His eyes widened and his back straightened as he realized she was not an SSS member. They had not met before. She had not been following him. No . . . she had been *waiting*.

His eyes narrowed and his shoulders hunched when he realized she had not heard of him. She simply *knew* he would be coming. "How?" he asked.

The steel in her hands began to roll around her fingers again. She looked down at them like a loving mother. "I know death when I see him," she said. "I have slept with it. I have embraced it. I love it."

Le Moissonner almost turned and ran for the last time. But death cannot turn and run. It can only go forward and claim its prize.

"I *am* death," he said, his arms going out slightly from his side, his palms toward her. He took his first step down the hall as the tiny steel tongue snapped out from under his left palm.

Her head jerked when she heard it. Her eyes gleamed when she saw it. Le Moissonner was astonished. She looked radiant, almost deliriously happy. She laughed with total delight.

"No, you are not," she answered him, turning. "But you'll have to do."

He was enraptured as she came at him. Her body moved like a lithe belly dancer's, twisting and dodging as her arms waved around, the blades still spinning around her fingers. They swept at his head, meaning to carve two channels in his skull.

He ducked to the right, feeling the blades parting his hair, as he punched with his left hand, meaning to tear open that flat, perfect stomach of hers. His back arched out and his fist disappeared inside her coat. Somehow she had contorted out from under his blow. His fist hit the cloth, and then her knee came up, smashing him in the side.

He was propelled into the right wall. He let his shoulder cushion the blow and swung his right arm around, sending her back.

It had all happened in a second. Suddenly they were back the way they had started. She stood a few feet away, spinning her blades. He stood by the stairs.

He put his right hand up and motioned her toward him. In turn, he walked toward her.

"Come along," he said. " 'Death calls ye to the crowd of common men.' "

"I am not a man," she said as she went at him in the narrow hall.

The first Hanzo Razor shot from her hand and sped at his face. He went under and caught it with his wrist-knife as his left arm shot up. The spike sank into the corner where the wall met the ceiling, but he kept coming. He grabbed her still bladed left wrist with his right hand, practically falling upon her.

She couldn't get the other Razor up, and his knife was coming down at her throat. Her empty right hand came up instead, her hand curling around his forearm. She blocked the knife blow and slammed her open palm on his nose. He nodded, blinking, and she grabbed his coat sleeve.

She stepped up, putting both feet on his stomach, and wrenched herself back. She landed hard and kicked out, sending him over her. He flew across the floor, somersaulting in the air. He smashed to the tile on his back.

Rhea ran in the opposite direction. The Reaper turned over immediately and vaulted off the floor. She was not going to get away now.

She jumped when she reached the first stair, stepped on the wall, and propelled herself up to the ceiling.

She grabbed the stuck Razor, hit the wall, bounced, and twisted her body around. She *bounced* off the wall and came down at the Reaper.

He brought his blade up, meaning to slice across her front as she fell on him. She straightened her body, diving over him. She spun as she landed and rolled to her feet, her back to him. He pushed his blade at her kidney. She pivoted so her side was to him. She swung one Razor down to block him.

He didn't slow. He let the momentum of her blow bring his right arm across her head. He propelled her into the left wall. She hit it face first, her arms up. He came in for the kill, meaning to push her face through the soft, weak wall.

Her left foot went back, just under his knee. She almost collapsed, the flat of his hand slamming into the wall just over her head, leaving an imprint. She whirled around, wanting the Hanzo Razor to slice him just over his belt, letting his intestines spill out.

He pulled his torso back at the last possible second, feeling and hearing his shirt rip. He felt his kicked leg collapsing, so he let it move his body away, toward the stairs. He rolled and came up, kicking the blood back into his numbed limb. He brought his knife arm up, making sure she kept off him. They faced each other again.

He moved his arm from side to side. The Hanzo Razors danced in her hand.

She was fast, he thought, but not strong enough. He might risk a slash, but he *could* kill her.

He was death, she thought. The mirror image of her hated love. *The* mirrored image, up to and including the blade on the opposite arm. If she could kill him, then maybe she could kill the demon.

He ran at her again, knowing she didn't realize what he planned to do. She practically went down on one knee to move below his blade and brought her left arm up to punch the Razor under his sternum and into his heart.

He *caught* her left wrist with his right hand and twisted.

Surprised, she brought her right hand around to cut him away. He caught that wrist in his *left* hand and twisted.

He was incredibly strong. He had both her wrists and was twisting her arms. Her body contorted sideways, and he drove her face into the wall. He slammed downward, knocking her torso to the floor. He stepped on her neck.

Rhea was wedged in the narrow hall. Her feet were flat

on the left wall. Her face was pushed against the right wall, her neck bent.

He was tearing her ligaments and muscles. He was breaking her arms. He was crushing her neck. He was choking her. Oh, God, his left hand was moving. He was trying to get the metal tongue to cut her wrist.

She was weakening. She couldn't keep her right wrist far enough away from the wickedly pointed blade. She felt it nick, just missing her vein. He was pushing his shoe through her neck. She couldn't breathe. He was ripping her arms out of their sockets, tearing them off her body. . . .

Feet flat on the left wall . . . ?

Rhea ran *up* the wall.

She let her feet run up the wall from her prone position. She kept her legs running until there was no more wall. But they had gone fast enough that they sped through the air and smashed the Reaper in the throat.

The toe of one high-impact shoe smacked into his neck, and then the other into his Adam's apple.

His head hit the right wall. His fingers opened as if spring-released. She spun away from him like a coiled rubber band.

He stepped back, choking and coughing, holding his neck with one hand, the other going into his coat.

Rhea vaulted to her feet and turned, triumphantly.

Her smile disappeared when she saw the Walther P5 in his hand. He was leaning on the right wall, still gagging, but the arm was coming up. She was too far away and too slow. He would be able to fire once before she threw the Razors. And once would be enough. At this range, the 9-mm bullet would tear open her head or excavate her chest cavity.

Daremo had taught her well. She could see the finger and wrist muscles contracting on his hand. She knew it was coming, but she couldn't dodge it.

But she could try, dammit.

The two sword blades came out of the wall. They were side by side, but their edges were laid opposite to each other. They came out of the wall like nails, moving like spears. They hit the side of the automatic and pushed the barrel to the left as it fired.

The boom was deafening in the enclosed space. The gun leapt in the Reaper's hand as Rhea flattened herself on the right wall and brought her arm around in a short, choppy arc.

The Reaper's head snapped back as the gun's report echoed up the stairs and down the street. The bullet went through the left wall, across a tabletop, and lodged in a brick on the side of the building.

The Reaper stepped back to keep his balance. His right eye was wide and staring at the woman. His left eye had a spike stuck to it.

That was what it looked like. It looked like one of the handles of the Hanzo Razor was glued lengthwise across his eye, because the Hanzo Razor itself was stuck all the way through the socket and into his skull.

The Reaper's left hand came up, as if to grab the intrusion and pull it from him. His right arm did not lower. His breath did not stop. He stood there and fought the shock and pain.

He pointed the automatic at Rhea like an accusing finger. She spun around, her leg up. She knocked the sleek P5 from his hand with a roundhouse kick. It slammed against the left wall and fell to the floor with a clatter.

Rhea did not stop. She planted her feet, then seemed to erupt off the floor. She climbed up his body, kicking him. Her foot went to his knee. Her other foot stepped to his opposite hip. She brought her first foot up and around, into the side of his face.

He jerked, like a yanked marionette, to the left wall. He slammed into it head first. But still he did not fall. He could no longer see or hear, but he did not fall. Instead he brought his left arm up, holding his blade out defensively.

Rhea threw the Hanzo Razor. She nailed his left forearm to the wall. She leapt at him, right foot first. Her feet sank into his stomach. She grabbed the Hanzo Razor in his eye. She stepped up into the air. She somersaulted backward, yanking the blade from his head. She landed on her feet.

Only then did he start screaming and jerking, his free hand over his face, blood pumping through his fingers. Only then did he try to run away, pulling on his nailed arm like a leashed dog eager for escape.

Rhea watched until his cries became inaudible and he sank to the floor. She waited until his right hand fell limply to his gore-caked lap. Amazing, she thought. He was still alive. His lips were moving.

" 'The glories of our blood and state are shadows, not substantial things; there is no armour against fate; death lays his icy hand on kings. . . .' " Le Moissonner, the Reaper, tried to smile before he died. He failed.

Rhea sliced down with the Hanzo Razor she had pulled from his eye, the blood splattering on the wall behind him. His left coat sleeve was suddenly open. She sliced across. The thin, tight buckle holding the wrist blade to his arm snapped in half.

Rhea watched carefully for a few moments. She started to straighten, smiling. The smile died when a thin line of red appeared where the blade harness had been.

"Shit," she muttered. Broke the skin.

She reached down and retrieved the Hanzo Razor and the Reaper Blade, anyway.

She kicked the door of the apartment open. Daremo was still standing against the wall, holding his bandaged side with his left arm. His swords were strapped to his right. That arm rested against his side. The hole he had made in the wall with them was behind him.

"Come on," she said, picking his blood-dried clothes off the floor. "We'll have to go. We made enough noise to wake the dead."

He didn't move, in obvious pain. "Rhea . . ."

She finally stopped and looked at him. They looked at each other until they heard noises in the rooms around them.

"I didn't want to take any chances," he said. "I didn't want to lose you."

She held her hand up. " 'Koibito,' no . . ."

"I never wanted to lose you," he said, his voice stronger. "I'd do anything . . . I *did* anything . . ."

"You'll never lose me," she whispered.

He was dead. She had killed him in the hall. She held up the wrist blade, the mirror image of his swords.

"Look what I brought you."

Daremo looked down, trying to accept all that had happened. It was not possible. It was all so unnatural. Now they'd have to go someplace else in the city . . . they'd have to keep hiding out . . . until he recuperated . . . until Cristobal was ready. . . .

"Well," he said with a sigh, "there goes the neighborhood."

15

"The ninja knew collapse," Napoleon said, swirling the remnants of the Louis Jadot Macon-Villages La Fontaine Chardonnay in the bottom of his glass. "Don't be fooled. They *represented* collapse."

It was his sixth dinner with Jennifer Hemphill of Admiral Seaworth's office. Each meal seemed to get more elegant and romantic than the last. The first was a calm, business-like supper in a small, plain restaurant on the Right Bank. She impressed him with her listening abilities there. She was a seasoned, smooth, interviewing professional. She asked him one question, then fed him encouragement, and, sometimes, inspiration.

She knew when to comment and when to analyze—remarkable traits in anyone, let alone an attractive woman. It was his experience that attractive women wanted to discuss nothing but themselves. If they spoke of the world, the attractive woman would want to discuss how the world affected her.

The meals continued through the weeks, each finding time in their busy schedules to meet. Most often they talked, but on the fifth occasion they danced. They had been in an exclusive supper club—she had lured him there, Napoleon realized—and when the small, quiet orchestra started, he felt compelled to make use of it.

She found his feet as capable as his mind. He did not step on her shoes or lurch around the floor. She enjoyed his warmth and strength. Later, she found his kiss as assured as his speech. But that had been it. He had dropped her off, accepted her good-night kiss, returned it, they had embraced, and he had left. Hemphill had stood on the top step, fists clenched, trying to fight the frustration.

She could not help but wonder whether he was homosexual. After all, no man had resisted her charms this long. She also never saw him in the company of anyone else, man or woman. He always answered the telephone personally whenever she called.

Even so, she found herself excited when he called her again. She played it cool when they talked over the phone but was interested to note that he asked her to wear evening, not office, clothes on their next date.

So here they were, at their sixth dinner together. The setting was opulent. He had taken her to a lovely, private restaurant in the sixteenth arrondissement, nestled between the Seine and the Bois de Boulogne—those beautiful woods and gardens covering two thousand acres in southwest Paris. She was dazzled and dazzling in her gown and matching jacket, mingling the colors silver and aqua.

He surprised her even further when the maître d' led them through the handsomely appointed room, past tables where she recognized ambassadors, generals, and even secretaries of state, to an enclosed balcony. The maître d' had opened doors—French doors, naturally—and presented them with a beautiful table and a breathtaking view.

To the left was Le Bois itself, and to the right was the City of Light and *le fleuve civilisateur*, the civilizing river. It was not some place a homosexual took a woman. Hemphill felt flushed when she sat down, but an electric thought went through her mind as he held the chair for her.

Tonight was the night.

They had dined royally on nouvelle cuisine and Napoleon

had personally ordered the wine. First a bottle of Joseph Drouhin Bourgogne Laforet, then the La Fontaine. By the time the conversation got around to the ninja, as it always did, Ms. Hemphill had an extremely comfortable "fur" of alcohol covering her brain.

"I thought they were the mortar that kept feudal society together," she replied.

"Ah, but what did that society consist of?" Napoleon retorted. "Men who swore by a strict code of honor, living a life they either consciously or subconsciously knew was dishonorable."

"All they had was honor," she countered.

"All they had was something they *called* honor," Napoleon corrected, sipping the wine. "Every society has an excuse for the evil they do. TSR. The Supreme Rationalization. Hitler's Nazis are the most obvious and extreme examples. At least the samurai had bushido . . . but they also had ninja. The completely honorable and the completely dishonorable. How could one truly exist with the other? Answer? They could not."

"But they did."

"Exactly," Napoleon told her proudly, toasting her with the last gulp in his glass. She joined him. "More?" She nodded, so he poured and continued. "Bushido demanded that the samurai do honorable things, so they had to hire ninja to do the dishonorable—never admitting that the act of hiring ninja was, in itself, dishonorable. All bets off, null and void."

"Do not pass go, do not collect two hundred dollars," Hemphill said, sipping the wine. "But the ninja had their own elegance . . . that is, their own style. They were tragic, romantic figures, were they not?" She looked at him over the lip of the crystal.

"Ah," Napoleon said, waving that away. "If you read the histories and the legends, the one overriding quality is of chaos. Ninja suffering enormous indignities to infiltrate and assassinate. Ninja drowned in offal, ninja skinned alive, ninja boiled . . . in water, mind you. Not oil. Boiled in water until they died."

"It's the price they paid for capture." Hemphill shrugged.

"That wasn't just it," Napoleon mused. "The ninja represented the collapse of the feudal society, and therefore were a living exaggeration of it. The samurai's strict, violent code of honor was unknowingly satirized by the ninja, who took every vendetta with deadly, almost disgusting, seriousness. They delighted in devising masterful plan after plan, which found loopholes within the bushido system, to do in their enemies—who, more often than not, were other ninja."

"Why was that?"

"I think they had an intrinsic fear of their employers, and their employer's enemies. The ninja were scum, remember."

"Weren't they noble warriors fighting for ideals?"

"Of course not. What noble warrior would become a ninja? Ninja were the violent trash of society. They had to be, or else they could not do dishonorable things. I think they became ninja for the same reason Germans became Nazis. To have an excuse to do the unspeakable. To terrorize with abandon. Remember Zanjanko."

"Yes," she breathed. They had spoken of it before. The supreme ninja code meaning, "Anything done on a mission is moral." It thrilled her to think about. To have that much power and to wield it . . .

"Read the histories. Pore over the details as put down by the objective archivists—Baron, Meyers, Inagaki, Schreiber. They did not purposefully exaggerate or glorify. They did not set down lore as fact. They incorporated their knowledge of the Japanese feudal psychology and mentality into their annotations."

"Not like the others, I'd imagine," Hemphill extrapolated. "Who had need of fine-tuning or whitewashing the human truths in hyperbole and self-gratification. Either to protect themselves from reprisal or to consolidate new power, I suppose. Better to paint a picture of misunderstood artists than reveal the insects under the stone."

Napoleon nodded proudly. "If there is one thing all ninja 'history'—and I use that term loosely—has in common is the sects' ultimate descent into an insular, painful, private war with each other. A secret battle within their secret wars, as it were. By the seventeenth century almost every mission, almost every infiltration and assassination, had an ulterior motive.''

''Which was?''

''To lure, expose, and exterminate rival ninja.''

''Similar to the Mafia,'' Hemphill noted.

''Yes? Go on.''

The woman continued gracefully, the thoughts complete in her mind. ''As crime became consolidated, subsidized by the public, who required gambling, prostitution, and drugs, the mob had only two adversaries. One, law enforcement, which could easily be subjugated through violence or money. But two, other factions of the Cosa Nostra. That is, other crime families who wanted a bigger share.''

''And units of crimes,'' Napoleon added.

''I beg your pardon?''

''In the modern world it is no longer just the families who control, or seek to control, portions of the underworld. Other units, such as street gangs, have infiltrated.''

''Granted,'' Hemphill said smoothly. ''It does not change the initial hypothesis, however. What they are fighting is each other.''

''But why?'' Napoleon asked her. ''You mentioned profit. But I believed that is only the exterior motive. An excuse masking the real reason.''

''They hate each other's guts,'' Hemphill suggested.

''Yes. But again, why?'' he countered.

''If I could answer that, I'd have the panacea for violence.''

''No, no,'' he said, correcting her, ''you would have only an answer, not the solution. Seeking the solution to human violence is like seeking the answer to human existence. Some things mortals cannot know.''

''Oh? Are ninja mortal? Are you?''

He ignored the compliment, spoken in a warm voice. ''It could be argued that every move the various sects make is for a twofold result. To consolidate their own power and to weaken their competition.''

" 'It isn't enough that I succeed,' " Hemphill quoted. " 'You have to fail.' "

"Yes." Napoleon smiled. "A concept carried through to this very day. But back then, in a regulated, impossibly strict police state, extreme acts of violence were conceived and required to strike at the heart of the enemy."

"The heart of darkness."

"Yes!" His enthusiasm and energy was as intoxicating as the wine. More so, in fact. She could see the animal beneath the civilized veneer when he spoke like this. The animal she wanted to unleash. "The heart of darkness. To invade the darkest heart, one's heart had to be as black. The greatest works of destruction perpetrated by the ninja were to destroy other ninja. As if only in the vanquishing of equals was there any satisfaction.

"Look at any of the great ninja confrontations of the 1600s to the end of the Shogun era. The Chiba sect poisoned the water of the town that headquartered the Shiomi on the day of their annual waterfall festival. The Toei sought to disgrace Kamui Sanada by sabotaging his village's grandest market on trading day. And, of course, one of the grandest strokes in ninja history: the Kohga kidnapping of the Shogun's heir to exterminate the Ega clan in one fell swoop."

The woman had heard the stories before. He was merely reminding her of the wealth of plot and counterplot that went into the sects' labyrinthine schemes. She remembered how the Ega frustrated the Kohga's plan by slowly infiltrating the Kohga castle and cautiously cutting away at the supports for a period of weeks until the Ega jonin attacked. Then, when the superior Kohga forces were about to succeed, the Ega chunin pulled the rug out from everyone by knocking the weakened building down.

"The vanquishing of equals . . ." Hemphill mused. She held up her glass. "To equals."

"I'll drink to that." They clinked glasses and emptied the remainder of the vintage. Napoleon turned the bottle upside down in the iced decanter, and they both surveyed the beauty of Paris at night. Hemphill wished there was not a table between them. So thinking, she stood, and went over to the balcony edge. She was pleased to find him standing beside her within moments.

She leaned against him. He put his arm around her shoulder. "Fascinating," she murmured. "So powerful yet so pitiful."

"Not pitiful," he said. "Necessary. It is a violent world, always on the verge of collapse. The samurai denied it. The samurai class was destroyed. The ninja corroborated it."

"And?" she wondered. "Did *they* survive? Do you think the ninja have . . . 'other units,' as you called them?"

Napoleon felt the thrill he always felt during conquest. That he shared with his diminutive namesake. It reminded him of his feelings when he saw the results of his grandest manipulations. He remembered the initial shock, then the surge of power that came with accepting responsibility for one's actions.

How many had died? Many dozens that he knew. Many hundreds he did not. Thousands. It was hard to completely realize. He had set up the targets that were to be attacked or protected, depending upon which side the SSS operative was on. He had done it six times. Three times the team marked "Us" had successfully prevented sabotage. Three times the "Them" team succeeded in crippling its objective.

The targets had been all over the world. In America, Europe, Asia, Russia, Australia, and India. It was interesting: The more intricate and desperate the secret battle, the less bystanders were hurt. In America only a few died as a result of a year-long game of intensely difficult infiltration and manipulation. In India thousands died as a result of the simplest and most instinctive of moves. In Russia the final tally would not be known for generations.

He looked down at the woman, his expression mixing power and pity. She had no way of knowing why he didn't need her. But like all women, she was attracted by his total assurance. People wanted only those who didn't need them. He needed no one when he had the fates of millions in his hands. This he could share only with others who understood . . . others like him.

"Other units?" he wondered. "You mean organizations not descended from the ninja but dedicated to their goals?" He held her tighter. "What do you think?"

She looked up at him and thought about the world. She considered the religious wars being fought for no tangible reason—in Iran, in the Middle East, in Ireland. She thought about pollution—of the air and water, as well as of the human body and soul. Drugs, cigarettes, alcohol, automobile exhaust, and all the other common poisons people lived with. She thought about money. She even thought about what she was wearing . . . the bra that lifted her breasts, the uncomfortable garter belt, and the high heels that defied all reason.

She opened her mouth to reply. There was a knock on the door behind them.

Napoleon whirled around, the expression on his face telling the woman that he had left instructions not to be disturbed. Then Hemphill saw his features change to concern, something approaching worry, and then . . . nothing. No expression at all.

"Excuse me," he said. "I'm terribly sorry."

He went to the door and opened it a crack, leaning his head out instead of letting the other person lean in. Hemphill could only make out the person's whisper, not what was said.

When Napoleon returned to her, his blank expression was even stiffer. Jennifer Hemphill's growing elation started to blacken and crumble, like burned ash. The magic had seeped out of the evening. Whatever he had been told had driven thoughts of her completely from his mind.

"Where were we?" he wondered idly, hands on the balcony banister. "Oh, yes. You asked me if I thought ninja had any contemporaries."

"But . . ." Hemphill began, about to answer his original question, but he just kept speaking.

"Yes, I think so. As long as humans exist, there will be the constant war of good and evil. Not good and evil on the battlefield." He waved that away impatiently. "The war within ourselves. We constantly balance what we know is right and what we know is wrong inside our minds.'' He placed his forefinger on his temple like it was the barrel of a gun.

"All those killers,'' he continued, ''all those serial murderers? They're lying and they know it. They killed because they wanted to, because the evil inside them won out. Not because their dog told them to, or they heard it on a record. They made a choice, and now they're too cowardly to admit it. Not when society is offering them a way out. 'Just tell us why and we'll forgive you.' You know why they demand motive? Because even the accusers and executioners cannot bear to think that they're capable of such infamy themselves. They want to think it's something that *isn't* in everybody.''

Hemphill was stunned by his intense vehemence, and the way he spat the words out with quiet fury. She had never seen his emotions so raw and exposed before. It was the sort of passion she did not like.

"Frightened children,'' he went on, shaking his head, ''refusing to accept responsibility for being human. Refusing to accept responsibility for eliminating evil. Not punishing, eliminating. The ninja killed each other, the gangs kill each other, the Mafia kill each other because they know who they are. If they could, they would kill themselves, but they cannot. So they kill each other because they hate themselves. 'Scared of their own shadows . . .' ''

"Charles,'' she said, laying a hand on his arm. That was the name she knew him by. Charles Bonner, a variation on the name of Napoleon's father, as well as the name of the nephew who had died at birth. "What is it? What's the matter?''

She was shocked by the look he gave her. For the past weeks he had always been attentive and attractive but distant. But now he looked at her with only vaguely disguised suspicion and paranoia. It was as if she were seeing Dr. Jekyll turning to Mr. Hyde.

"A friend,'' he said, ''a friend of mine was killed tonight.''

"Oh, no!''

"Murdered. He was found murdered."

"Oh, my God, no. Oh, Charles, I'm so sorry."

"Yes," he said, looking out at the city. "Well, Couldn't be helped. It's a violent world. . . ." He stared at the flowers and the trees and the glorious architecture and saw only stone and dirt. " 'A little trust that when we die, we reap our sowing; and so . . . goodbye.' " He looked at her. "George Louis Palmella Busson Du Maurier." She stared at him, a hand to her mouth, her eyes wide. "Come," he said, his arm out. "I'll take you home."

She was stunned when he pulled her to him in the car outside her door. At first she was slightly afraid, but his passion and need could not be denied. His hands gripped her, his arms embraced her. His lips found her ear, then her neck. When he reached her mouth, she was ready.

He had kept her off-balance. She had started the evening certain that it would end this way, and ended the dinner certain that it would not. When his desire became clear, it took her a few seconds to comprehend. But he gave her that time, and when their lips met, there were sparks in her mind.

She was foolish to think she could control him. She wanted his strength, feeling that she could make it hers— that she would do the commanding and he would do the jumping. It had happened every time before, with every other man. They had fallen in love with her, so she had called the shots. They had wanted her body, and she used it as a reward for meritorious service.

And, of course, she soon became bored.

This time he was driving her. His grip was rough. He didn't give her time to breathe. He moved her the way he'd move a mannequin. Her embrace soon became the actions of a woman holding on. She grabbed his sleeve, his hair, and his sides. Then she was pushing.

He was overwhelming her. She was drowning in him. She was like a novice surfer thinking she could tame the bonsai pipeline.

"Not here," she finally gasped. "Not here in the street. Please. Come in. My bedroom . . ."

She tried surging ahead of him, getting a little distance in which to think. But his long legs and her high heels kept him at her shoulder. They seemed to fly up the stairs, and when she got the key in the lock, he didn't even let her put the lights on.

Her back was against the wall next to the door. His lips found hers again as his hands slipped between her coat and dress. He pulled it off her shoulders and let it fall to the floor. She didn't notice he had held on to her scarf.

Instead she concentrated on matching him in intensity. Damned if this man was going to overpower her again. She saw only two possibilities in her addled mind: to reject him or to equal him. Damned if she was going to reject him.

But he was still surprising her. She had not expected him to be so rough. He still pinned her to the wall in the dark apartment, and he still kissed her as if he wanted to occupy that space. She had been looking forward to his caress, and she was not disappointed when it came.

She was shocked. His hand gripped her breast through the dress. It was not a gentle touch. He gripped it as if he meant to have it. She felt the jolts she was hoping for, but his fingers pinched when she wanted them to fondle.

She jerked under him, but he wouldn't stop. Her fingers sank into his suit sleeves as he did it again and again, his lips and tongue still gagging her. She rubbed herself against him, her right leg bending, trying to gather her thoughts, but he maintained the onslaught.

Finally his lips left hers and began their descent down her body.

"Please," she gasped. "Please . . ." But the words degenerated into gasps and moans as his head went down her throat, and his hand went up her leg.

He fooled her again. Just as she thought she knew what he was going to do, she felt herself lifted as if she weighed no more than a child. She was swung around. She was about to cry out in surprise when his hand was at her face, the scarf still in it. It muffled her shout, and she all but flew through the living room door into the bedroom.

She fell face first to the bed and bounced. Before she settled, his hands were on her again, whirling her around, pushing her onto her back, throwing up her skirt, and, incredibly, tying the scarf in her mouth. She found her teeth clenched on the knot.

"You talk too much," he said, undoing his pants as he kneeled between her legs on the bed. "The words give you balance and control. Not now, my dear. You don't want either of those things tonight."

Her hands went to her mouth. He fell on her, pinning them to the side. Within minutes her arms were across his back, holding on to him as if she were dangling over a cliff. She was glad the scarf was in her mouth, because she was screaming.

Jennifer Hemphill was nothing if not a considerate neighbor.

Napoleon put her to sleep when he was through. She lay beside him, her clothes on the floor, her skin warm and creamy. She was already drifting into sleep, but he helped her along with a thumb and forefinger on the proper neck veins. She hummed contentedly and sighed. He got up, dressed, and left.

Le Tenter was waiting for him on the street outside. It was late, and the sidewalks in this wealthy residential area were deserted.

"I hope you had a good time," he said sarcastically as Napoleon came around the car.

"You've had yours," the SSS leader grunted. Le Tenter was nonchalantly opening the passenger door of the car—a door that had been left locked—when Napoleon strode by him. "Let's walk."

The Place Furstemberg was quiet now, its famous cafés and bouquinist art kiosks closed and shuttered for the night. The men walked near the walls, under the trees, their voices low and furtive.

"What did you find out?" Napoleon asked.

"The life and times of Moe Dare," said the Tempter. "A

lot of chits were called in on this one. I don't think I have any more favors left in this town."

Napoleon glanced at his associate's handsome features. "You'll get more."

Le Tenter smiled with pride. "As near as anyone can tell, Moe Dare hasn't become a cliché yet. He appears to have a Superman–Clark Kent relationship with one Anthony 'Joe' Anthony, a Washington D.C. operative."

"Anthony? Code name Joe?" Napoleon echoed. "I did research on him a year ago."

"Possible recruitment, no doubt," Le Tenter supposed. "He was kind of strategy for a while there ... their own little wonder boy. The head office was grooming him for big things, but he wanted to stay in the field."

"I saw no apparent promise." Napoleon sniffed.

The Tempter shrugged. "But he was really cruising for a while there. Successfully located a terrorist training camp funded by the Russians in Central America. Suggested a possible reason why Israeli security suddenly went balmy, which turned out to be correct—"

"Which was?" Napoleon said, interrupting.

"A nuclear installation in the desert had been breached by an Arab terrorist."

"What?" Napoleon exclaimed. But then he recalled the incident and calmed. "Oh ... oh, yes. The terrorist was found dead."

"Yeah. But then this Joe Anthony stalled. Word has it that he's putting together some sort of counterespionage masterstroke. Something involving the Chinese, the Russians, the Africans, and the Japanese."

"The Japanese?"

"Yeah," Le Tenter repeated dryly. "What is it? Sex make you deaf?"

But Napoleon had stopped walking. He stood at the edge of the sidewalk, his eyes flitting inside their sockets. The Tempter stopped a few paces away and waited.

"How many operatives are there available?" Napoleon suddenly asked.

"You would know better than I," Le Tenter replied. "I

suppose everyone not on your . . . exercise." He spoke the last word like profanity.

"That exercise requires only one operative each evening," Napoleon explained, still thinking. "And if it succeeds, it will be the ultimate statement of the futility of existence our organization can make."

"Whoopee," said the Tempter flatly. "Then what do we do, knit socks for the rest of our lives?"

"Oh, come," said Napoleon warmly, stepping forward and putting his arm around his associate's shoulders. "We will embark on another recruitment drive, replenish our numbers, and return to the game board as before." He was showing the sort of charisma and leadership that had started the SSS in the first place. "Are you telling me you don't enjoy your time off-board?"

Le Tenter thought of *le grand jeté*, and of the little girl he'd seen in the corner café for three weeks running now. The girl with the pouty, Kewpie-doll lips, and the wisps of blond hair coming from beneath her cap. . . .

The Tempter smiled, but then the image of his last conquest burning to death in the car wreck superseded the previous vision. He saw the man in gray and black leaping again, catching the pipe bomb with perfect rhythm and throwing it with exceptional strength.

"I want the one responsible," he said coldly.

"So do I," said Napoleon. His thoughts were of the Reaper. He would never find his like again. "As I always have. But now I know how to get him."

"How?"

Napoleon looked at his new, closest associate. The man who would have to take Le Moissonner's place. The man who now had the responsibility to put Napoleon's grand designs into action.

Napoleon suddenly got a flash of déjà vu. He felt content, completed, after years of searching. He no longer saw his organization as a small, select group of the world's finest espionage operatives struggling to find meaning for their existence. He saw them as they actually were. The "other unit." And he was their Hanshi.

He had found the rival Hanshi. He was here, in Paris, disrupting their plans, plotting against them. He would have to be lured, exposed, and exterminated. Napoleon swelled with determination and expectation. Now he not only had an enemy who was an equal, he also had an enemy who would *understand*.

He looked at Le Tenter. "How? By entering into our finest game, with our very best players?"

"But we're already—" the Tempter complained.

"We're not changing that," Napoleon said, interrupting. "We are making it complete. That exercise, by itself, was not a game. There was no 'us' and 'them' involved. It was a training exercise designed to test infiltration and sabotage skills.

"But now we need not designate a 'them.' It is waiting for us. And this time the goal is not to destroy a target but to terminate the enemy. Terminate with extreme prejudice."

Napoleon stepped forward on that dark, deserted street, feeling every inch the conquerer. This was what he had been born to accomplish. Survival of the fittest. Kill or be killed. He would become master of the martial world. He would destroy the planet's greatest assassin.

"Project Masterstroke," he marveled, remembering Joe Anthony. "It is a masterpiece. It is a plan linking the past with the future. It starts now. It starts tonight." He turned to Le Tenter. "Contact everyone available," he instructed. "We must scour the city. We shall paint this town red."

The Tempter looked at his leader skeptically. "With blood?"

"No," said Napoleon, who swore to himself that Le Tenter would never look at him that way again. Soon—and forever—all the SSS would look at him with obvious respect, if not awe. "Graffiti. 'We find great things are made of little things, and little things go lessening till at last comes God behind them.' Robert Browning."

"Desist." Le Tenter groaned, putting up his hands before walking away. "The Reaper is dead, remember?"

"Yes," Napoleon said to himself. The Reaper is dead. The heir to Hittori Hanzo had killed him. " 'Then bless thy

secret growth' ''—he quoted Henry Vaughn as an epitaph—
" 'nor catch at noise, but thrive unseen and dumb; keep
clean, bear fruit, earn life, and watch till the white-wing'd
reapers come!' ''

We will get him, my friend, Napoleon promised Le
Moissonner. *Either he will die . . . or everyone else in Paris
will.*

16

I

Inspector Dugelay had much on his mind. He was hoping
that the fall and winter would be easier on him and the force
than it had been. He was hoping that the foolish terrorist
attacks would diminish and essentially disappear as the skies
grew grayer and the air grew colder.

Inspector Dugelay sighed. It was not to be, it seemed. Souls
darkened along with the weather, he surmised. The anger of
these weekend anarchists seemed to grow as the sun disappeared.
Their rage grew as the cold grew in their bones. They were not
as quick as they had been in the heat, but they were as
thorough . . . and as damnably difficult to catch.

It started small, as it always did. The first few assaults
seemed like tests to see how far they could go. Each time,
the attacks grew bolder and more violent. First, vandalism
in a block of offices near the Opéra. Next, a gas bomb in the
Métro, at the Charles de Gaulle station. Next, gunplay at the
Quay des Artistes, with a weapon fired into a crowd from a
speeding automobile. Finally the explosion in the intersection near Menilmontant.

They still had to discover whether the car's occupants
knew of the bomb they were carrying. They had found out
the identities of the driver and the passenger. He was the

son of an area politician, and she was the daughter of a shopkeeper. They had been in the same school classes together. Neither had shown signs of resentment, according to their parents. But parents never wanted to admit that sort of thing, Dugelay thought.

He tsked for the third time and took off his hat to run his fingers through his sparse, stringy hair. He touched the bloody tile with his toe again, hardly able to believe that the pathologist's boys had pulled that wreck out of this place just a few hours ago. And here they were, still interviewing the apartment dwellers—all of whom knew nothing, naturally.

"How could they know nothing?" Dugelay had exploded, waving his long arms. "He had a knife stuck in his eye! He had been pounding his head—or having his head pounded—on the walls for minutes! He fired a gun." Dugelay made a gun with his fingers and let his thumb be the pin striking the shell.

The coroner told him that the corpse's internal injuries were prodigious . . . and not just from the head wounds, either. "Internal organs were ruptured," said the doctor. "Like they were stepped on."

"Stepped on?" Dugelay had echoed.

"Tromped on," the doctor had corrected. "Leapt on with both feet from a height."

And these people heard nothing? This had not been a small man, and his lithe frame was deceiving. There were coiled muscles beneath the fine clothes. It had been truly a clash of Titans down there.

And now look. They had not been away from the site more than a few hours, but there was that sign on the wall. Here, on the other side of police lines. Dugelay had seen them all over town. They hadn't been there night before, but he saw them everywhere the next morning. On curbs, on walls, on posts, on poles, even on trees. It was a simple graffiti but effective. Eliminate one of the lines, straighten the ends, make it a cross figuration, and it would have been a swastika symbol.

But as it was, it consisted of three interlocking lines, like an asterisk. But at the end of each line there were six shorter lines, coming back at an angle of about forty-five degrees. They were like stick-figure representations of spears, with an arrowhead on each end. They made a sort of star—a little star that would roll down the road on its points, if it was to be animated.

And they were everywhere. Well, Dugelay thought, it was no matter to him. The custodial staff would handle it. Not impossible to wash off, but still, it piqued his curiosity. What could it mean? Maybe an advertising symbol for a new musical group or movie. If it was, *les flics* would no doubt have something to say to the record label or producers when the product premiered.

Again, it wasn't his concern. He had to turn his mind back to his disagreeable task: interviewing the blind, deaf, and dumb to get a lead on another seemingly motiveless crime. There were too many of them nowadays for Dugelay's liking. If only they had found some drugs on him so they could attribute the murder to "death by misadventure" and close the file. Just like they did in the United States.

Inspector Dugelay stretched, trying to get the numbed sensation out of his muscles. He could no longer deny it. He had a bad feeling in his bones. It always came with the fear that there would be no answer to this one.

And that the deaths weren't over.

II

Rhea took her first step on Califlorida land. That's what it felt like. She paid her twenty-five hundred francs, went through the gate without harassment, and left France completely behind. It wasn't California and it wasn't Florida. It was Califlorida. It was the Paris Disneyland.

Her feet were on the same light gray slate that made up the path into the Magic Kingdom everywhere else. She still stared down Main Street, with quaint shops lining both sides, and saw Cinderella's Castle in the distance. She might as well have been in Anaheim or Lake Buena Vista, except for the manner in which she arrived.

This was not Disneyland, nor DisneyWorld. It was a

Gallic combination of both, placed in Roissy, northeast of Paris. Rhea had gone from the romantic city streets to the industrialized outer edge of the area and through rustic farming towns to reach the amusement park.

Yet she felt no thrill. She was not returning to her youth but descending deeper into her hellish present.

They had slept together for the first time in months the previous night. For the first time in months they more than occupied the same bed. She held him without sleep, hugging her rediscovered love to her. She had killed his mirror twin and purged herself of much hate by it.

She had helped him through the streets prior to that, following his directions to another cellar apartment in the eleventh arrondissement. He always seemed to have at least three empty places to go in any given city. This one had more amenities than the others, but all he cared about was the bed. He lay upon the mattress and started sweating.

"Come here," he had told her. She had obeyed. She had no questions, but he needed to tell her answers. "I don't know who that was. I don't think Cristobal has betrayed me. I don't think that was a black marketeer."

"I can tell you what he said to me."

"I heard. 'When the enemy attacks,' " he quoted Musashi, " 'remain undisturbed. Observe. Join in with his movement. Do not allow the enemy's head to rise.' "

"Who was it, then?"

"I do not know," Daremo said. "I don't care." Then he fell asleep.

The next morning Rhea had returned from a nearby market to find him awake. "The streets are marked," she said, "with the symbol of a shuriken."

"Which?"

"Chiba."

Daremo had smiled wanly. "The enemy is challenging us," he told her.

Rhea took another step into the Paris Disneyland. The Chiba sect. Each ninja sect had their own shuriken design that distinguished them from the others. The throwing stars were not just poisoned weapons, they were calling cards made to instill fear. The shuriken would be seen, and the legends of that sect would leap into the forefront of the witnesses' minds.

Warlords assassinated. Ninja disappearing through walls. Industries destroyed. Ninja disappearing in a puff of smoke. Entire villages poisoned.

"What day is it?" Daremo had asked. "All Saints Day," he had translated after she told him the date. "Cemeteries visited and graves decorated." He laid back and spoke to the ceiling. "The Chiba challenged the Shiomi to show itself by poisoning their town's water supply on the day of their greatest festival."

"They're going to poison water fountains near cemeteries?" Rhea said sardonically.

"Hardly a grand enough gesture. What's the greatest festival around here? I'll give you a hint. It isn't All Saints Day."

It was fitting: to poison the water of the city's greatest festival on the Day of the Dead. Once the horror and amorality of the act was accepted, it was only logical.

"What should we do?" Rhea had asked him.

"Nothing," said Daremo. He settled deeper into the mattress. "I don't know who these people are."

"Ninja!" she exclaimed.

"The ninja are dead. Was that ninja you killed last night? *Another* hakujin ninja? He was probably a friend of the man who followed me from the café bombing."

"Of course." It all came together in the woman's mind. "We have uncovered a terrorist group."

"Great," Daremo mumbled. "A terrorist group who can speak ninja."

"They are going to kill hundreds of people and are daring us to stop them," she realized.

Daremo remained still. "We are weak. We are not prepared. There isn't enough time."

"Let those people die?"

"The Chiba . . . may be bluffing."

"They may not."

"Who are these people to us?" Daremo said evenly, still looking at the ceiling. "People die all the time."

"You saved those people at the café. . . ." The apartment was silent for a time. When his voice came, it was empty.

"I saved myself."

So she was in the Paris Disneyland. He had begged her not to go. He said it was useless. He said it was a meaningless gesture. "There is only one reason they are doing this," he told her as she reached the door. "To force us out into the open. To lure us into a trap."

"You don't understand," Rhea had replied, halfway out the door. "I want to go. I want to be lured. I want to be trapped." She remembered the sensations of all those nights hunting on the streets of Paris, waiting for the man who had wounded her hated lover. She remembered the feeling the previous night when she had kicked, punched, and stabbed that man to death. It was elation. It was exhilaration. It was an explosion of energy that had been building since she was born. An energy that had been *burning* since she had been held captive and brainwashed . . . twice.

"Let them kill me," she had said. "If they can."

"Kunoichi," he had said, cursing her in a feeble voice from the bed.

"Eta Ninja," she called back at him. Then she was gone.

So she didn't see him sit up painfully and reach for the clothes on the baseboard.

Instead she saw the elegant fairy-tale spires of Cinderella's Castle in Fantasyland. " 'Become the enemy,' " said Musashi. One way was to think like the enemy. She knew it wouldn't be desperate, pathetic psychotics she would be fighting. The man she had faced in that hallway was not a wild-eyed bomb thrower. These were terrorists of means. In other words, elegant, educated psychotics.

But there was another way to become the enemy, in Musashi's words: " 'People always think the enemy is strong and so tend to become cautious. He who is shut in is a pheasant. He who enters is a hawk.' " Rhea would not become the enemy by putting herself in the enemy's position. She would, instead, literally become the enemy. Switch from being the hunted to being the hunter.

She was not trapped in Disneyland with them. They were trapped in Disneyland with her.

Rhea got her bearings. She had picked up maps on the way here and pored over them. The setup was not much different than the California amusement park. Tomorrowland was east and Adventureland was west. The need for water was centralized to her left. The Jungle Cruise, the 20,000 Leagues submarine, Tom Sawyer Island, and the Pirates of the Caribbean adventure all needed a steady flow of water.

Rhea moved quickly down Main Street. She had come at mid-morning during one of the slowest times of the year, but the park was still teeming with children and their parents. There were enough Asians so that she didn't attract too much attention, but the sooner she reached her destination, the better she'd feel. She passed the Penny Arcade, the Cinema, and the Railroad Station, then crossed the bridge. Suddenly she was out of Califlorida and into South Nowhere.

She stood amid a chaos of cultures: date palms from the Canary Islands, honeysuckle vines from Africa, Chinese hibiscus, hanging sword ferns, and spider plants. It was as if Daremo were still watching over her and laughing. Even the flowers bore evidence of his influence.

The buildings were designed in a mixture of the Polynesian, the Caribbean, and Southeast Asia. The New Orleans villa she stood near seemed to drip with humidity and moss, even in the chill of November.

Rhea leaned on a palm and watched the weaving line of people outside the Southern mansion. Disney had been brilliant, attentive even to such details as the science of standing on line. Rather than have people stare woefully down a seemingly endless expanse of long-suffering humanity, he designed "people gates" that compacted the waiting into neat groups and always gave the impression of movement. He built the anticipation, rather than dissipating it, by making the wait part of the adventure, and always giving the waiters something to look at.

The people passed Rhea's eyes. All shapes of heads, all

heights, all expressions, all sizes. Each had their own stories, their own joys, their own tragedies. Each had come here today to escape for just a few hours. To enter a genius's world of happiness and equality where the imagination was lifted and all was controlled. The control of the seemingly uncontrolled. Measured thrills that would stimulate without scaring.

Rhea was distracted by a fuzzy movement beyond the bobbing heads. It was a purposeful movement, not in keeping with the seekers of pleasure. This movement was part of a job, not an escape from one. She watched closer as the people on line went by. There were eight rows of them moving back and forth in front of the mansion. She looked carefully at the farthest row. There was a blur, a black spot between heads. As they went by, another stationary head appeared.

Rhea stepped closer. The head was moving. It was jerking back and forth as if signaling a combination of yes and no. She looked behind that head. In between the people on line, she saw an arm. It was moving up and down. It held a brush. It was rubbing the white stucco wall these people were passing.

The head and arm belonged to a Disney staff member. It was part of the Disneyland custodial team. Each of the amusement parks had an army of workers, set up and run like the best military force in the world. Each segment of the staff population had a uniform. This was the white-and-red-striped uniform of a cleaner.

But it wasn't the cleaner who most interested Rhea. It was what he was cleaning. It was a piece of graffiti on the wall of the entrance to Pirates of the Caribbean. It was a stick design of the Chiba shuriken.

Rhea stood stock-still and perceived. She could not locate any of the Chiba sect members watching her. She was fairly certain the man she had killed had not described her to any associates. The sect members were probably already in place, waiting for her to enter the trap. They couldn't be here long. The custodians were only just cleaning off the graffiti now.

She watched the line of visitors and counted. She waited until the timing was right and entered the line itself. What she heard around her was not important in detail. What was important was that those words made her feel she was doing the right thing.

She had renounced the Ega and was living her own wretched life. The Ega had done things Zanjanko and gold had dictated. She did things because she wanted to . . . and felt they were correct.

These people did not deserve to die. Even if the problem were located and eliminated within minutes, none of these escaping innocents deserved to die that way. Let an accident take them if it was heaven or hell's will, but not these Chiba pretenders.

The innocent should not die because Daremo would not.

Each boat held twenty people. Rhea positioned herself to be the twentieth. Last person, last row, left rear seat. As she went, she memorized the mansion's interior. They went through a wide hall, then down a huge ramp to a cavern. They passed an indoor restaurant made to look like a grotto bistro. She saw a footbridge across the first water sluice, and heard the sound of shoppers.

It all jibed with what she had studied. This adventure ride was part of an indoor-outdoor plaza that also housed an exclusive hostelry. There were visitors who paid a premium to stay at the Pirates' residence. That meant an extraordinary inner system of tunnels and machinery.

The quick, attentive, professional boat wranglers helped the returning riders out, and the prospective riders in. This was Rhea's first major test. She moved as part of the group, separating from it at the last minute. The wrangler turned to help the last rider on . . . and she wasn't there. He turned back to the boat in confusion to find it already pulling away, filled to capacity.

"Did you see that?" he asked the wrangler behind him.

"See what?" she answered, making sure the next boat slid in properly.

"Did you see that?" he asked the wrangler in front of him.

"See what?" he said.

Rhea let herself grin. This was an adventure, right? She looked down at the little boy beside her, who was looking up at her in wonder. Rhea looked at the boy's parents, sitting beside him. They were laughing, pointing, enjoying every detail. It was their first trip here. The boy was along for the ride.

"Did you see that?" Rhea asked the child, pointing to the skull and crossbones at the top of the incline up which they were being pulled.

"You just . . . poof," said the boy.

"Watch closely," Rhea said. "I'll do that again."

But then they passed the crest of the incline, where the legend read: "Dead men tell no tales!"

The boat flew down the water-covered metal runners, throwing up liquid on either side of the man-made cave. Everyone screamed and laughed, waiting for the wonders to come. They all heard the song, designed and sung to be the tale of pirates long dead.

"What terror lurks in the mind of stouthearted seamen . . . battling the angry seas?"

The boat, powered by jets of water, came around a curve in the mock cave to find a panorama to their left. It was a ghost ship, destroyed by years of battle, helmed by a skeleton in the remnants of a pirate's garb. Rhea counted how long it was before they left this sight and the boat following came upon it.

"A man of delicate taste, the captain . . . his quarters rigged with the finest furnishings money did not buy." Rhea looked over the boy to see a skeleton sleeping in a magnificent bed, surrounded on both sides by dust-covered booty. She suddenly noticed the little boy was not oohing or ahhing along. She looked down to see him looking up at her.

"Look," she said, pointing behind him, "you'll miss it."

"I want to see you . . . poof."

"Look and you'll see," she promised.

He resolutely stared at her until his eyes watered, wavered, then bugged out. He was looking beside her.

"Pretty baubles," the ghosts sang, "and a king's ransom in gold. Aye, blood money, and cursed it be."

Rhea turned to look at a skeleton sitting atop a mountain of riches. She leaned back so the child could view it completely. Treasure chests, wine vats, thick doubloons, jewel-encrusted plates, rubies, sapphires, diamonds, and silver coins to dazzle the eye.

"Did you see that?" said the boy to the empty seat beside him. "Did you . . ." He did a miniature double take. "Mommy, Dadda, the lady disappeared!"

"Yes, yes, dear," said the mother, already turning to take in the next diorama. "Watch this, you'll love it."

Rhea got behind the pile of fake gold coins in one leap, staying alert for security cameras. The park management had to keep apprised of any problem on the line. She had waited until she was in the deepest shadow possible and made the transition in one soundless movement, so hopefully the screen watchers were blinking or having a coffee break or something.

She kept her steps light, praying the designers weren't so thorough as to have "tilt mechanisms" built in to gauge weight. She also wasn't going to wait until she saw another piece of Chiba graffiti. No reason she had to walk into the trap with an apple in her mouth. If they had the manpower to surreptitiously guard each of the exhibits, then she was sunk, anyway. Musashi said one man can beat ten, but he never said anything about eleven or more.

The Hanzo Razor was out from under her jacket and in her hand. It was just another flashing jewel among these fake riches. She heard the boat behind hers go by as she put a long, vertical slice in the "rock" wall of the cave. It was a painted canvas and plastic drop, of course, which the knife went through like butter.

Hey, everybody, she called silently. *Want to see a ninja walk through rocks? Hey, guards. Want to see a wall grow a woman?* Rhea put her leg up and pushed one half of her through.

It was another sort of wonderland on the other side. A magnificent network of metal scaffolding held up the wall, as well as cunningly designed and placed speakers so the different stanzas of the song didn't mingle in the boaters' ears. The skeletal figures were animatronic robots, but they were powered by electronics and hydraulics on this side of the world.

Rhea stayed near the wall, in the shadows, looking for the tiny red eyes that would signify cameras. It occurred to her that one well-placed infiltrator in the security staff could contact unanchored operatives by watching the video monitors, but that would mean the Chiba sect members had planned this for months.

She doubted that. They were probably in the same boat as she, if you'll pardon the expression. They were moving forward as per Musashi.

" 'Holding down a shadow,' " he called it in *The Book of Fire* within his *Book of Five Rings*. This was the third ring, the fighting ring, the interlocking ring. If she could succeed her, they could move on to the final phase. " 'Soak in,' " he said. " ' "Become one with the enemy." ' "

Will do, she thought, reaching for the first metal scaffolding support. Rhea put the Razor away and pulled herself up like a seasoned gymnast. She climbed and swung, just out of view of the red eyes, until she was close to the ceiling. Then she climbed across, hearing the final stanza of the song fade out.

"Strike your colors!" she heard from around the corner. She carefully sneaked a look as she heard the reply.

"We will never surrender!"

"They needs persuasion, mates! Fire at will!"

It was a pirate battle at sea. The cave emptied out into a cavernous room, large enough for a baseball field. The little boats were floating between two full-size Spanish galleons, one flying the skull-and-crossbones flag. As she watched, the cannons began to speak, booming and belching huge white smoke rings. The walls shook as the water shot up in torrents, and the enemy ship's mast was cracked in half.

The scaffolding area opened up as well, becoming one with the cave. Rhea slipped down and let herself sink into the water up to her chest. She bent her knees until her eyes were level with the surface, then started walking across, behind the pirate ship. She moved quickly, letting her feet and legs feel for the pipes and metal tunnels that the battle necessitated.

She hardly needed her ninja skills, since no one was looking at the water's surface, anyway. She made it to the far side and climbed onto the scaffolding again. The boat riders, and she, were about to enter the world of pirate plunder.

The song took up again, and Rhea noticed that the new scaffolding was sandwiched by another brown canvas wall. She put a slit in that and peeked through. Inside was the waterworks. She saw a huge pit, like a gramophone speaker held straight up, over which were two parallel metal catwalks and regulating switches. Some switches were the knife-handle sort, which moved up and down. Others were steering-wheel types, which were twisted around.

The area appeared empty, but Rhea knew shadows better than most. She could see these shadows, in the corners of the room, *breathing*.

There were crow's-nest type platforms midway up where the walls met. No more than little, lying, metal fans upon which to stand. There were no doors behind them, so Rhea gathered that they had to be climbed onto. It was a semi-perfect place for ambushers to wait. Anyone who wanted to poison the water would have to come here.

Rhea climbed to the floor, between the sweeps of the red eyes, and slipped off her coat. "'Injure the corners'" Musashi had said. Injure the corners she would. She heard the pirates taunt her from the room beyond.

"Pipe the lubber aloft, matey! Speak up, you bilge rat. Where be the treasure?"

A shapely leg erupted from the wall behind the first shadow. It slammed into the center of his back and sent him flying down to the first catwalk across the water funnel. The kick and crash were swallowed up by the water, as were the thuds and coughs of the three silenced automatics coming from the other corners.

They were dressed in black, with blackened faces. They

had worn the black clothes under lighter coats and kept the black makeup in their pockets until they had infiltrated the ride. No one expected anyone to be so crazy in Disneyland.

The man in the opposite corner spun when he heard the noise behind him. It was too late. The slit in the canvas already had been made, and the leg struck again. It kicked him from his perch and sent him to the other catwalk, arms flailing.

The men across the room fired again, their silenced .380 and .22 ammo spitting around the wall and scaffolding. The .380 slugs ate up the silencer's innards, and the .22 bullets were wildly inaccurate. It couldn't be helped. They couldn't have smuggled the larger guns inside, nor could they have contained the power in here with any anonymity.

The man in the far corner cursed. They didn't know who or what they were looking for; they were just supposed to kill it. Whoever it was must've climbed the scaffolding on the other side, kicked, ran, and kicked again. He could only now imagine the strength, grace, and speed of their target: to soundlessly slice a hole behind the first man, kick out with enormous force, drop to avoid the bullets, roll, come up running, leap to a scaffold, swing to the second perch, cut and kick again.

A body erupted from the center of the brown canvas wall, leaping at the first man, who was trying to get up on the catwalk. The men in the far corner fired on it.

"Don't shoot!" the first man tried to shout as the coat and a bullet hit him at the same time.

Another figure leapt onto the lip of the water funnel and jumped onto the first catwalk. Rhea had hurled her sopping-wet coat out of a third slit in the wall, then ran back to the first corner and cut a horizontal slit in the canvas near the floor. She had slithered into the room during the confusion and waited for the second wave of confusion to hit before making her move.

The first man had been hit in the shoulder. She grabbed him and held him up as the second man stood on the other catwalk, parallel to her, and fired.

"No!" the wounded man yelled as the bullets struck him.

He was too weak and shocked to fight her. As more bullets struck, he felt something clawing at his gun hand. He wrenched his arm away, but his fingers came up empty.

Rhea shot the man in the far corner behind her—the only one with a clear view.

He saw a woman in dark red, with dark blue on her arms and legs, and dark black on her feet, pointing at him. Then he felt God slap him, and he saw nothing.

The others saw him dive to the floor, his arms by his sides, his gun still clutched in one hand.

Rhea grabbed her dying shield by his wounded shoulder and held him up. Her slim figure was well covered by his bulk. The others would have to go through him to get to her. They had tried and failed. Now they froze, stunned.

"All right!" she boomed over the roar of the water. "I'm here! What do you want?"

Before they could answer, metal doors in the side and back walls slid open. Park security officials in dark green and white poured into the room. They had massed and charged the moment the technician had seen the action on the red-eye screen.

They surrounded the water funnel and blocked both ends of both catwalks. Rhea could see they all had gloves, some had clubs, and a few had stun guns.

"You fool!" the man in the far corner shouted.

"This isn't Paris, idiot!" Rhea shouted back. "This is Disneyland! Now what are you going to do?"

They showed her what they intended. Before the guards could say or do anything, the man across from her pointed his gun and fired while reaching into his pocket. Rhea held her now dead shield up as the guards surged onto the walks. But only she saw the vial in the other man's hand.

She didn't have time to warn the guards. With concentrated strength she threw her shield at the man, vaulted the catwalk, put both feet on the banister, and dived across.

The guards reached the man a second before the woman did. They grabbed his gun arm. Rhea grabbed his free hand. She ripped open his pocket and fell. She dropped into the raging whirlpool, feeling the tiny, unopened glass bottle in her grip.

The guards overwhelmed the Chiba sect member on the second catwalk. He opened his mouth and roared, his head and shoulders wrenching back and forth over a human anthill. The man in the last corner brought his gun down and shot him in the back of the head. The .380 bullet went through the top of his skull and out his mouth. The report was loud and echoing, the silencer's interior completely eaten away.

The mob of guards spun in his direction. They watched him leap from his perch and drop down between the catwalks, between their reaching arms, into the raging water funnel.

III

Hands slapped onto the switches and wheels, but one voice was louder than the water and the shouts and the guns' echoes.

"It's too late!"

The others stopped what they were doing, as stiff as the animatronic pirates, and turned to the man who had yelled. His face was grave. "There's nothing we can do. The current'll carry them to the grates. The grates'll grind them into chopped meat." He turned to the guard nearest the rear door. "Tell the technician to put the filters on extra fine."

Rhea was sucked into Neptune's world. Her body was spun like a top. Invisible hands turned her torso at different times than they turned her head, hips, or legs. But she held on to that damn vial. That's what it was all about, wasn't it? She wasn't going to let the Chiba sect members get away with their two-edged trap.

Her eyes were open, her chopped hair too short to obscure her vision. She was glad her heavy coat was still on the catwalk. It would have weighted or strangled her. She watched as she whirled, looking for a way out.

She needn't have bothered. The water carried her along. It pulled her down and around, hurling her under the French

"Caribbean." She saw the smooth cement walls going by, and exulted in the breath she held in her lungs.

She had been submerged as a baby. She had been held under the water for longer and longer periods with the passing days. She was held down with a choice: Live or die. The one who held her had not cared which.

Hari... The name echoed in Rhea's brain. Hari, the goddess-demon. The bitch-monster. For the very first time Rhea wondered whether Hari had killed her husband . . . and Rhea's father.

When the man's body struck her, she almost screamed, letting out the precious air. He had fallen into the whirlpool after her. He had wrenched his body around. He had dived into the unknown. He had spotted her ahead and swum toward her, his teeth clenched.

He clawed at her now, his hands gripping her hips and pulling her to him. His hands gripped her throat as she punched him in the crotch. It wasn't hard enough. His fingers closed on her neck, and they embraced.

Rhea kneed him the second time. He let go. Rhea put a foot in his stomach and kicked, as much to damage him as to push away.

She shot forward, like a torpedo fired from a submarine. They flew like superheroes through the straight tunnel. She looked ahead, seeing nothing but a steep decline. If she could just hold on long enough, she'd make it to wherever this emptied out. At this speed the odds looked good.

But the man was still conscious. His eyes were still red, and his teeth still clenched. He clawed through the water toward her.

Rhea kept her body straight, her arms at her sides. Maybe she could stay ahead of him because of her lighter weight and sleeker form. No such luck. He was gaining steadily.

Okay, she thought. Let him come. There was no stopping him. He reached out, his fingers scratching the soles of her running shoes.

She daren't kick. She didn't want to expend unnecessary oxygen. He was using up energy like crazy. Why didn't his lungs burst? Why didn't he die?

He grabbed her ankle. He pulled her toward him. He climbed up her. She looked down. The coursing water was cleaning his face. As she watched, the black makeup was being washed and chipped off. It was like a reborn insect breaking out of its used shell.

His hand slid across her thigh. She reached down to grip the handle of one Hanzo Razor in its waist scabbard. His hand went down to his belt.

What was he trying to do? Rape her? Here?

His hand came up, holding a Beretta 87 automatic.

"*Merde*," Rhea said, swearing. She had forgotten about the gun. If the shell casing was tight enough, the gunpowder wouldn't get wet and the weapon would fire. He could shoot her under water. He wouldn't miss at this range.

She kneed him in the chin, pulled the Razor out with her free hand, and stabbed at him. He surged away but didn't drop back. He was above her.

She couldn't throw the blade now. But he could still shoot her. He sailed above, his teeth still clenched, but his lips pulled back in a horrible Sardonicus death grin.

That bastard Napoleon hadn't told them about this. That bastard Napoleon had lost all grip on who they were. The SSS weren't hired hit men. It was like asking a master chef to make franks and beans. There was only so much one could do.

He was asking masters to do shit work. He was asking brilliant painters to do picket fences. He had lost all grip on reality. This was not infiltration. This was breaking and entering. This was not sabotage. This was vandalism.

He would kill this bitch, and then he would kill Napoleon. He would take over the SSS. They would return to the game. Enough exercises. If they had needed more practice, they wouldn't have been asked to join in the first place!

The man forced his arm up. It took astonishing effort against this tide, but he raised it. He used all his considerable strength to keep it raised and pointed at the woman's body.

He was just close enough. It made no difference how slim she was or how she spun herself. The bullet would hit. He was a marksman. He could hit a hummingbird at this range. His finger squeezed the trigger.

That's when they hit the grate.

The guard had not identified the obstruction properly. It was not so much a grate as a cell door. Metal pipes had been vertically affixed parallel to each other. The two slammed into them.

Rhea had been spinning her body. Her left shoulder hit first. The man had been arrow-straight through the water. His head went between poles, both shoulders smashing into them.

His shoulder blades were immediately broken. His fingers jerked spasmodically, the gun being torn away from him as it fired. His body surged up. He slammed into the pipes a second time, lying on his back, looking as if he were standing on his head.

Rhea's body was pulled sideways, wedged between the bars. She had held on to her air but just barely. She was only becoming aware of what had happened when she felt fingers in her hair.

They gripped and pulled. She looked up. The man was staring down at her, his mouth open. He was yanking on her scalp. She took the Hanzo Razor and started cutting his hand with it.

She saw his silent scream. She saw the dark blood swirl and get swept away by the raging torrent. She felt her lungs burn and her body being pulled between the bars.

Again and again he had noted her slimness. She was almost completely muscle but just slim enough to get through. He felt his lungs start to tear apart. He felt the water pouring into his body. He held on to her hair.

Rhea's body popped through the grate. She was jerked back and held in place by his bloody hand. The water was screaming around her, her brain was screaming at her, and her scalp was just screaming.

She plunged the Razor into his wrist. He did not let go.

His lungs burst. He felt them. The inside of his head filled with water. His organs lurched. He died. But he did not let go.

Rhea sliced her hair off. The water took her.

She windmilled her arms toward the surface. There had to be air pockets at the top. There had to be, or she would fall into hell just after the Chiba sect member.

Her cheek scraped the top of the concrete tunnel. Then she hit another grating.

It was different this time. The bars were set horizontally. It had not been too far from the first grating, so the punishment to her body was not as severe. But the surprise was greater this time, and she lost what remained of her air.

She forced her head up and gulped. She did not get liquid, Buddha be praised. She played chicken with the water to get three more gulps. Then she slid between the bars like a mermaid and swam for her life.

17

Daremo had liked the Mickey Mouse sweatshirt she had worn home. It was the insulated, reversible sort, with one red side and one blue side; each with well-delineated designs of the cartoon character in his glory years. Daremo also noted the light brown duster—that long coat made famous by cowboys—which she had bought in Adventureland. Thankfully they'd accepted the wet money she'd taken from the waistband of her bicycle pants.

Daremo nodded in tired appreciation of all the skills she had utilized getting out of there. Ultimately the channel had emptied out into the jungle ride where she had slammed up against a submerged rhino animatronic. Dragging herself to the shore, she rested amid thick plastic and real plants. Then she avoided the suddenly plentiful guards on the grounds to find a rest room, where she sat under the hand drier for almost a half hour.

There followed more stealth and new clothes buying until she could sneak out an exit, head held low and eyes darting.

"Where did you put your Razors?" Daremo had asked, marveling.

"In the arm pads. The spikes showed but just barely. I think everyone thought I was a punk."

"With that haircut I don't blame them." Daremo's handiwork, cutting her from a crucifix in Japan, was enhanced by her recent hack work. The longest section, cut on a diagonal by Daremo's sword, was now cut across, short, with a sort of layered look.

"Welcome to the wonderful world of ninjitsu." He sighed with exhaustion, putting his head back on the pillow. "Exciting, isn't it?" And he stayed there until Rhea came in a few days later with more news.

"More graffiti," she had said, sitting at the table and drawing a buzz-saw type configuration on the paper bag holding the bread. "Toei."

Daremo closed his eyes and put a hand across his brow. "Not another one," he said with a groan. "What is this? Has Paris become the pseudo-ninja capital of the world? Are there going to be challenges from Aunt Ninja on your father's side? Where will it all end? Did you bring the wine?"

He was feeling better. He was drinking again. She handed him the bottle of Côtes de Ventoux. "The Toei sabotaged the Sanada market day," she said.

"I know," he complained.

"What are you going to do about it?"

He used the corkscrew he kept on the floor by the bed to open the wine. He took a long swig before answering. "Same as before."

Rhea silently watched him drink until he felt compelled to speak again. It was a singsong poem he told to the ceiling—a part of the apartment he had become quite friendly with. "The spider waits in his web for us to do his bidding; he waits till everyone is dead and eats all in one sitting."

"Who said that?" she asked.

"I did."

Rhea rose and collected her things. "Well, I'm not going to sit here and listen to your brain melt."

"Where are you going?" he asked without interest as she put on her new coat.

"Shopping."

He stopped her at the door with his voice. "This time," he asked of her, "kill them all, will you?"

Rhea felt slightly queasy when she saw the rows of stuffed Mickey Mouses. She had taken the Métro to the Opéra station and walked the three blocks to Galleries Lafayette.

The graffiti had been cunning. Where once there had been Chiba insignia, there was now the Toei shuriken drawn over white spray paint. But if one knew what one was looking for, the directions were painfully clear.

The signposts were much like the ones prescribed in the Boy Scout manual. Rhea found the new graffiti on untainted telephone poles, lamps, and walls plainly pointing to the huge department store, which took up one and a half city blocks.

The shopping mania spread throughout the area. In addition to the tiny shops crammed together all around the bricklike building, the inner courtyards and alleyways were filled with carts and open-air displays. It was much like a carnival—much like the Sanada Market Day, in fact, where feudal craftsmen and salesmen from all over Japan would sell their goods. The same town that housed many members of the Sanada sect.

To draw them out the Toei had created intricate explosives, disguised as different products, then slipped them amid the regular goods. The bombs the Sanada couldn't find would kill them and their sympathizers. These bastards who were jerking her around obviously planned to do that in Paris's largest department store.

Rhea had walked from one end to the other, watchful for any graffiti. Thankfully the place was only three stories tall, and she all but eliminated the cramped top floor after a careful examination. With all the furniture and other heavy goods there, any explosive wouldn't have much killing effect. Better to concentrate on the lower, more central levels.

She rested in the toy department, leaning on the mezzanine's banister. She looked around, feeling elation and concern. This was the spot. It had to be. Not only was the area crawling with children and easily sabotaged stuffed animals, but this was the store's focal point.

The toy department was next to the juniors' fashion department (plenty of young girls to hurt there), which was next to the housewares department (young housewives). But it was all set in a large circle, on a balcony overlooking the expansive and expensive perfume and makeup department on the first floor. And above . . . above was what the Galleries Lafayette was most famous for. There was the gigantic, breathtaking domed ceiling made entirely of stained glass.

A bomb planted here would reach every level, since every level opened up here for a magnificent view of the Lancôme and Chanel displays. Everything below Rhea sparkled with silver-and-gold glass. She could just imagine all of it blowing apart and speeding in all directions, like so many Toei shuriken.

Rhea gripped the banister more tightly. She had surveyed the first floor, and there it was, moving through the crowd. It was the Toei shuriken.

It moved across the off-white marble floor, between booth after booth of lit glass. Rhea strode around the balcony, following the path, trying to get a clear view as to what made it move.

A woman made it move. No, a girl. Rhea saw a young girl, couldn't have been more than twenty. She was small and blond, with a china doll's face and Kewpie-doll lips. Her eyes were big and blue. She wore a pleated black skirt, a thick black jacket, and a beret. The Toei shuriken emblem was on the jacket's back. She carried a big book.

It was a hardcover book, otherwise known as a coffee-table volume. It was ten inches wide, twelve inches long, and two inches thick. Rhea suddenly felt ill. Who knew how much gelignite could be crammed into that thing? Who knew how it was detonated?

God. She had put herself into this, so she had to act quickly. They had already proven that what they really wanted to do was kill her, so she doubted bombs had already been planted everywhere. No, she told herself, no. The man in the water funnel had shot his associate. The news had told her that. They were classic ninja: draw no attention to themselves, commit suicide if captured. They would try to kill her and be gone. They would only draw attention to themselves by killing others if she did not appear.

Rhea looked around, found no one watching her, and leaned over the banister. She grabbed the lacy black metalwork at the base and swung herself over. She hung there a second until the floor, sixteen feet below, cleared. She dropped straight down.

She landed with hardly a thump, bent her knees, and began walking toward the girl. Three women around her started, because it seemed she had appeared out of nowhere. But then Rhea was past, still heading quickly toward the blond girl's back.

Here's the plan, she told herself. Grab the back of the book, yank it from the girl's grip, run for the exit, hit the street, drop it down a sewer, hope for the best. Maybe even tap the blonde in the stomach, neck, or kidney while passing to keep her from yelling "Thief!"

Rhea was getting closer. Yeah, it might work. But maybe, if she got the correct sensations, she'd just throw it out the window. Hurl it like . . . well, like a shuriken. She kept her attention on the girl but let her eyes pick out possible Toei sect members. Maybe they planned to kill her as she approached. Silly boys. Plug her at this range, with this many unknowing interceptors in the way?

Still, it paid to be careful. Paid in blood. Use the blonde as a shield. Rhea kept moving, looking everywhere. Would they try overkill? Watch from a distance through binoculars, wait until she got close, then detonate the bomb? No, she didn't think so. She *hoped* not. No matter how they attempted to get her, they had a warped sense of honor about it. Again, like the ninja. The honor of dishonor. The honor of no honor.

She was almost on the blond girl now. She could see that the blonde was as nervous as she felt. The blonde kept looking around furtively, clutching the book to her side. Rhea was some five yards away when the blonde looked over her shoulder and saw her.

The kunoichi was not prepared for what happened next. The blonde stopped in the middle of the floor, stiff as a board, and started screaming at the top of her lungs.

"Help! Help! Help me! Please help me!"

Rhea started to step forward, ready to join the throng "soothing" the girl. She would then grab the book and run. But as she moved, the blonde started pointing directly at her.

"Don't let her near me! Help! She'll hurt me! Help!"

Merde, Rhea thought. There had to be a fifth Chiba sect member at the amusement park. One placed specifically to memorize her features.

But then, why weren't more killers waiting for her at the Disneyland exits? Unless . . . unless there weren't enough Chiba *or* Toei sect members to go around. . . .

A crowd of shoppers had gathered quickly. The prompt, attentive sales and security people appeared as if by magic, trying to calm the hysterical blonde, who was still pointing and shrieking at Rhea.

The kunoichi took a step away, then remembered the Toei sabotage. They were counting on her not walking away from possible mass murder. Everything she had been, however, told her to run, to escape, to protect herself, *to covet ninja secrets*.

So she planted her feet and told her tortuous training to go fuck itself.

This is my life now, she thought. *To throw away if I wish.*

"Her! Her!" the blonde was crying. "She hurt me. She tried to rob me! Stop her!" The crowd had moved back to make a semicircle around the girl. They all stared at the beautiful, harmless-looking Asian woman in the long coat.

One of the four security guards who had appeared approached her calmly, his hand out, aiming for her arm.

"Please, mademoiselle . . ."

Oh, well, Rhea thought. "There's a bomb in that book," she told him so the others wouldn't hear.

His calm visage was shaken for a second, but his unctiousness soon returned. He put his hand on her arm. "Mademoiselle, please . . ."

They were all around her. Rhea could practically smell them. The Toei sect members. Cut and run. They would be just like other shoppers until they brushed by and the knife or bullet would go through their coat pockets and into her.

Rhea remembered. The last of the great ninja vendettas. The Toei had killed Hiriyoki Sanada as the old man was seeing his grandson off at a railway station in 1910. He was waving good-bye as an obsessed, ancient Toei man slipped behind him with a cast on a supposedly broken arm. . . .

"Sorry," Rhea mumbled as her head went down. She started moving.

Witnesses were astonished. The police kept getting reports of people suddenly defying the law of gravity. Shoppers would tell them that the security guard suddenly dived forward, somersaulted in the air, and landed back first on a counter.

When asked what caused it, all the witnesses could recall was a sudden gust of energy, as if a shock wave had erupted from the floor.

It was Rhea's muscles. They even shocked the blond girl into silence as she cowered. Rhea spun the guard's arm like a hurdy-gurdy handle, and his body had to follow or his muscles would be torn in half. He went flying, and Rhea kept moving.

She did not discriminate. Anybody near her with hands in pockets of their coats. There was a man behind her, to her left side, with a light, long overcoat, hand in pocket. One of Rhea's legs stayed on the floor; the rest of her body became the top of a *T*. Her foot went flat into the man's torso, where his chest met his stomach.

He whoofed and went back, arms and legs straight out,

into a jewelry display. The pearl-and-diamond earrings fell around him like tears. She didn't stop. The same foot swung around and up, to catch a guard running at her from the front. The top of her foot hit him from the ear to the back of his neck.

He didn't know what happened from then on, but the blonde saw his feet sweep out, and he did most of a cartwheel in the air . . . without hands.

Rhea brought the foot back to slap down another man coming forward. His hands were up to grab her, out of his pockets, but that couldn't be helped. The bottom of her foot, just below the toes, smacked him across the brow and nose. He went down to his face as if sledgehammered from behind.

Each blow had been incredibly strong, the prodigious power of all Rhea's leg, hip, and stomach muscles behind it. Each strike was accompanied by a burst of dust and lint from the clothes and shoes, and each had its own sickening sound of effort and contact.

Everyone stared at the violent vision for a shocked second. She had just been standing there, and suddenly four men were down in the wink of an eye. The three remaining security guards looked at each other, then someone shouted, "Get her!"

The three men left the blonde and charged Rhea. She had heard the battle cry, all right. It had come from behind the girl. From some bastard Toei mastermind who wanted her distracted.

The guards had billy clubs. The first man was swinging it down at her head as she watched. Rhea reacted the way Daremo had taught her. She had seen him do this once. She plucked the man's club hand out of the air by the wrist and twisted. She turned the arm so the club blocked the second club the next guard was swinging at her.

" 'Church door,' " Daremo had called it, because it made the two attackers' bodies into a slightly open doorway. It took lightning-fast reflexes, but Rhea was capable of that.

She kicked through the opening of the "doors," into the stomach of the third guard coming up. Then came the move that really wowed them: Her leg snapped back, out from the door, behind her, and into the side of a man reaching into his pocket. *At the same time* she put the back of her free fist into the second guard's face.

The second and third guards went down, the second on his back, the third on his face. Done right, it all looked like one continuous, incredibly quick, motion. It had been done right.

The first guard was still paralyzed by her arm hold. The silenced automatic in the pocket of the sect member behind her went off, the bullet hitting the floor. Rhea turned, twisted, and pulled. She vaulted the first guard over her back, over her shoulder, and used him as a club to knock down the gunman.

Another Toei sect member came at her from the side, from between perfume displays, the knife out of his pocket and held low. Rhea spun around, her leg up. Her foot smacked the knife hand, sending it wide. Rhea kept spinning, bringing the first leg down and the other leg up, higher. That foot struck the knifer's face. He spun to the floor like a corkscrew.

She came all the way around, checking the positions of the others. A man some ten feet away, opposite the blonde, was taking no more chances. He was standing by a mirrored post, the gun unconcealed and held at arm's length—reflected three times, making him look like a firing squad. He was treating Rhea like a target shoot.

Her turn wasn't even completely finished when she used the energy as a springboard to dive to the left. She went over the Chanel counter as he fired. A huge display bottle of Number 20 cologne burst, sending the amber liquid to the floor.

Rhea didn't land normally. All the exercise inside the cellars was paying off. Her muscles were like coiled springs now. She landed on her open hands. She vaulted herself over, snapping onto her feet with bent legs. She grabbed a display bottle of Number 5. She turned and threw it like a backhanded Frisbee.

The thick, rectangular bottle shot across the room, past

the man's outstretched gun arm, and into his chin. The bottle shattered as if it had been struck by lead. The thick glass felt like a two-by-four to the gunman, whose head went back into the mirrored post.

That was taken as a cue. *All* the Toei sect members started pulling their guns. There was one behind her, to her left. Another was coming through the crowd, next to the cowering blonde. A third was running at her from directly in front.

They were going to box her in and pump metal into her like a pincushion. She needed shock. " 'Move the shade!' " Musashi demanded. " 'See the enemy's attacking spirit!' "

Rhea spun behind the counter. Her shadow leapt into the air, toward the blonde. It was enough. The two men nearest her changed their aim to kill the "duster" coat she had whirled from her ducking form.

Then the Hanzo Razors were out. They spun in two directions, like crystalline snowflakes the size of basketballs. A spike sank into the side of the first sect member's neck, on a diagonal. The blade itself then cut across his throat, from the side of one chin to his shoulder.

The second one hit the third sect member in the top of the head. His fingers twitched, shattering the Chanel display with bullets, but Rhea was already gone. She had jumped through the swinging partition that separated the booth from the shopper's area, her hands filled with more big bottles of sinfully expensive perfume.

She smashed them into the face of the second, the one by the blonde. The glass broke on his face, and the acidic liquid poured into his eyes, mouth, and cuts. He threw his arms up, screaming, as Rhea executed a flying kick. One foot went into his stomach just before the other went across his face.

If it was possible, he went down and to the side at almost the same time. He smashed into a display of luggage, twitching.

Rhea spun to face the blonde, who reared back in fear from the wraith with the twisted face and white-knuckled fists.

The man next to the blonde tightened his hand *inside* the girl's jacket. He gripped the Astra A75 automatic he held there. He was certain the woman didn't see it. It looked like he was just a shopper who was comforting the hysterical girl. He had gone to the blonde's side as soon as she'd started screaming, kneeled with her, and slipped the gun into her pocket as soon as the violence had begun.

The woman would come close and the man would kill her.

"Give me that book!" Rhea snarled, leaning down, her hand out.

A battering ram hit her shoulder. She was literally thrown off her feet and sent flying west. She smashed into a fashionable female mannequin and took her down.

The Astra bullet went up and killed an innocent-talking Teddie Ruxpin on the second level. Its head just burst. All the shoppers had hit the floor when the shooting started.

The final Toei man saw a foot swing into his vision from the side. It was covered by a man's shoe. Then it filled his vision, and there was some sort of wet noise, an explosion of red, white, yellow, orange, and finally black.

The man skimmed the floor on his back and hit a trash can headfirst.

"Daremo!" Rhea gasped, springing to her feet.

"Close," said Yasuru. "Let's get out of here." He turned as Rhea reached him, but there was no time for a heart-warming reunion.

"No!" said the woman, rushing forward and grabbing the blonde by the hair as she turned to run. Rhea yanked the book out from her arm. Yasuru saw the Toei shuriken design on the girl's back. "How is this set?" The girl just stared at her in fright and pain. "How is this set?"

Rhea threw the girl into Yasuru's arms, grabbed her coat off the floor, and pounced on the sect member she had clubbed with the guard. He was still barely conscious. She yanked the glass bottle she had torn from the chiba sect member's grip at the water funnel and held it against the man's teeth.

"See?" she yelled at him, shaking him by the lapel.

"See? This is poison. I'll smash this in your mouth if you don't tell me how to defuse the bomb!"

There was no doubting her veracity. "You . . . you can't," he sputtered. "It's a time bomb. If you tamper with it at all, it'll go off." He raised his head and shouted the rest. "There's enough explosive to kill everyone on the floor!"

Rhea was instantly standing, stepping on his solar plexus. He curled into a fetus position, groaning.

"How much time?" Rhea yelled at them. "How much time?"

The man below her grunted out the words. "You've . . . lost. 'Us' wins!" Rhea kicked him in the face.

"Sixteen seconds!" the blonde screamed, holding out her arm where a watch was strapped. "He told me to get out of the store by eleven! Run!"

Rhea put the book under her arm and sped toward the nearest door. The book was plucked from her as she passed. She skidded to a halt and whirled to see Yasuru holding the book in both hands, staring at it with complete concentration.

Rhea was about to shout when she noticed he was speaking.

"Ten, nine, eight, seven, six . . ." he was saying. At five he brought it down in his left hand. At four he positioned his body. Everyone shrank away from him. At three he threw it.

People screamed and scattered. The blonde tried to get to her feet and run, but Rhea swept her legs out from under her with a kick. The blonde landed face first on the marble floor.

Yasuru's artificial left arm used its hydraulics to send the book up three stories and through the thinnest section of stained glass near the crown of the dome. Only one panel was broken by it.

"One," said Daremo's student.

The bomb went off above the streets. Shrapnel rained down, breaking a few more panes in the dome and slightly wounding several pedestrians. There were a few auto accidents because the noise of the explosion scared some motorists. There was one heart attack, but the elderly victim survived.

By the time Inspector Dugelay heard about it, Rhea and Yasuru were well away. They were gone when the blonde regained consciousness, her nose bloody and front tooth broken. They had run out before the first bystander had gotten to his feet.

"You know," said Rhea, "we'll never be able to show our faces in this town again." She stopped in the alley and looked in every direction. "Which way is Switzerland?"

"Not you too?" Yasuru groaned. "I've had enough of the flippant jokes from him! You haven't started drinking also, have you?"

"What are you doing here?" she asked, more to the point.

"What do you think?" he answered, moving ahead. "Hama sent me. We found out some things you ought to know. What on earth was all that about? I step out of a taxi, and the first thing I see is some graffiti of a Toei throwing star. I followed it to the store . . . !"

"Later. You won't believe it."

"I'll believe it. I don't *dis*believe anything anymore."

"Let's just get back before 'le dragnet' starts."

They moved through the side streets and alleys of Richelieu-Drouot and Strasbourg Saint-Denis like it was ninja stamina training. They reached Oberkampf and Saint-Ambroise in record time. The exhilaration had still not worn off the woman. She was feeling alive, young, and most importantly, free. The stigma of the last year was being burned out of her. She was making personal choices that weren't quite killing her. Her violent satire of women's lib was working.

"You'll never guess what I found walking the streets," she announced from the doorway. "Ta-da!" She put her arm out and Yasuru walked in.

"The Chinese Moshuh have taken over for the Kohga ninja, sensei," he said quickly. "An informant was called *mei li*, the pinyan word for beautiful and . . ."

His rapid explanation trailed off as Rhea closed the door and turned around. They both stared in amazement.

The bed was empty.
They were the only two people in the room.

18

"It's beautiful up here, isn't it?"

The antique car had come through Charles Bonner's window. Daremo had been behind the wheel. It was a suitably outrageous entrance, befitting the vision of the madman with Napoleon's name.

Daremo had gotten onto the roof opposite Bonner's building, climbed along the wires, cut the wheels' supports, and let the thing slide. He saw it as a test of his recuperation. If the skin didn't pop after that, it wouldn't until it was sliced the next time.

The office had been empty, but the fireplaces were all working. The files were burning. Daremo imagined that he could check the furnace pipes for all sorts of weapon parts that would slowly melt over the next few weeks. Even if they were retrieved, there'd be no evidence to cull from them.

The only thing that was left unbroken was a single paperweight in the middle of the desk. It was a dark steel shuriken, shaped like a snowflake, lying on the green felt desk blotter.

Kohga design.

"Yes," said Daremo. "It is beautiful up here."

Paris at night. The Seine was all around them. Daremo could take one step to his right and miss it by that much. They were on one of the two islands made where the river split, Ile de la Cité. The other was the Ile Saint-Louis.

To the south was the Latin Quarter and the Pantheon. To the north was Marais and the National Archives. The city, in all its gray, eccentric glory, was spread before them.

"You know," said Napoleon, "a bronze star set in the parvis marks the starting point of the main routes out of the city."

Daremo didn't bother looking for it. His side still ached from climbing up here. "You shouldn't have sent them after me."

Napoleon finally turned to face him from the other side of the tower at the top of the three-tiered facade. "You *would* say that." There was defensiveness as well as bitterness in his tone. He held a small stick in his hand, atop which was a red button. A wire went from the bottom of the stick to a black box attached to his belt.

Daremo shook his head sadly. "They were spies. If they do their job right, no one dies."

"They were . . . *are* . . . operatives," Napoleon corrected, the moon high in the night sky behind him. "They should have . . . been . . . capable of any requirement."

"Spies," said Daremo.

He had followed Rhea out that first day, but instead of going to Disneyland, he had gone to the morgue. He had infiltrated and read the coroner's report concerning the man killed in the cellar hallway near Menilmontant.

"No fingerprints . . . possibly burned off" tipped him off. There were only two kinds of people with no fingerprints. Criminals and secret agents.

"Irrelevant," said Napoleon. "They were my men."

"They're mine now," Daremo informed him. "If I do *my* job right, *everybody* dies."

"Yes . . ." Napoleon mused, keeping the ninja master occupied.

They stood atop the north tower of Notre Dame, about fifteen feet across the slightly inclined dome from each other.

"You are ninja?" Napoleon asked.

Daremo shrugged. "Or something like it."

"Why did you come?"

They were sixty yards off the ground. The wind was brisk, pulling at Napoleon's fine suit and Daremo's gray denim jacket. The sounds of Paris came to them. The citizens on the streets below went about their business obliviously.

Daremo had slipped up the roped-off stairs and picked the locked cloister door to reach the top of the turret, which allowed sightseers during visiting hours. But the main section of the hundred and thirty yard long Cathedral had been closed for hours.

"You invited me," answered Daremo simply.

The Kohga shuriken signified the collapse of that sect, knocked down during the final battle with Ega. They had fought in the castle the Kohga had occupied for hundreds of years—the focal point of their history. Cathédral de Notre Dame de Paris was this city's equal. It was also their greatest tourist attraction besides the Eiffel Tower.

"Do you know why?" asked Napoleon.

"I don't care."

He had called Hama and asked to be put in contact with Agent Anthony. That was when he discovered the man's death. Instead he was put in touch with who he heard one agent refer to as "the broad with the thick wrists." They had to be, the way she used weapons.

"Hello," he had told Moser Grzyzga, "this is Moe Dare."

"You are standing on the site of Operation Masterstroke," Napoleon told him. "Do you know who I am? Who I truly am?"

Daremo thought about saying "I don't care" again, but it would have been a lie. Truth was, he *did* care. His whole wretched life made him care.

"Yes," he said.

Agent 1 After 909 did some checking. After a thorough file investigation she was finally able to come up with some names and code names, addresses, and "last seen in the vicinity ofs."

"I'm not talking about names!" Napoleon said.

"Neither am I."

"Oh? Who am I, then?"

"You're the pathetic fool who *wants* to be ninja."

Napoleon ignored it. "I am the man behind the worst

'accidents' of the last decade!" he announced. "and I'm not talking about plane crashes or forest fires. I'm talking about the political accidents. Accidents that, if they were revealed to be sabotage, would start World War Three."

"I *have* killed all your people," Daremo noted. "You've no one left to talk to."

"You mean 'we,' don't you?" Napoleon said, verbally counterpunching. "We know about the gook girl."

"You mean 'I', don't you?" Daremo replied casually. "Everyone else is dead."

Napoleon paused. Daremo fought the urge to crouch. The silence could be interpreted in two ways. The SSS leader couldn't think of a retort or everyone else *wasn't* dead.

Daremo didn't feel the cross hairs on him, but he imagined he could sense them.

The man at the café. The one who had orchestrated the bombing. The one who had come after him in the subway. Was he dead? Had Rhea gotten *him*?

"Don't you understand?" Napoleon demanded. "The major powers *knew* these weren't accidents. They *knew* they were sabotage. But still they didn't go to war!"

"Maybe they also knew the 'enemy' wasn't responsible."

"Impossible," said Napoleon. "What else could they think? That ninja did it? That a secret secret service did it? Who would believe that? No rational man!"

"That's for sure," Daremo agreed dryly.

"Don't you see, then? It's all a farce! All the espionage, counterespionage, move and countermove is useless, ridiculous! The superpowers will *never* go to war, because they both know it will mean total destruction!"

"Cooler heads will prevail," Daremo interjected.

"So what's the point?"

Daremo shrugged. "Great. You've proven your point. Can I go now?"

"Stay where you are. There is still Operation Masterstroke."

Daremo sighed and started toward him. "I think you should change the name to Massive Stroke. The assault on Mickey failed. The attack on All Saints shoppers failed."

"Keep your distance," said Napoleon, moving to the

edge of the tower, his back against the restraining wall. "I'm holding a signaling device."

Daremo said, "No shit, Sherlock," but he slowed and stilled.

"War of honor," Napoleon told him. "The secret battle. That is what this was all about. That was all the ninja had. That is all we have. The personal knowledge of a job well done. If anyone stopped to question what we were doing for a second, the pure, useless insanity of it would be clear."

"So?"

"So I created an organization based on that very insanity! It was the only thing to do! Create your own side or go mad."

"I don't think the word *or* is really operative here," Daremo advised.

"You should know."

"I told you before," Daremo complained. "I was forced into this. You wanted to do it. You *chose* it." He took another step forward.

"Freeze!" Napoleon demanded. "Not one more step. I'll push this button." Daremo rolled his eyes, threw up his hands, and walked away. "It was natural," Napoleon said after him. "I was utilizing my talents to the greatest extent. 'Better it is to dare mighty things, to win glorious triumphs, than to take rank with those poor spirits who neither enjoy nor suffer much. They live in a gray twilight that knows not victory nor defeat.'" His eyes were glowing. He was on a cathedral top with no one, spewing Theodore Roosevelt quotes, and happier than he had been all day.

"Yeah," said Daremo. "'Better to be vile than vile esteemed.' 'Better to forget than remember and regret.' 'Better to give than to take.' 'Better to reign in hell than serve in heaven.' And 'better to know nothing than know what ain't so.' Henry Wheeler Shaw. Two can play at this game."

"I have dared," said Napoleon. "I have triumphed."

"You're alone," Daremo countered. "You had an army in your mind. They're dust."

"As you shall be. As shall we all."

"Okay," said Daremo. "Impasse. I came up here to see what I was dealing with. Now I know. I don't have time for this. I'm sorry I got in your way. All I wanted to do that day was save myself. I couldn't care less about you or your friends or anybody else. I told my chunin to leave you alone, but she didn't listen. You know what kunoichi are like, right? Good-bye." He turned around.

"Every night," Napoleon said sternly, "for the last thirty nights, one of my men has climbed onto one of this cathedral's flying buttresses." They were the winglike structures coming off the spired roof and attaching to the top of the first tier that encircled the church. "Each one lay a thin line of explosive across the support wing, effectively slicing the buttress in two."

Daremo turned and stared at the man with the button in his hand. "Ega knight to Kohga king," he finally said. "Check."

"And mate," said Napoleon. "Yes. I have recreated the Chiba poisoning, the Toei bombing, and now the Kohga collapse. I have done it all for one simple purpose: to play a game with *you*." He strained to make Daremo understand. "No professional wants to play with amateurs. A master seeks . . . wants, needs, desires . . . another master."

"I repeat," Daremo said. "We're not in the same category. Apples fighting oranges. Intrinsically unfair, unequal, useless."

"I disagree. I *am* in your league. The SSS was—is—the modern version of the ninja. It will be so again. There are always more agents. More people who need the thrill, who crave the excitement, who are better than the rest and need an environment in which to prove it. We spy. We infiltrate. We assassinate. How do we differ from you?"

If Napoleon was expecting Daremo to repeat the force-versus-choice line, he was disappointed. Instead Daremo smiled and wandered back, looking at his hands. He was holding them by his side, palms up.

"I'll tell you how," he said mildly. "We kill. With our bare hands. You do not."

Napoleon blinked. "We kill," he said harshly. "There is

the blood of hundreds—thousands in the Asian hemisphere alone—on our hands. Can you claim that?

"You kill with technology," Daremo continued quietly. "You use machinery. Whether it's a gun or a bomb or a securing ring on the outside of a retro rocket, you use science. We use our souls."

Daremo turned away from the man, taking in all the beauty of the city. "You can't know what it is like to die. To you death is a clinical exercise. There's no passion. No *com*passion. You use your minds. We use our blackened, diseased hearts. We kill with everything we are."

He turned back to the amazed man with the button. "You kill with nothing. No, we are not the same. We're not even close."

Napoleon could think of nothing to say for minutes. The two men just stood at the very top of Notre Dame, now no more than seven feet away from each other, silent—almost motionless.

Napoleon finally spoke. Each word was measured and temperate. "I suppose you think that you're better."

Daremo laughed. "You learn nothing, either," he said. He looked at Napoleon over his shoulder. "It's over. You've won. I give up. Happy?"

"How did I win?" Napoleon retorted angrily.

"Or you lost," Daremo answered mildly. "Take your pick. It makes no difference to me. Like you said, it's all meaningless."

There was no more time to waste. Daremo had to get to Cristobal. There were borders to cross.

"I still have this!" Napoleon announced, holding up the button.

Daremo grinned, turning to face the man. "Okay. We can make a decision. I'll make you a bet. You win . . . and you've won. I win . . . I won. Okay?"

"What is it?"

"I bet you can't press that button." Daremo pointed at it for emphasis.

Napoleon's mind said, *What? You're joking!* but his lips stayed still. He looked at the button, then back at Daremo.

What was the ninja master doing? Committing suicide? Taking Napoleon with him? If he pressed the button, the explosives would crack the thirty flying buttresses, and it was an even bet that the entire cathedral would collapse.

He had wanted to wait. He had wanted to wait until the mass on Christmas Eve and the rush of the thousands to cram the ancient, delicate, glorious building. Then the implosion would seem like just another accident. It would be the Secret Secret Service's ultimate insult to the world. No one would ever be able to prove anything. And if they could, to reveal the organization would be to call the superpowers' bluff.

Collapse . . . the ninja signified it. The SSS represented it. Yes . . . Yes, it was fitting. Either way the ninja master died.

And if Napoleon was to go, he wouldn't mind taking the thousand-year-old symbol of France with him.

"All right," he said, and pressed the button.

19

I

Daremo blurred.

He moved faster than Napoleon thought people could move. It was as if all the inactivity of the last few months had built up inside the man for one burst of mind-shaking speed.

Napoleon let his thumb up. Nothing had happened.

He looked at Daremo. There were swords coming over the man's right fist. They had not been there when he'd started to move.

Napoleon looked quickly down at himself. There was no apparent damage. No slits across his stomach or throat. There was no puncture in his chest. He looked at his hand. His fingers were all still there.

He looked back at the blades. They were unstained.

He pushed the button down again. Nothing happened. He clicked the button three more times. No explosions. No collapse.

He looked down again. The wire connecting the button to the transmitter was cut. It hung from his waist.

He looked at the ninja master. "I pressed the button," he said.

The ninja master let his smile grow slowly. "Then I guess you win."

The bullet went between them. They both felt its passing at the same moment, and then it struck the wall harmlessly. Then they heard the distant, innocuous cracking sound.

Daremo had kneeled before Napoleon could even look back in the direction from which the round had come. He stared, openmouthed, for several seconds before he realized no more bullets were being fired.

"He missed!" Napoleon said in amazement. "Perfect vantage point, perfect target, perfect weapon . . . and he missed!"

Daremo remained kneeling. "Not the perfect weapon," he said. "That's the difference." He clenched his right fist twice. The swords slipped back into the scabbard strapped to his arm, and he punched Napoleon in the solar plexus.

The man doubled over, gasping, as Daremo hit him repeatedly in the stomach. That way the abuse wouldn't show when some inspector found him. It would be a shame to mess this beautiful structure with four pints of blood.

Daremo stood, slipping behind the man just in case any more bullets were forthcoming. "You cheated," he whispered in Napoleon's ear. "All bets off. New bet." He grabbed the man by the collar and the belt. "Heads, I win; tails, you lose."

Daremo hoisted the paralyzed, breathless man up onto his shoulders, then dumped him over the tower wall.

Napoleon got just enough air back to start screaming before he hit the sidewalk.

II

Daremo stood there for several moments more. He stood on the tower, staring at the only place from which the shot could have come. The roof of the Gare de Lyon, a few hundred yards away.

He stood, as if daring the sniper to shoot him and put an end to this misery.

On the roof of the Gare de Lyon, Asao Katsu wiped the ceremonial tanto blade on the already bloody garments of the Tempter. The Tempter lay slumped on the wildly expensive Heckler and Koch 5000 sniper rifle, blood pumping out of the wound in the top of his skull and the slash in the back of his neck.

Asao Katsu leaned carefully across the corpse and unscrewed the scope from the weapon. He stood, putting it to his eye. He saw Daremo walk to the cloister door, then take one last glance back in this direction.

Asao Katsu had tracked him across Asia and Europe. He had gone to Hong Kong. He had traced the businessman from whom the yakuza was to get the smuggled money. He had trailed the various illegal shipments. He had seen the boxes the police had taken. And he had heard about the secret shipment to Paris.

He had seen the graffiti. He had followed. He had watched. He had waited.

The Ichi gang would not be denied its retribution. The Gaijin's time would come.

"When you have mastered the way of strategy,
   you can make your body like a rock,
   and ten thousand things cannot touch you."

—Miyamoto Musashi

"To die with honour when one can no longer live with honour."

—Samurai Sword Inscription